FRANCESCA CATLOW
in the heart of Suffolk, C
Europe with her French l
two young children. Of all the places she's been, it is the Greek
islands that have captured her heart.

The Little Blue Door was Catlow's first novel – written
during the lockdown of 2020 while feeding her newborn in
the early hours

In 2023, Catlow was shortlisted for the Kindle Storyteller
Award. We'll find out in November whether she has won.
www.francescacatlow.co.uk

F:@francescacatlowofficial
I:@francescacatlowofficial
TikTok: @francescacatlow

For trigger warnings visit: francescacatlow.co.uk/trigger-
warnings/

The Little Blue Door Series in order:
Book 1: The Little Blue Door (2021)
Book 2: Behind The Olive Trees (2022)
Book 3: Chasing Greek Dreams (2023)

Standalone novels related to the series:
Greek Secret (2023)
Found in Corfu (2024)

Novellas:
For His Love of Corfu (2021)
One Corfu Summer (2022)

The Last Christmas Promise

Francesca Catlow

Gaia & Fenrir Publishing

Published in 2023 by Gaia & Fenrir Publishing

Copyright © Francesca Catlow 2023

First edition

ISBN: 978-1-915208-31-6 (paperback)

ISBN 978-1-915208-30-9 (ebook)

British Library Cataloguing in Publication Data A CIP catalogue record for this book is available from the British Library.
www.gaiaandfenrirpublishing.co.uk

*This book is for 'French Boy', or as my brother
likes to call him, The Camembert Kid.*

Acknowledgement

As well as The Camembert Kid, I would like to
thank my copy editor. She's such a talented and
kind individual. Thank you for helping me to get
my manuscripts up to scratch.

Thank you to my mum and Gemma for being
brilliant alpha readers! You always push me to have
faith in my stories, as well as making sure I see
everything from the all important reader point of
view. I'm so grateful to you both.

Part One

Chapter 1

Ralph

Four Years Ago

'Look, we'll get you over her. Actually, I think you'd be better off over *her*. Shit. Look at those two.' Benedict's eyebrows shoot up and disappear under his mop of hair. He excitedly bites down hard on his lower lip. I turn in the direction of his dipped head towards two girls in tight dresses strolling towards the bar in the throbbing nightclub.

'Yeah, I mean, they're hot, but, Bennie, I've gotta level with you, if there's a chance of getting back with Holly, I don't want–'

Benedict pulls me to one side, tugging at the lapels of my jacket as he presses our heads together.

'We've just had a bottle of free wine *each* from that mug Joe and his shitty Christmas do.' Each word is punctuated with a short slice of his hand. 'Let's not waste the momentum, bro. Don't let Holly and her weasels ruin your happiness. Now's the time for freedom. Keep moving. Keep being happy without them. Now's the time to enjoy yourself, yeah? Not tie yourself up in knots over some–' He hesitates, and I know he wants to call her a bitch, but he's better than that. '–over some girl.' His eyes dart about into the music around us before narrowing back on me. His lips descend on my ear to cut through the music. 'I need you to make me a promise. We *have* to have fun, yeah? If it's not fun, stop. Walk away. Promise me you'll stop letting these girls walk all over you? I've seen enough of it with my dad. You'll actually try and have some fun? Right?'

Laughter trickles from my lips. 'Yes, bud. I promise.'

Bennie releases his grip on my jacket and instead presses the weight of his thick arm around my neck. 'Look around you, mate. There're so many girls. *So* many. Now come on, let's find ya one for tonight. You've promised me now. It's all about the fun.'

Bennie puts his left hand forward with his little finger standing up in my direction. I'm right-handed, he's a leftie, but this is something that was born before we knew that you're supposed to shake using right hands. I meet his little finger with the little finger of my left hand and we wrap them together in a pinkie-promise, following it with our usual fist bump. I guess now I'd better stay true to my word and have some fun. Move on from Holly. He's probably right. Benedict's usually right, even if his ideas on girls and relationships are a bit wonky.

Fuelled by alcohol and bravado we walk up to the bar to top up our buzz and to scan the room for potential women to go with for the night. I'm taller than Bennie by an inch or two and have been from our first day of school until now. We've grown in sync and stuck together like brothers, even working at the same jobs and living in the same flat. Although he's got some distorted views on relationships, I think for tonight at least he might actually be right. I need to cut the ties between me and Holly, and there's one very simple way to do that.

Benedict can always talk to girls, always could. I'm still sure I'm built for a relationship. I hope one day he'll feel the same, but I guess as long as he's happy that's all I really care about. In my twenty-three years I've had two relationships, both lasting two years, which is the opposite to Benedict who's clocked up at least two girls for every one of his twenty-three years, I'm sure. No, it's probably more than that, thinking about it. But tonight, I'm going to try to be a little bit more like Bennie. I'll do it for him. I trust him. Bennie's never without a smile on his face. Never worrying about women in the least. Maybe it's time for me to live a little vicariously myself.

When I was sixteen, I sort of fell into a relationship with a girl I really liked. We had just started college and I fell for her hard. It was only when we went to different unis that it kind of stopped. That's when I met Holly, and Bennie went on a rampage of finding any girl he could get his hands on. That's how we ended up living in Exeter. Benedict always wanted to surf and do science and I had no idea what I wanted, so I took media. Now the plan is, he'll teach people to surf in the summer, and I'll help him with his promo videos. At the moment we work with a health food place to pay the bills. Although it started as a joint interest, the job now feels completely boring.

The bass of the music is stabbing in my chest and making the hairs on my arms stand on end as a girl with flowing black hair and long silky legs comes to stand next to Benedict at the bar. A sharp probe from his elbow finds my ribs. His lips move next to my ear, but he still needs to speak up to be heard.

'I'm going for a smoke. Talk to this one. And remember, you promised to have some fun.'

Before I can argue, he turns and disappears into a group of people, like he was gobbled up by the music.

She's a sweet girl with round pouting lips painted the colour of Real Madrid's pink away kit. She's studying to be a vet. I forgot her name as soon as she said it, too distracted by the way she looked up at me from under her mass of fake lashes. I know they're fake because no one has real eyelashes like that.

I get her a drink, then her number. Things are still hazy around the edges. She's coy and not looking for a one-night thing. Instead, she says she'll meet up with me another time and asks what films I'm into. It's a start, but not what I promised I'd be aiming for. But she's a step towards freedom from Holly's grasp. The high of talking to a pretty girl lingers in my chest, giving me the confidence that I'll find someone to spend my night with.

I check my watch, and find that almost forty minutes have passed. Bennie normally checks in with me. Even when he pulls, he sends me a message to say he's left. I pick my phone out from the back pocket of my skinny jeans. There's nothing on my phone from him, but there's a message from Clarissa, Benedict's little sister:

Hey you. Bennie said you were going to the U. Are you there now? Thought I might join you. Xxx

Clarissa moved here as soon as she could, setting up a life for herself away from their parents and close to Benedict.

I scan the sections of dancers, arms waving under the pulsing blue lights like sea grass swaying under the waves of music. I skirt the pit that's the club's dance floor. Maybe Benedict's got talking to someone outside. Knowing Bennie, he's got more than one girl's phone number already and another about to leave with him.

As I step out of the thundering club and into the corridor towards the street, the frozen December air slaps me so hard it nearly steals my breath. With the doors at the end open, this part of the club might as well be outside.

I march forward.

A sound slices above the bass and cutting rap lyrics playing behind me. I'm sure it's a girl crying. It's obligatory though, isn't it? To have some girl crying out the front of a nightclub. So standard you would almost think clubs paid them to hang about vomiting and crying at the feet of the smokers.

This is different though. This one's shrill tone is bordering on hysterical. It pulses with the music from a shrill whistle to a guttural snort. This one's going to be messy.

On the three steps out to street level, two bouncers in thick black overcoats and neon armbands come into view. They're completely blocking the entrance with their combined width. The taller of the two – shaved head with a fake Santa beard tucked under his chin – turns to face me.

'Stay here for a bit, fella. There's been an incident.'

Anxiety nips at the bottom of my lungs. Something in the air feels wrong. That girl's screaming, muddled words weaving in with her tears. They are blurred so badly they're no longer intelligible. It's like trying to catch a snowflake without melting it on a hot hand.

I lean one way then the other trying to see through the floor-to-ceiling windows either side of the glass doors. Something glistens like oil on the pavement, like a thick black mirror reflecting the streetlight. I scramble to make sense of it.

A car wouldn't have been parked outside on the kerb tonight surely. There couldn't be an oil leak on the pavement.

What spilt drink would be as thick as that?

Maybe a smoothie slowly oozing along?

Paint? How could there be paint?

It takes me a moment to confirm in my own mind what it could be.

Blood.

I thrust my weight with force between the two men in front of me, managing to wedge myself between them long enough to follow the trail of blood. My eyes adjust to see where the viscous liquid's oozing from, and the girl that's howling.

Chapter 2

Félicité

Present Day

My thumbs punch my phone so fast my joints ache.

Can you please keep me updated? Do I need to come back?

I study the screen, waiting for a reply. When it begins to dim, I slap my thumb back on the screen again to keep it lit, not wanting to miss an incoming message. This happens three more times before I get a response from Henri.

I can handle it. I'll message later.

I can handle it. I repeat his words over and over again in my mind. Not that that was my point, but I'm not sure he can. Maybe when I get off the train, I should turn around and get one straight back. My phone buzzes in my hand while I mentally plan my journey back to Carnac. It's Henri again.

Do not come back, Félicité. I'm not incapable, he's my son too. I'll message later.

Tilting my chin to the ceiling, I dig the back of my head into the seat, and exhale hard through my nostrils. That's the problem with living with someone for more than three years; they get to know you much too well. Even if we were practically children ourselves when we were together.

I know I need to let Henri get on with it. That's not easy though. I've found it impossible to trust him and I've made no attempt to hide it. As the train begins to grind to a halt, my teeth grind just as hard. I should trust him. I *have* to trust him.

I don't want to trust him.

I exit the train, with a healthy mix of tourists and commuters brushing past my shoulders, and make my way into the city of Rouen. The city of a hundred bell towers. It was once my home and now it'll be my home again for the next two weeks. The same as every December for many years.

It used to be a trip bursting with family and friends, but for the past few years, it's just been me and my mamie, my grandmother, for most of the time I'm here. At least everyone will make the effort to come this year for her birthday at the start of next week. This year she'll be turning eighty-five, and no one wants to miss it.

My feet eat up the pavement and my suitcase rattles along behind me as I make my way through the city. I march under the bright-white Christmas lights hanging above me, that line every street. Their glitter draws my attention with ease, but they can't keep it. All I am thinking about is how Henri might not know which bowl to use when Milo is sick, or where the flannels are kept, or which toys will give him the most comfort.

I stop in the middle of a cobbled street and a couple nearly walk right into the back of me.

'*Désolée.*' I automatically speak in French. I'm French and this is France, after all. They say 'sorry' in return and the woman blushes as she passes me.

Maybe I should tell Mamie I've had to get a train back to Carnac. It's a five-hour journey. I hesitate, my feet tapping back and forth. No. I need to at least go to see Mamie and explain. I can always book a train back on my phone.

I weave my way into the city, slotting between buildings that have been standing for hundreds of years, and eventually find myself at the door of my grandparents' eighteenth-century town house.

The exterior is a faded yellow that now looks almost crème and the beams that hold it all together are a chalky black. Without any hesitation, I let myself in through the squeaky old door. She's expecting me, so I know the noise won't alarm her in any way. Plus, she's quite deaf now and she might not notice that I'm there until I call out.

'*Salut*! Mamie? I'm here.' I prop my bag against the worn-out wallpaper in the square vestibule. There's no answer. I slip off my fur-trimmed boots and step into the lounge.

The smell of pine fills my lungs. She's got her tree up in the corner of the room and the box of decorations is waiting next to it. That's been our little tradition ever since Grand-père died. They used to have everything ready and waiting for me and my brother, Pierre, and our cousins. We would all take turns putting decorations on the tree. Now it's just me and her each year. It's hard for us all to get together now.

I call out again, louder this time, and I'm nearer.

'I'm in the kitchen, *ma petite chou.*' A smile glides over my lips. *Petite chou* – little cabbage. It's a traditional nickname, and one she has been using for me from before I was born, so I've been told anyway.

|Passing through the living room, I bound towards the long kitchen diner. The other side of the dining table, she comes into view, pottering in the corner of the room. The smell of warm cider fills the air around her like a sharp apple cloud mixed with spicy cinnamon and fresh orange.

Mamie places down her spoon and moves from the counter to kiss my cheeks. Her skin is even softer and more wrinkled than when I last saw her. She's so delicate and downy that she reminds me of a tiny newborn. Once she would have walked at a speed I couldn't match, and played tennis like the racket was a rocket launcher. Now she's slow to get to the shops, but I'm always impressed at how well she manages on her own without Grand-père holding her hand the way he used to.

It only takes a moment to exchange pleasantries, before she's pulling off my coat and telling me to sit.

She asks after Milo, and without a thought my brows knit together and I shake my head. 'What is it? What's wrong?'

'He's got a temperature and vomited twice in the past hour.' I pull out my phone again and check for an update from Henri. Nothing.

Mamie lets out a deep groan. 'You want to go back to him to see how he is.' She begins to ladle the cider into the festive mugs I bought from the Christmas market last year. They say "Rouen" and have holly and stars all over them. 'You mustn't, ma chère. Unless he is very ill, you should leave them to work it out. Has Henri said he needs you back?'

'No, but–'

'Félicité, he might not be the best dad, but you have to let him try.'

She's right. She's always right. I know that of course, but it doesn't make me feel any better.

I make my way to the kitchen table and slump down onto one of the old wooden chairs. Mamie edges a coaster with a kitten on it closer to me and places a mug of hot cider in front of me.

'Drink up,' she says as she pulls out a chair and eases herself into it.

'I still find it hard to trust him.' Instead of picking up my drink, my fingers dig through my hair and gnaw at my scalp. 'What's that noise? Have you left the tap running?'

Mamie rolls her eyes behind her glasses.

'It's okay,' I jump up. 'I'll get it. You stay there.'

It's only a few steps further into the room to get to the sink, but I don't want to see her pull herself back off the chair for something so trivial.

'I know you don't want to trust Henri, and you have good reason, *ma petite*, but he has never let down Milo.'

Other than leaving him in the first place, that's true enough. No matter how many times he has said he isn't ready for a child *since* Milo's birth, if he said he would be there, he has turned up. I'll give him that.

It's only me who was let down by Henri. Before Milo was born, he called the baby our *new adventure*, and told me he was *excited* to have a child. Only to tell me just after Milo had turned six months old that he didn't want our life. He wanted to travel again. It was as though he thought I *didn't* want to travel the world anymore. As though I liked being vomited on and being stuck indoors feeding a baby. No. Half the time it was exhausting and depressing. Being forced to stay awake when all I wanted to do was sleep turned me into a miserable zombie.

I've loved Milo since I found out I was pregnant, but that doesn't mean I wanted to stay rooted to the spot. I wanted it all and knew I couldn't have it, so I chose Milo over Henri because

I love him the most. From the moment he opened his big amber eyes to the world, I knew he would always be first in my heart.

Henri left to travel without me, settling back into his old life that had once been *our* life. He's back teaching English or French to children all over the world. However much he stole my heart from my chest and crushed it under the weight of his heel when he walked away, I can't take Milo from him. Henri still wants to be a part of his life, even if it is only for four weeks in the year – two in December and two in the summer. Milo is almost six now, and adores his father. I can't blame him, who wouldn't adore an adventurous stranger who brings gifts.

I pick up the mug of cider and drink deeper than I should, leaving my tongue fuzzy from the heat. The pain nips at me but releases the tension in my chest from thinking about Henri. He's there in my house in Brittany where I let him stay with Milo. I don't like to be in the house when he is there. Not since he's had a girlfriend, someone new on his arm. Not so new now, I guess. Naomi and Henri have been together for two years. This year she is staying with them. Milo met her in the summer. He liked her well enough, and however much I was pleased they got along for Milo's sake, the thought of them all playing happy families makes me feel as though someone is scrubbing my skin with pine needles.

At least Henri isn't alone dealing with vomit, I suppose, although I've never had anyone holding my hand through it all. I've had to deal with everything alone. From squirming through impossible-to-put-in eyedrops to screaming meltdowns in supermarkets.

Mamie cuts through my thoughts. 'Is there someone you could ask to check on them to put your mind at ease?'

'You know, that's a good point. I'll message Léa.'

Scooping my phone off the table, I type out a message to Léa. She's a student teacher in the school where I work, and she only lives a street away from us. Milo knows her well enough because we have been commuting together since she started in September.

Mamie asks who Léa is. I'm sure I've mentioned her before, but I explain, and she nods. Her curly heather-grey hair bounces over her mug as she sips.

My phone buzzes. It's not Léa.

It's a stomach bug. It's coming out both ends. We're making sure he drinks plenty of water. I'll message if anything changes. He'll be fine. Say hello to Noëlle.

'It's Henri. He says it seems like a normal stomach bug. He says hello.'

She doesn't tell me to say hello back. Instead, she makes a low noise at the back of her throat before sipping her cider. I do the same, hoping the alcohol will settle how on edge I'm feeling, while also knowing my mamie has probably cooked all the alcohol right out of it because it's piping hot.

'You know what you should do? Send a friend round to check on them. That'll help settle your mind.'

My head tilts and I feign a smile. 'You've already said that. I messaged Léa, remember?'

Her umber eyes roll and she shakes her head. 'Course you did. Has she checked on them yet?'

I tap my phone screen making it come alive again. 'No message back yet.'

My phone vibrates and lets out a contradictory squeal to alert me to a message from Léa.

'Oh, brilliant. Léa's coming back from the gym and she's happy to check up on them for me. She's already armed herself with a good excuse so I don't seem neurotic.'

Mamie nods. 'Well, that's decided then. You're staying. There's no point in you moping here all evening until you hear whether or not Milo is well yet. And he will be well soon, I'm sure. You can take me out for dinner. I don't feel much like cooking and you, *ma petite chou,* need to get out more.'

'No, I don't!' I bury my face in the dregs of my cider and the slice of orange that's lingering at the bottom of the cup.

'When was the last time you went out anywhere for fun without Milo?'

It's not something I actually have to think about. We both know the answer. I just don't want to say it out loud.

Mamie clears her throat, signalling that she actually wants me to give her an answer. A heavy sigh expels itself from the depths of my lungs.

'When I was last here without him,' I mutter.

Mamie purses her lips, and the decision is made that we are two women, one in her twenties and one in her eighties, who are going out on the town.

Chapter 3

Félicité

Mamie is so determined I will enjoy my time that she makes me message Bernadette, my best friend from school. However much I tell Mamie that with two school-age children the chances of Bernadette being free at late notice are pretty remote, she doesn't listen and makes me send a message.

Bernadette knows I'm visiting over the next two weeks, and we have promised to make time to see each other. A reply bings on my phone saying that as long as Manu, her husband, is home on time, she could make it out for a drink when the kids are in bed. Mamie beams as I tell her, and links her arm in mine.

'Let's go to La Belle Cuisine. They've got a new girl working there. You'll like her. She's English.'

'Okay, but only if it's my treat.'

From what I remember, the prices at La Belle Cuisine are a little steep. Last time we went there it was, perhaps, three years ago. Pierre lives right next to the place, when he is home that is, and he had suggested we should all go there. He insisted it would be fine with Milo, but it really wasn't the sort of place for small and overly tired children. The staff were kind and patient, but I did feel sorry for the couple next to us celebrating their engagement with a three-year-old watching their every move and moaning that he was hungry. Milo was desperately wanting to ask the couple next to us questions, even though their French was at best passably conversational. I think they were Russian; I can't remember now. He wanted to look at the woman's new shiny diamond-and-emerald ring.

'No, no,' Mamie protests. 'I said we should go out, so I'll pay.'

'Wait,' a thought strikes me, 'how often are you eating at La Belle Cuisine that you know when someone new has started working there?'

'She's not that new. Perhaps she's worked there two, no, maybe three months now.'

'You didn't answer my question.'

Mamie is slower on her feet than she was even a year ago. A while ago she slipped, embarrassingly, on a dog poo, right outside her house. She didn't break anything, but her hip and her pride haven't quite been the same since. It knocked her confidence, making it more surprising that her new haunt is her local, fancy à la carte restaurant.

'Your mother told me to get out more. That I was wasting my life sitting indoors. Easy for her to say from all the way in the south where the sun is always shining.'

As our arms are still linked, I'm not looking at her face, but I can hear the bristle in her tone as we meander under the glittering white lights that line every millimetre of the city this time of year. I love this street. It's mostly eighteenth-century timber town houses, like Mamie's, and hidden shops with offbeat treasures.

It's enough to distract me from the mention of my mother, Carole. Or at least turn a deaf ear to her being mentioned. She'll be here in a week, of course, and we'll get on well enough, then barely speak for another year while she absorbs herself in the life that she chose without me. Honestly, for a long time I've been glad she left Papa, and in turn me and Pierre. I think we were better off without too much of her narcissism growing up.

'Normally, I'd say not to listen to a word Carole says, but I think perhaps she was right about going out more.' Mamie flinches a little as I call my mother Carole, but it was she who insisted we call her that, I think to make her seem younger, like she was Pierre's and my older sister instead of our mother.

'Anyway, Pierre introduced me to this girl, Ruby's her name. I was hoping she was a new girlfriend of his, but apparently she's just a lodger.'

I let out a little noise to suggest my suspicion on the matter.

'*Non, non, non,*' Mamie reassures me. 'I think she's hung up on someone else. I could be wrong.'

I scoff again only for Mamie to squeeze my arm. '*Non,* Pierre hasn't been home for a month or more. He has been teaching in South America for six months now. Won't be back for a while.'

'He'll be back next week for your birthday. And I'm pretty sure he hasn't been in South America for a few years now. He's in South Africa.'

'That's what I said. South Africa.'

I know she didn't say that, but it was an easy mistake, they sound similar enough. We all make mistakes.

We round the corner into the little square. It's busy, everywhere is busy. Not packed with people, but an old couple are sitting on one bench and a small group are chatting on another, all wrapped up in scarves. Dog walkers pass by in all directions and lovers walk hand in hand looking for somewhere to settle in for dinner.

I glance up towards Pierre's flat. His building has a modern façade, but behind it there's another eighteenth-century building hiding away like a secret only for those who know about it.

All the trees here are dotted with lights for the festive season and we follow underneath them all as we head for the restaurant. Even though it's cold enough to make my toes in my boots begin to lose all feeling, there are chairs spilling out on the street under the shelter of a maroon canopy with plastic windows. It doesn't give much shelter from the December weather, but there are heaters to help.

Each empty black chair has a perfectly draped crème coloured blanket on it. Only one of the outside tables is taken. Two men dressed in smart overcoats are sitting there smoking hand-rolled cigarettes and loudly discussing politics.

A girl with short, thick hair opens the door. She's attractive with full lips and a spattering of freckles over her nose. As I move closer, I see the glint of a vicious scar on her chin, but it in no way takes away from her beauty.

'*Bonsoir, Madame Noëlle.* How are you this evening?' The girl holds the door open for us with perfect poise.

'*Bonsoir*, Ruby. This is my granddaughter, Félicité, Pierre's sister.'

I turn to my mamie as Ruby takes over, carefully settling her into the room and removing her shawl followed by her heavy winter coat with the fur collar. 'I thought you said she was English?'

Ruby smiles across at me as she carefully folds Mamie's coat and shawl over her arm and gestures for mine. 'My father is French.'

I return her smile and address her in English. 'Well, your French is good. How is my English accent?'

'Good.' Ruby slips into English too. The tilt of her head suggests something other than good though.

'I know. I still sound a little French. I find the accent impossible to entirely lose. I have tried and failed many times.'

Ruby laughs. 'In many countries a French accent is desirable.'

Mamie interrupts our chat. 'No more of this English. You both know I have none of it. I didn't come here just to be cut out of the conversation.'

'*Désolée,*' we both chime. Sorry.

'We have a special guest here tonight,' Ruby continues in French. 'Would you mind if I place you next to him? I know I can trust you two to reflect well on the restaurant.' There's a playful note in Ruby's voice that I appreciate. If I were to guess, I'd say she is perhaps my age – late twenties or early thirties – although likely without children as she lives with Pierre, and therefore seems younger somehow. I suppose it's the gift of sleep and rest that makes our child-free counterparts seem a touch younger than we parents.

'Oh, well, I can't guarantee that. You know me, Ruby, always the loudest in here.' Mamie's lined lips twist into a girlish smile and Ruby joins in playfully.

'Ah, in that case, I'll have to ask you both to be on your best behaviour.'

This woman, Ruby, has a pleasant aura. I like the way she doesn't treat Mamie like an old lady. That's not to say she isn't an old lady; I know that she is. I'm not completely blind to her ageing, however much I'd like to ignore it – and since Grand-père died Mamie seems to have aged at an accelerated rate – but Ruby isn't treating her like a flower that could drop its petals at any given moment. Nor is she disrespectful. She's kind and friendly and treating Mamie as an equal, which is just what Mamie needs around her.

'Who's the guest?' I quiz as she leads us through the restaurant. It's lined with square tables, with delicate napkins and sparkling cutlery waiting for someone to give them life and purpose. About half the tables are still empty at this early hour. I'm sure they'll all be filled soon enough.

'He's from an English magazine. He reviews restaurants and eateries around the world and posts videos about them, as well as writing articles for the magazine itself. To be honest, he seems more interested in chatting to his phone than much else. I think he's reasonably popular online. You might recognise him if you watch those sort of things. He has been on morning television in England too, apparently, talking to chefs and trying their food.'

'Even if I did recognise him, my dear, I wouldn't be telling him in English.' Mamie's voice booms a little over the buzz and chatter in the restaurant.

'Good point,' Ruby says over her shoulder to make sure she's heard in her more hushed tone.

It's obvious who she's talking about as we close in on the table, but equally obvious he has little or no French, as he doesn't bat an eyelid at our conversation about him. He is, as Ruby said, chatting away to his phone which is propped up on a small tripod on the other side of his table for two, instead of a person. His face is shining back at him from the phone's screen. Even as we pass behind him, he doesn't flinch. The man is perfectly presented, though, with dark styled hair and an elegant pink shirt.

I should've changed before we left the house. I'm still in my beige jeans and crème boots and matching crème cashmere jumper. Plain and simple but not really dinner attire. Not that it matters of course. Since having Milo I'm sure I've become invisible to men. It's as though they can sense they would never be my priority, so they just aren't interested.

We place ourselves down, Mamie almost next to the man with her back to the restaurant, and me sitting with my back to the wall in line with his camera.

Ruby asks us what we would like to drink, and Mamie orders a bottle of house red and table water before I can even open my mouth.

Mamie stretches her face to present wide eyes like shining Christmas baubles and tilts her head towards the man before saying, 'What a strange creature, chatting to his camera over dinner.'

I snigger and agree as I pick up my menu and look across at him. He looks over at me at the same time and I do my best to divert my gaze back to my menu.

'*Bonsoir*,' he says and smiles across at us both.

The tables are packed in snugly, and I could easily reach across and pick up his phone if I had the inclination to do so.

'*Bonsoir*,' we both return, and this time I look him intentionally in the face. I can see why he is popular for a women's magazine or television, or anything really. He has a sharp jawline like it could cut open a heart and ruin it, with cloud-grey eyes that seductively muse to the camera.

I'm about to return my gaze from him to my menu, when Mamie asks him a question. 'So, young man, Ruby tells us you're from a magazine. What magazine are you from?'

'I'm sorry, erm... *Je ne comprends pas,*' the man stutters.

Mamie looks a little taken aback, as though she thought he would reply to her in French, even though I'm sure it was obvious he wouldn't.

I decide to save them both. 'She asked what you're doing.'

I didn't want to ask exactly what Mamie had asked, for fear of getting Ruby into any kind of trouble.

'Nice to hear some English.' The man exhales with some relief then catches himself as my eyebrow slips up into my forehead. 'No,' he stutters, 'that came out wrong. I love France, love French, but it's also nice to be able to communicate outside of ordering food.' A slight blush crosses his cheeks and I have an urge to laugh, but I maintain my calm exterior.

He coughs before continuing. 'I work for a magazine called Future Calling. It's all chic lifestyle stuff about creating the "you" of your future. I'm the food guy. I get sent around the world and try anything from street food in Thailand to French food here in Rouen, and I write articles about the restaurants. And the Christmas market in this case.'

'What's he saying?' Mamie has been squinting at the man's mouth this whole time, as though she might be able to understand him if she really studies his lips.

'He works for a magazine called Future Calling. It's all wannabe stuff.'

Mamie's mouth turns down, as she shrugs and nods at my explanation. She looks back at her menu only to mutter about her glasses, before diving into the handbag she's placed on the back of her chair.

'Well, it was nice to meet you–' I pause, hoping he will fill the gap with his name.

'Ralph.'

'Ralph. I'm Félicité and this is my grandmother, Noëlle.' I gesture towards my mamie who's sliding on her spectacles. Her eyes now look like saucers under thick maroon rims.

'Enchanté, enchanté.' Ralph gives a smile filled with painfully white, straight teeth.

Mamie smiles at him but addresses me. 'Do people really say this? Is it trendy? Or is it just foreigners?'

'Non, they don't, but it's nice that he's trying.'

'*Oui,*' Mamie shrugs off her agreement.

I return his smile, taking him in for a longer moment before saying, 'It's nice to meet you, Ralph. We are also enchanted.'

Chapter 4

Félicité

'Handsome, loves to travel... Perhaps you should have a drink with Ralph after dinner instead of Bernadette.' Mamie doesn't look at me; she keeps her eyes on her menu.

'Mamie! He may not be able to speak French, but I'm quite sure he can understand his own name in any language.' Without turning to look I can't be sure, but I have a strong suspicion that Ralph glanced up at us as Mamie said his name.

As I've decided on my order, I place my menu down in front of me. Ralph has removed his phone from its tripod and he's fiddling with it intently. I can't help but wish Mamie was right, and I was meeting him for a drink after our meal. I haven't been with anyone since Henri left me.

It's not from lack of wanting. I am human after all. But I'm also a mother and a schoolteacher. Most of my colleagues are women or married, and the few that are single and straight I have no interest in. And as I don't hang about the school gates looking for single dads or have the luxury of going out without a five-year-old shadow, it's been a tough few years.

At the insistence of Bernadette and a few of my friends in Carnac, I joined a dating app a year or so ago. I managed to meet one person while Milo was on a play date. Sadly, he asked far too many questions about Milo and by the end I was determined he was part of a paedophile ring. I should never have put that I was a single mother on the app. He might have been perfectly nice, but he made me feel uneasy and it put me off.

Milo comes first, so I have only had that one date in all the time since Henri left. Ralph would be the perfect plaything, I'm sure. He's probably married though, with two or three beautiful children at home with his enchanting grey eyes. They're likely always clean and in matching clothing, unlike Milo, who loves to catch bugs and play in mud even when I beg him not to. Just the thought of him lifts my soul. I can see him so clearly begging me to look at the latest spider he has found and whether or not it is radioactive and will turn him into his favourite superhero. Milo is worth having no social life for. Although, in a perfect world, I'd be able to juggle both.

A waiter arrives to pour our wine and take our order. Mamie orders the salmon and I order the pork in Calvados. A different waiter brings over Ralph's meal. Pork in Calvados. I don't say anything, although I am tempted to start up a conversation with him, because I really have nothing to lose, but at the same time, I'm here to focus on Mamie. We raise our glasses and toast to December and to being together.

Ralph takes photos of his meal and films his first reactions to his food. It's highly distracting. He's extremely animated for someone talking to himself, lifting his plate and inhaling before describing the smell, then moving on to taste the dish.

'I think I'll message Henri again, and see how Milo is feeling now.'

Mamie nods and openly watches the entertainment on her right that is Ralph. He continues to chat away to himself. I send a quick message and get an even faster response from Henri:

Your message woke him. He was sleeping. I'll message in the morning. H

My stomach clenches. I've pissed off Henri and upset Milo. It's not like I was trying to be selfish, but I suppose I'm not helping Milo by messaging. I'm wanting to settle my own nerves, I suppose. Another message makes my phone vibrate and chime on the table.

Sorry if that was abrupt. He's just fallen asleep again. He has had water and hasn't been sick for the past hour. I think he's improving. Hopefully it's a twenty-four-hour thing. I'll stay with him in your bed overnight to keep an eye on him. H

Me: *Thank you x*

I don't normally sign off my messages to Henri with a kiss. But he'll know it's my way of showing my appreciation for his kinder second message.

'I have something I want to talk to you about, but I'm finding this man–, What was his name again?'

'Ralph.' I lower my voice as much as possible to say it, but Mamie is talking in her usual measured and clear tones.

'Yes, that's right, Ralph. He's rather distracting.'

I look about the room. It's filling up, but Ruby has left the table the other side of him free. He's having to chat to his phone over the noise in the restaurant. Maybe that provides a more authentic atmosphere. Mamie and I are both staring as Ralph reaches forwards and stops the recording. He gives us an awkward smile.

'I hope I'm not bothering you.'

I automatically translate for Mamie.

'Tell him not at all,' she says with a smile. I look her over the way a stranger might. Knowing someone else is watching Mamie makes me see her as if for the first time. She's wearing a smart red jumper with a black-and-red silk scarf tied around her neck, and although she's given up on make-up over the years, her hair is neatly curled and a shine of lip balm glosses her slender lips. She looks elegant. Warmth encompasses my chest as I repeat her words to Ralph in English. I add, 'We're not ruining your footage by talking, are we?'

'Not at all.'

Ruby appears and asks how Ralph's meal is and whether he requires anything else. She smiles across at us and checks on us in French. Some sort of in-joke is shared between her and Mamie before she leaves. A niggle tugs at my heart. It's a little sad that Pierre isn't interested in Ruby. She seems nice.

I catch sight of Ralph watching her walk away before turning back to his plate. He's eating the rest of his meal without a camera fixed on him. There's a scratch in the depths of my chest, one I haven't felt in a long time. The lime shades of envy tinge my insides as I wish Ralph, or anyone, would look at me that way. I'm invisible. I'm as beige as my jeans.

Exhaling the thought as best I can, I turn back to Mamie. 'What did you want to talk to me about?'

'Oh, yes. I want to gift you my house.'

Chapter 5

Félicité

'What?' However much I know my mouth is hanging open, there's no way I'll be able to shut it anytime soon.

'I have thought about it. You know the inheritance laws here are strict, and I don't want your maman to get it all, since your Uncle Marcel passed. The "usufruit" – the gifting now – it makes sense. You will own the house, tax will be paid now at a better rate, and I will live there until my death.'

'But...' Words curl and ripple over my head, knotting up like used Christmas lights turning into a balled mass of confusion. 'What about Pierre or Michèle or Rachael? Why just me?'

'I have already explained it to them. Over the years I have given them large sums of cash. They all own their homes, but you rent. You are the only single parent. And anyway, I want to gift it to you. No matter what anyone else says or does.'

Food is elegantly placed down in front of us, and we both automatically smile up at the waiter, who seems to be familiar with Mamie. Ralph catches my eye. For a short moment I'd forgotten he even existed. He smiles across the table at me before nodding towards my plate and saying, 'Good choice.'

'*Quoi*? I mean, what?' Stuttering over my words seems to have destabilised his confidence. My voice did come out a little sharp I suppose, although it was completely unintentional.

'Your food. We have the same.' His smile lingers on his lips but has disappeared from his eyes. 'Anyway, enjoy.'

He looks back down at his lonely plate. Guilt crackles through me, and in the same way that chilli lingers on the tongue, it burns me. There's nothing I can do to mend it.

My attention turns back to Mamie. 'You can't gift me the house. It's a house. You just can't.'

I watch as Mamie picks up her polished cutlery and starts to flake off a piece of salmon. Before it makes it to her mouth, she says, 'Of course I can. I'm old, I can do what I like. It's the only good part about getting old. You no longer care what anyone thinks of you.'

I continue to watch her, but she doesn't even look up at me. People move about the restaurant and the table the other side of Ralph gets filled as Ruby directs a young couple there. My eyes dart around as though I'm about to drown and I'm looking for someone, anyone, to throw me a lifeline and save me from my swimming head.

'Aren't you going to eat, *ma petite chou*?'

'Mamie–'

'I'll keep living in the house, but you will own it. I've had all the paperwork drawn up. There's nothing much for you to do. *Joyeux Noël*!' A smile spreads across her face as she wishes me a

Merry Christmas and suddenly my eyes are stinging and a ball the size of a child's fist feels as though it's lodged in my throat.

'Mamie, I–' My voice is strangled and barely audible. Her knife and fork clang down onto her plate and she weaves her hands between the glasses and finds mine. I dip my head and let the dark strands of my hair fall about my face to cover it. 'Thank you.' My voice comes out strained but clear. I know her hearing isn't what it used to be, and I want her to know I am grateful, even if shock is the overwhelming emotion.

'Nonsense. Now eat your food before it's cold.'

It takes me a moment to gather myself and to slot back all the pieces of my bewildering puzzle. I've just inherited a house and my grandmother isn't even dead.

I don't even want to imagine her not being here. It's been hard enough since losing Grand-père. Mamie and I have always been close. I'm close to my papa and my stepmother too –they brought us up after all–but Mamie and I have always got on well. It wasn't because we were related and the fifty or so years age gap didn't matter, we liked the same films, books, colours, and she would always buy me clothes I liked whenever we visited. We could talk. We *can* talk. God, this announcement has got me thinking in terms I really don't want to. She's still here–in front of me–and she'll still live in the house. Her house. Because even though it'll be mine, it'll always be hers first and foremost.

We continue to discuss how it'll work. It seems as simple as she says. I will own the property and she will live there to her dying day. There's no inclination of this being morbid or sentimental on her part. This is a sensible transaction, and in her eyes one she should have organised much sooner.

During our conversation I see a message pop up from Léa telling me that all seems fine at my house. Naomi opened the door apparently but everything was peaceful. I feel silly for asking her to go round there now. I just wish I could see everything with my own two eyes. I quickly send a message back with thanks and tell Léa I owe her one.

As we finish our meal, Ralph begins chatting to himself again. His dessert has arrived, an *île flottante*, a floating island. As it's Christmas they've put it on the menu as *oeufs à la neige* – snow eggs. They're soft balls of meringue floating in a bath of smooth crème anglaise. Although I still don't know why a French-style custard is called crème anglaise – English cream. It's nothing like the custard my stepmother makes. We've adopted lots of English traditions over Christmas time, and although she enjoys crème anglaise, it's nothing like the stuff she slathers onto her Christmas pudding.

I get to hear Ralph describe how the crème anglaise tastes of subtle vanilla, and how it feels like silk on the tip of his tongue. It becomes impossible not to eavesdrop on his intimate conversation with his screen. Heat rises up under my jumper and it's taking all my willpower not to sit and watch him eat. No wonder someone pays him to do this. I can imagine women all over the world watching his videos, hoping for him to lick his lips one more time.

When he finishes, I couldn't be more pleased, and with perfect timing Mamie declares she's full. I'm more than happy to skip dessert after Ralph's show has made me feel sweatier than I've been in years.

We call for the bill and Ruby comes over for a chat as she passes it to us.

'How was the meal?'

'Delicious as always, my dear.' Mamie beams up at her.

'That's always good to hear. And yours, Félicité?'

'Magnificent.' I then slip into English, in part because I love to chat to a native speaker in their language. Teaching English is one thing, but using it is another. 'Now, before we leave, tell me, how did you end up living with my brother?'

Ruby lets out a short laugh. 'He is friends with Rob, the head chef here at La Belle Cuisine. I've known Rob for years. He got me my first waitressing job in London.'

'No interest in my brother then?'

Ruby splutters and under her tanned skin a rouge tint blossoms in her cheeks. 'No, I–, erm. I've sworn myself off men for a while. Bad experience and all that. I haven't really thought about Pierre like that. That's not to say he isn't attractive, but–'

I hear Ralph snigger behind her. Now that our conversation is in English, he has the cruel fun of hearing her embarrassment.

'It's fine, Ruby. I was not trying to embarrass you in the slightest. It would just be nice to see him happy.'

Ruby's brows slightly furrow but she doesn't get to continue the conversation as a waiter comes over and whispers something into her ear.

'There's something I need to deal with. Have a lovely evening. *Bonne nuit.*'

We join in with pleasantries as she turns to move away. Moving between our table and Ralph's, I pull out Mamie's chair. It's heavy wood with a high back and black velvet upholstery and I don't want to see her struggle to push it back.

Pressing her hands into the table, she stands and I step back to let her get past. I wonder if I should say something to Ralph. I was a little rude to him after Mamie's surprise announcement. Before I can collect my thoughts, Mamie loses her footing and grabs for Ralph's chair.

'*Désolée,*' she cries. 'I don't know what came over me. It must be all that wine.'

Ralph asks whether she's alright, but I cut over his English with my French.

'Are you okay?' My hands grip Mamie's shoulders. They're somehow both angular and yet gently rounding her posture.

'*Oui, oui.* I'm fine, *ma petite chou.* Tell the young man I'm sorry.'

'Please, let me help you.' Concern pours out of the Englishman as he slips out of his chair and carefully takes Mamie's arm. He then goes into French. '*Ça va, Noëlle?*'

'Well, I thought he was English?' she says to me. Then turns to Ralph. 'Yes, thank you. Just all the wine. I'm sure I'll be fine.'

'She says it's the wine,' I tell Ralph. Something niggles at me even as I say it. Between us we didn't finish the bottle and I can feel her trembling under my hands. A waiter comes over, his face wrinkling with questions; but she is adamant that she's fine.

'I'll walk you both home, just in case.' Ralph asks the waiter for the bill. '*L'addition, s'il vous plaît.*' His accent is pretty good, not perfect, but I like that he's trying even though he claims not to speak French.

I raise an eyebrow at him and smile at his words.

'I can order food and pay for it in at least ten languages. That's pretty much it though, so don't be too impressed. Now let's find your coats.'

Chapter 6

Félicité

Although I initially said no to having Ralph walk us the five minutes back to Mamie's town house, she insisted that he should. Her reasoning was that it would be the first time since Grand-père died that a good-looking man had walked her home. She went on to add that it would be the first time in fifty years since a good-looking *young* man had escorted her home who wasn't one of her grandsons. So, I relented. Now, as it turns out, I'm pleased. Even with our usual slow pace, the short walk wouldn't normally take this long.

Mamie has spent the whole time talking about Ralph, and not *to* him. He's tall, and walking a little hunched so that Mamie can hold on to his arm. I'm the other side of her. It's quite sweet to watch his face in the warm glow of the Christmas lights and the shop windows. His eyes dart from my mouth to Mamie's to figure out what's being said, or waiting for me to translate.

When we eventually make it to the door, Mamie turns to Ralph and thanks him – which he seems to understand without my translation – then she tells me she'll see me tomorrow.

'What?'

'You're meeting Bernadette remember. If you don't leave now, you'll be late.' Mamie grabs both my shoulders and kisses my cheeks only to loudly whisper in one ear, 'Talk more to the handsome man. It'll do you some good.'

I couldn't be more grateful that Ralph's French is that of a schoolboy, because Mamie's whisper most certainly belongs on a stage.

'I should come in with you, see you upstairs–'

'I'll have you do no such thing. I live alone, Félicité. Don't you think I manage the other days of the year? Now off with you. Go. *Bonne nuit.*' And with that I'm gently pushed back out onto the street to stand next to a confused-looking Ralph. Mamie smiles and closes the door behind her.

'I thought you said you were staying with her? Did I misunderstand?'

'I am. She's kicked me out to meet a friend for drinks.' Tugging back my coat sleeve, I look at my watch. 'But we aren't meeting for another thirty minutes at the earliest.'

'Do you know Rouen well?'

Turning to face him, I can feel my face lift at the mention of my city, the only place I still think of as home. 'Yes, I grew up here when I was very young. I live in Carnac now, but I always visit Rouen for Mamie's birthday. Other times too, of course, but always for Mamie's birthday.'

'If you have some time to kill before meeting your friend, I'd love to be shown around.'

Tilting my head to the side, I shrug my shoulders. 'In thirty minutes there is only so much I can show you, but I will try.'

We walk back the way we came, along the narrow street and towards the warmth of the festive lights. 'Have you been to Rouen before?'

Ralph shakes his head, 'No. I've been assigned to Paris, obviously, Strasbourg two Christmases ago and a few places in the south. Never Rouen.'

'Have you seen the clock?'

'No, not yet. I only arrived this morning and I slept most of the day.'

I glance up to see him bite his lower lip, before he pushes his hand over his hair to smooth it down. Even though it was still perfectly smooth to one side.

I might be mistaken, but I could swear there's a pink glow across his cheeks as he owns up to a nap. As though I care what he does with his time. His eyes meet mine, and I don't let the moment linger. I need to keep my eyes forward. I don't want to trip on myself and fall into his shining pewter eyes.

There's silence apart from a group of teens laughing somewhere not far away and the click of our boots on the cobbled streets then we both speak at once. I'm telling him how long it'll take to walk to the clock, and I don't quite catch what he says. There's a beautifully awkward apology as he asks me to continue.

'I was just saying, it's only a short, perhaps ten-minute walk.'

'That's fine with me. I was wondering what you do?'

'English teacher to high school students.'

'Okay. That explains your impeccable language skills.'

A laugh hits at the back of my throat before I suppress it and manage, 'Thank you.'

'I guess English people always tell you they love your accent.'

'Usually.'

A memory flickers of a time when I was teaching English in Mali. An American teacher was obsessed with my accent. So much so that Henri wanted us to move on from working there as soon as our contract was over.

'What can you tell me about Rouen that I don't know already? I need filler for my shoot tomorrow.'

My eyebrows lift and draw together automatically. 'You're just using me for filler?'

'No, I don't want to just use you for that.'

This time the laugh spits out of me. 'So, what *do* you want to use me for?'

A low laugh rises up from Ralph as he hangs his head and thrusts his hands in his pockets. 'That's not what I meant.'

'Hmm, good to know I suppose. To answer your question, I'll tell you what I know about *Le Gros-Horloge*, or to you English tourists, that big gold clock.' He acknowledges this remark with a smile before I continue. 'It is one of the oldest working clocks in Europe. The mechanism was made in 1389. It's part of a beautiful Renaissance street arch. You can do a tour inside to see the belfry and the tower if you are so inclined. And of course, you would be surprised how many people you see tripping over as they go underneath it, breaking their necks on the cobbles to study the beautiful gilding underneath. That is all I remember.'

'I'll try to remember not to break my neck. That seems like the most important fact to note down.'

'Yes, please share the information far and wide. More people need to know how to protect themselves from the aggressive beauty of the clock and the arch.'

We share a smile, an acknowledgement of humour without stepping all over it. A flutter fills my lungs and my stomach at how relaxed and easy our conversation is. If only my situation were as light and easy as talking to Ralph. For now, at least, I can imagine myself being carefree. Without the burden of vetting any potential suiter with Milo in my mind. Not that it should even be a thought. Ralph would be a less than ideal suiter, but potentially a perfect source of fun.

As we get closer to the cathedral more and more people spill out from every side road, many with cups of mulled wine. Stalls come into view, and the sounds of the market chime around us as we edge ever closer.

The whole market opens up before us in front of the imposing Gothic cathedral as we stroll into the square. Ralph stops walking, removes his hands from his pockets and crosses them in front of his chest.

'Wow,' he breathes, 'that cathedral's stunning. I love old buildings. Religious ones in particular, because they always have so much spent on them. This market looks great too.'

Following his eyeline, I look across all the matching white, wooden chalets in neat rows in the Place de la Cathédrale, with blankets of white fairy lights joining together in romantic light tunnels. Enormous Christmas trees that pale in size next to the soaring cathedral frame the picture-perfect market. I still remember the market's days of mismatched stalls with half as many lights, although there was just as much festive cheer. I adored it as much then as I do now with all its polish and sparkle.

Ralph continues to scan the scene before an audible exhale leaves his chest. He looks down at me. 'Shall we continue on to the clock?'

Nodding, I follow on, weaving us between the hordes of smiling people queuing for *une gaufre*, a waffle, slathered in Nutella and strawberries, and the groups gathered to buy roast chestnuts. I know exactly what's on offer with my eyes closed. The air is filled with the sweet smell of sugar. I can almost taste it on the tip of my tongue, so much so that it feels as though you could rot your teeth without taking more than a bite of the air. It's wonderfully indulgent and calorie-free as far as I know.

Banking right past the crowds, we arrive at the main street that leads to the clock. We don't talk as we make our way along. The busy street doesn't make for easy conversation.

My phone buzzes in my pocket and I pull it out to read a message from Bernadette:

I'm so sorry. He still isn't back. Can we meet another time?

I reply quickly telling her it's fine. My stomach drops as I now have no time to kill. No reason to be out. A warm glow lines every street, and this one in particular, but a frozen wind whips around me, making me pull my coat collar tighter around my neck. I'll show Ralph the clock, then I'll get back to Mamie to check on her.

The clock is suitably impressive, and possibly not one of the sights he thought I would pick, such as the cathedral, the market or where Joan of Arc was burned alive.

Ralph coos at the clock the way most tourists do. He asks a few more questions, some of which I know answers to and some I don't. I did a school project on the clock many years ago and it's the only reason I know anything at all. He seems to like it, studying the intricate gold details, craning his neck to do so.

'What time do you have to meet your friend?'

'She has cancelled on me. She messaged me five minutes or so ago. In fact, I should get back and check on my mamie. If you're lost, I can walk you to your hotel. Where are you staying?'

'Wait, hold on.' Ralph's hands come up in front of him as though he wants me to slow down. Taken aback, I bite my mouth shut. 'Can *I* take you for a drink instead?'

I tuck a loose strand of hair behind my ear and take a moment to settle my tingling nerves. This is the closest thing I've had to a date in a long time.

'Sure,' I shrug.

The muscles in his face move into a relaxed smile as he asks where we should go and what I want to do next. I let him decide, offering two possible ideas for someone new to the city, back to the cathedral or towards the Joan of Arc area.

'How about here?' He gestures to the bright blue tables in neat rows under the clock and along part of the street. They belong to the Delirium Café and each table has their iconic pink elephant image on it. 'They'll do coffee, right?'

Folding my arms over my chest I move toward the only free table. 'French people don't drink coffee after lunch. We drink wine.'

'The English do. We enjoy being up all night.' There's something in his tone, something dark and rich. Flirtatious. He pulls a chair out for me. My eyes flick over his sharp features; his face is impossible to read. It's as though the tone I heard and the innocent face don't quite match.

No. It has to be my imagination. I'm projecting my desire for him – for almost anyone by this point – onto his actions towards me. Although, he hasn't looked away from my gaze as I sit down on the silver bistro chair. I'm not even sure he's blinked. It's worse than when I was fifteen and desperate to be touched for the first time. I look away and down at the pink elephant.

'So, you would like a wine?'

'No.' My answer is more abrupt than I mean it to be, but I want to have a clear head when I'm around this man. He already leaves me feeling intoxicated. I swallow hard at the thought of being closer to him. *Up all night.* Did I imagine him saying that to me?

'We're in Normandy, so I'll have an apple Minute Maid if they have one.'

Ralph smirks. 'Isn't that a kid's drink?'

'That's the joy of being an adult. You can do what the hell you like.'

Ralph's eyes flick up in thought as he nods at this idea. 'Hopefully,' he says. Then he turns away and goes into the café to get our drinks.

Chapter 7

Ralph

Four Years Ago

'I know we're not together anymore, but I really needed to see you. To see if you're okay.' Holly's voice is laced with the tenderness that can only exist between a couple who've spent real time together, loving each other and nursing each other's wounds.

She's shivering in the doorway, having walked all this way to see me without even a coat on. I want to pull her in and feel her soft skin pressed to mine, to feel her thaw me, and tell me everything will be okay, and for it to be true. In the same breath, she's holding back. Her shoulders are rounded and her block bleached hair is tightly scraped back behind her head where I can't see what it's doing. Normally we would kiss hello and I'd hold her to my chest. Instead, Holly steps forwards and briefly presses herself to me while patting my shoulder.

'Yeah. Come in,' I say into her hair, before she pulls away and walks past me.

I've been staying at Mum and Dad's since–

Nope.

Can't even think the words still.

For a week. I've been here, supposedly living here, for a week. I can't go back to our place. It would be way too tragic there, too quiet to sleep. I sent Dad to get my stuff instead. I've had Bennie's mum, Joy, saying she wants to go through his things to look for clues, but Clarissa told me not to let her. I was split; I'm the one with the key after all. Yeah, I might hate his parents for being useless, but they are still his parents, and I'm sure they probably love him in their own strange way, even if they don't seem to love each other that much. Or Clarissa for that matter. She's always been treated like a spider hiding in the corner that their parents allowed to exist.

Anyway, the police said this was random, that's what they've come up with so far. Random drunken attack, so there won't be any clues hanging about in Benedict's wardrobe. So, I've avoided letting Joy go there, and I've managed to avoid answering her, using the charm I know she always responds to. The right smile and redirection usually works with her, even with her son in hospital hooked up on machines. A shiver hits my lower spine, just thinking about it.

'Holly, dear, do come in.' Mum scuttles down the stairs and as soon as she reaches Holly, she kisses her cheek and holds her shoulder. 'It's good to see you. Perhaps you can talk some sense into our Ralph and keep him here for some dinner. Would you like a cup of tea?'

'Thank you, Margret. I'd love one.' Holly almost trips on the heeled boot she was carefully removing before Mum caught her off guard.

I haven't been in long. I need a shower and to get back to the hospital. At least Clarissa is there with him for when he comes round. Clarissa told me to get some sleep before heading back. I don't want to be too long though.

Reluctantly, I follow on behind Mum and Holly. Benedict thought Holly was no good for me. Mum sees someone neat and tidy, a put-together girl with a university degree and ambition. Who cares that nothing I, or anyone, ever did was good enough for her and her mates? They would all sit around and compare eyelashes and nails and the outfits of girls on Instagram they'll never meet. Probably compared all their boyfriends' dick sizes as soon as we left the room. Bennie never said a bad word when we were together, but I knew something about her made him squirm. If he spent time near her when she was with her mates, he got a wrinkle in his nose like a dog had farted.

She also hated that I wouldn't move in with her yet, but that was only because she wanted me to move way too far away from my work and be right outside hers. There was no middle ground.

Maybe with what's happened to Benedict, she'll realise that life could change in an instant and worrying about all these crazy little things doesn't matter. It's all I keep thinking about. One minute he was getting me to promise to have fun then... Then he... I need to swallow it all down. Just thinking about it too much makes a cold sweat gloss over my skin.

After all the love we shared, Holly and I, I don't feel loved now. There's a comfort about her face and the smell of expensive perfume that clouds the room around her, but I thought she might have said or done something to show the residue of her love for me. But right now, it feels like a random Sunday, and we've been invited over for dinner at Mum and Dad's. Holly still hasn't given me a comforting hug or said the right words; she's just trotted in after my mum. This is a woman I've spent so much time with, almost as much as Benedict in the last couple of years – and I lived with Bennie. You'd think she would know me better than this. Even if she doesn't want to be with me anymore, turning up here must mean she cares. So why not show it? Surely, she should show me a little more love than this? Or say some of the right words, whatever the hell they might be.

My fists ball at my sides, and Mum could use the heat in my chest to boil the kettle for the tea.

'How did this even happen?' Holly comfortably plonks herself down on her usual stool at the breakfast bar. 'I mean, I've heard people talking and read about it in the local paper, but really, *how*?' Her laminated eyebrows stay exactly in shape even when she presses them together. She had them done the day before she broke up with me, and got me to drive her there and back, likely knowing she was dumping me the next day.

I don't answer her.

I let my mum take the lead. She clicks the kettle on, coos, and agrees with Holly's indignation. Mum muses that it's just dreadful. Saying how horrid people are, how we all must stay positive for Benedict.

The thing is, something inside me has just broken. The way Holly sat down and asked the question. Something about the arch of her spine, the tilt of her head, tells me she isn't here because she cares. She's here because she wants to be involved. I'm guessing maybe this is what laser eye surgery feels like. I don't know, I'm a perfect 20/20 vision, or pretty much, but it's like I've been seeing Holly with soft fuzzy edges from the day we met until one minute ago. I was only able to take in the cosy nice bits, and now someone's come along and sliced a bit of my eye off, and I can see exactly who she is.

'I've got to go.' I look over at my mum, doing my best to avoid the sour pout I know will hit Holly's lips, soft lips I once loved and now, as fast as love at first sight, I loathe. Maybe Benedict was right last week to say I should avoid people like her. Look at her and her fakery. I can't believe I wanted her back, and said as much to Bennie. Why? Because she's pretty or smart? Comfortable? Is that enough to waste my life with someone who doesn't even care more than how to style pain?

'What?' Holly shunts the breakfast bar stool back, and stands to be as tall as she was sitting on it. 'But I've just got here.'

'And you're welcome to have tea with Mum. I'm going back to Bennie. He needs me.'

'But you've just got here.' Holly searches from my mum's pink face to my own.

'So?' Then it hits me and my body jars for a moment, stalled by a sudden thought. 'How the hell do you know that, Holly?'

'Know what?' Now it's her turn to look pink. Only it isn't from crying or honest sadness. Not to say she doesn't feel sorry for Benedict, I don't think she's that much of a bitch, only she can't help but frame it with her in the pain picture.

Holly stutters and stumbles over words before she can form a solid sentence, 'Can I come with you? We can talk in the car.'

'No. Tell me how you know that I just got back from the hospital.'

Not sure what is going on, my mum is awkwardly standing over the kettle as it begins to vibrate. Her hand hovers a teabag over a spotted red mug clearly debating whether or not she should drop it in or say something.

Holly's voice drops. Lowering her voice won't render her unheard, it only shows she's trying to hide her embarrassment somehow. 'I was checking where you were, on my phone. I wanted to see you, so I left mine when you left the hospital. I still care for you. You know I'll always love you in some way.'

Something about hearing love on her lips again stings. Only, now, being stung doesn't hurt. I'm maxed out on pain and anything she gives me is barely a notable graze.

'You've been stalking me out to make sure I was here? Not just popping over to check on me or Bennie. You planned it so that you don't have to come back and forth again if you miss me, I guess. Yeah, guess it makes sense. Is that why it's taken you a week to check on me? Don't answer that. I don't care.'

How didn't I see it sooner? I *know* that everything is a conscious decision with her. I've known that for so long and yet when it's aimed at me, I've somehow been rendered blind. Not now. I'm such an idiot. Hell, I spent enough time sitting on her bed scrolling my phone while she banged on about putting together the *perfect* outfit for each and every occasion. So, I know this visit took her hours to come up with. How stupid am I that I didn't see it at the door? She looks like a grieving widow with her frilly-necked black jumper on. Plus, it's freezing and she isn't wearing a coat, likely because she doesn't own one that looks *tragic* enough. She sucked me in with this bullshit. How am I this easy? Desperate for her to throw her arms around my neck and give me some kind of security and love. There's not one part of her that's truly capable of that, and now I know that I've been had.

'Clarissa needs me,' I confirm. I will sit silently next to her by Benedict's hospital bed. 'Thanks for your concern, Holly. I'll tell Benedict you are thinking of him.'

'I thought he was unconscious.' Holly tilts her head and crosses her arms as though she's annoyed he's up and talking and no one told her about it. Or annoyed that someone might have lied to her about Bennie's condition.

'He is. Guess I won't bother telling him in that case then.' My voice is deliberately monotone, and I let my eyebrows fall heavy over my eyes.

Her skin now represents the surface of the sun as I turn to leave.

'Bye, Mum. And Holly, don't be surprised when you can't see my location from now on. Please feel free to forget any and all locations I could possibly be.'

I leave the kitchen to the sound of Holly whining my name and my mum telling her to give me some space. Holly's whining shifts into crying as I pick up my keys.

If Holly is representative of women, then Benedict is right; it's better just to focus on having fun. Nothing serious, only fun. When he wakes up, I'm going to tell him I'll be his wingman until the end of time. No more settling. No more listening to women who hide who they really are just to trap you in a relationship until they've used you all up. Never again.

Chapter 8

Félicité

I don't want to lie, but I do not want to tell the truth either. I do not know this man. I do not owe him an explanation of my life. Ralph is nothing to me, not really, so I suppose I can say anything I like when he asks about my situation. In fact, I won't lie, I'll avoid showing him the whole picture instead.

'I was with someone for a few years. But now I am single. There's not much to tell.'

Milo sick at home sticks in my mind. I know he's safe with his father. Henri loves him in his own way and he will be looking after him, but I don't fancy explaining *that* situation, and the fact I have a son asleep in my bed at home four hundred kilometres away with his father, my ex, sleeping there next to him. No. That can all stay in my head.

'And yourself? No girlfriend back in England? I assume you live in England.'

'Sort of. Sort of live in England, I mean. I don't sort of have a girlfriend. I have a one-bedroom place, but I'm rarely there. And no girlfriend.'

Ralph nips at the sachet of sugar, shaking it a little before ripping it open and releasing the contents over the bowl-like cup in front of him.

'You're very beautiful, you know that?' With his chin tilted down he looks up at me from under his eyelashes. His hands are still working the sugar packet even though I'm sure nothing's left inside.

Placing my elbows on the vibrant aqua table, I rest my chin lightly on my fingertips.

'Maybe. But beauty is boring. This is why the English are only interested in the weather. Is it pretty outside? Here in France, we like politics and people with something to say. We don't care much for a pretty face.' I use my most delicate voice, but as I say it, I think of my beauty-obsessed mother. Everything about her is enough to leave a sour taste in any mouth.

Ralph laughs. It's not a raucous laugh or a puny chuckle. I can't describe what it is. But it's there as he shakes his head and brings his coffee to his lips before saying, 'Well, that, Félicité, is a first. Most girls like a compliment. Anyway, didn't the French invent the beauty standards?'

'Yes, but we've evolved, and we might like to look after ourselves, but this isn't Paris, and the women I know are more interested in breaking away from the shackles of standardised commercial beauty. I wouldn't want to be the same as all the other pretty faces.'

'Oh, don't worry, I'm quite sure with an answer like that, you're not.'

'*Bon*. I take it you've asked me to stay for a drink because you want to take me to bed? With your talk of my pretty face and single life?'

My heart is thumping so hard on my ribcage that it's making me lightheaded. I hold myself with poise because I can't let him see my nerves. If he sees them, they'll be real and I don't want to back out of this corner I'm putting myself in.

Ralph chokes down his coffee and grabs a napkin from under his cup and presses it to his lips.

'Yeah,' his voice rasps, 'I'd like that.'

'Good. Me too.'

He sits straighter in his chair, composing himself once more. 'You know, I thought I would have to work harder than that. You might be beautiful but–'

'But?'

He openly eyes me up and down and I lower my eyeline to follow the action and look over my clothes.

'What?' I demand.

'You look prim and proper. I half expected you to have a husband and kid at home.'

I pick up my can of juice and pour it into the glass, not wanting to focus on this assessment of my appearance. To him, I look mumsy. Attractive but taken. Who needs a badge when my demeanour tells the truth I'd rather hide? Although no husband at least, I suppose.

'As we say here in France, "the outfit doesn't make the monk".'

'Ha. I like that. So, in England we say, "you can't judge a book by its cover".'

My head bounces in recognition as I move my drink to my lips. I've heard this one from my stepmother many times.

'Yes, I know this one too.' I place my glass back down on the table.

There's a group of two couples on a table near to ours, and one of them has said something that's clearly hilarious. They all burst into laughter, snorting and clutching stomachs and slapping backs, before one of them swings an arm in what I assume is a continuation of the story, only to knock a drink over. The contents rapidly empty out onto their table and pour to the ground. Ralph and I watch the scene play out, the people groping for napkins while tears of laughter still roll down their cheeks as easily as the beer to the floor.

While Ralph is distracted by the mayhem, I watch him sidelong, studying his face. My pulse is still racing underneath my thick winter coat. The angles of his face are sharp, almost aggressively so even in repose, as he watches the chaos.

He smiles and turns to me. 'Looks like they're enjoying themselves.' His rich voice snaps me out of staring at him.

'Where are you staying?' The words spill out from a place of desperation. I'm afraid that any minute something will happen to stop what *could* happen, and I've waited far too long to miss an opportunity like this.

'You really do surprise me.' He sits back in his chair, confidence radiating from every pore. 'Drink up, and I'll show you.'

To get to his hotel, we pass under more romantic Christmas lights, joining the buildings together in knots of stars and glitter. There's something in the air around us, something like bravado, as though we are both playing a game of chicken, or we're on a mission to win a dare.

Before Henri, I had my fair share of fun, but nothing as processed as this. This almost feels like an arranged marriage with the wonder cut out. We have taken a step and decided our fate on the matter. *Il ne faut rien laisser au hasard* – as we say here – nothing has been left to chance. We have made our feelings clear and we know what is expected to happen next.

We have laid all our cards on the table. We are attracted to each other and simply want to act on those urges. This isn't a game I've played at any point in my life. Even so, even without the mystery and the subtlety, my body still feels electric at the idea of him. At the idea of what the night might bring.

As we pass the Musée des Beaux Arts de Rouen, an imposing building with seated statues either side of the thick wide steps, and tall windows facing out to the trees and greenery of the Square Verdrel, Ralph stops walking. I'm two steps ahead of him when I turn back to see why he's stopped. He takes a moment to look up at the sky. I join in with his gaze, expecting to see something up there, but there's much too much light pollution in the city to see anything of interest.

Something akin to sadness settles into my bones as I wonder whether he's regretting coming this far with me, and nothing has even happened yet. We haven't touched, haven't kissed. I'm beginning to doubt we will, as he makes no move from his position. It'll be another cold night for me, I'm sure.

'*Bonne nuit*, Ralph.' I turn to walk away, only to feel the tug of his hands on mine.

'Wait.' There's a laugh in his voice, as though I've said something amusing. 'It's beautiful here. You're beautiful. I wanted to kiss you.' He tugs me into his chest and smooths his fingers through my hair. 'If that's okay?'

I often feel that being asked if one would like to be kissed ruins the idea of it. I'm all for consent, but to me that's more about acceptance of a no. But, when Ralph asks me for a kiss, it doesn't feel awkward or a mood killer. Instead, it seems playful and oddly endearing, and almost sexy, that I have to give him permission to touch me, that I have all the power in this plotted world.

My shoulders lift in a shrug and laughter wrinkles the corners of his eyes.

I press myself closer to him. 'That's okay.'

Ralph's face moves towards mine, as slow as if time was warping and the moment might live forever. As though I might be suspended in time for eternity waiting for his lips to meet mine. The warmth of his breath tickles my lips before any contact is made, and he lingers without touching my skin for the longest moment. Then, his lips carefully brush against mine. Velvet isn't soft enough to describe their delicious sensation. It's like the smooth crème anglaise he described in the restaurant but more divine. Then it happens; he presses his lips to mine and carefully pours himself into me. My hands run along the arms of his coat, and I hold onto the lapels for fear my knees will give way and I'll collapse to the ground.

With a firm grip on my back, he presses me into him. Our mouths open to each other. I push myself onto tiptoe to meet him harder, pulling him in. And then the moment is snatched from me as he pulls away. He says, 'Come on. It's not far.'

'Wait.' I tug harder on the lapels of his coat. 'I need you to make me a promise.' His eyes shoot down to my hands then back to my face. 'We have to have fun. If it's not fun, we stop and we tell each other. No matter the relationship – even one that will only last a night like this one – there must always be fun and trust.'

Ralph's mouth hangs open a little and his eyes seem as wide as the moon.

I can feel his heart race against my chest, harder than before.

His voice appears like condensation in the air, as if his words are gossamer and easy to miss. 'I promise.'

Chapter 9

Ralph

Félicité has no idea what she's said.

No idea what she's just asked.

How she's turned my insides into nervous tatters.

I can't remember the last time I was nervous around a woman. Not since I made my promise to Benedict. I didn't care after that, it's all been about the promise of fun. The promise of not getting hurt. Now, four years later, and Félicité has just mirrored his words to me. Mirrored the promise I made to him that Christmas – to *have fun* and *to stop* if it's not. I wasn't nervous before she said that. I was pleased to have such a beautiful woman so easily agree to spend the night with me. She's quietly confident. Elegant. Put-together in a way that's normally unattainable. Originally, I'd had my eye on the English maitre d' in the restaurant, until Félicité came in. Her smoky, lingering eyes with minimal make-up on her snowy skin intrigued me.

She lured me into a false sense of security. Now she's quoting my best friend and it's impossible that she can know what she's done. How could she? Even people who know roughly about the promise I made don't know the exact words. She was way too close to them.

To distract myself from the open wound she's just dug her fingernails straight into, I pull her in and kiss her again, harder this time, as though I can pull the secrets from her tongue if I try hard enough.

I can't let her into my head. No woman has taken living space there since my promise, and I'm not about to start letting someone in now.

Her lips escape from mine and she begins to walk away. She calls a casual question over her shoulder. 'This way?'

Maybe she's the female equivalent of Bennie, notching up those lines on her bedpost from past trauma. He said that wasn't it, but it was. The stuff he had to live with when we were growing up, with both parents demanding of him, piling everything on him, and generally being miserable bastards. There's no way he'd want to settle or be like them. No way *I* can settle. Not ever. Keep moving. Keep being happy alone. Easier that way.

If you don't let people in, you can't get hurt. Love is an equation that always ends in a broken heart. There's no good way out. Either they leave or they die. Félicité is just another pretty face, so why the hell does the acid in my stomach feel like it's trying to burn me alive all of a sudden? I only have to promise one night of fun, so why do I suddenly care so much?

Chapter 10

Ralph

Four Years Ago – Christmas Day

'Will your parents be visiting today?'

I wait for Clarissa to reply while she wipes mayonnaise from her lips with the back of her hand and finishes the chunk of turkey sandwich in her mouth. She's shaking her head though, so I guess I already know the answer.

'Nope. I told them there was no visiting on Christmas Day.' A smug smile brightens her face as she pulls one leg up onto the hospital chair and leans on her knee. She eyes the thick sandwich in her hand. 'Nice of your mum to bring these though.'

'She wanted to bring Christmas crackers to pull. I shot her a look and she got it. I mean, Christ, it's not like we're here to celebrate.'

'Unless the banging would wake him up. Or, if he wakes up today, then you'd wish we had the crackers.'

We share a smile, but it fades quickly back into silence. We know the reality. The chances are, Bennie won't make it to new year. Brain-dead, they told us. Just the machines keeping him going. Clarissa went at the doctor, screaming at the poor sod like it was his fault. I held her back. Squeezed her round the waist so tight to keep her in. Eventually when she went floppy, I had to hold her upright. But today is Christmas, and we made a promise to each other yesterday that we would be positive. People wake up out of these things all the time.

'You know, Benedict made me promise him something, before–'

'If it was to do him a favour, and you haven't, I don't think he'll care.'

'Nah, I promised him to have fun.'

It sounds off now, sort of pointless to tell her. Seeing Holly again has got my brain on replay and thinking about everything Benedict ever said or did about girls. He never stressed about them.

'Don't you two normally have fun?'

'Yeah, no, I mean, it was more like I need to stop letting girls take the piss out of me. I need to have some fun.'

'I take it he meant *his* kind of fun.'

'Yeah. You've got to admit, Bennie could always find his way to the fun.'

'Hmm.' Clarissa dusts crumbs off her hands by rubbing them together then down her sage joggers. 'You know, not all girls will want to take the piss out of you. Just because Holly didn't appreciate what she had, doesn't mean we're all idiots.' Clarissa's eyes flick to mine before she gets up to throw away the cling film Mum wrapped the sandwiches in.

'I didn't say *you* were an idiot. But it's not like we're ever going to be dating, is it?' A snort puffs out of me at the thought of it.

'So, you don't count. I actually didn't say anyone was an idiot, anyway.'

Clarissa studies my face in a way that makes my skin burn. I can't place the look, but it soon passes as she says, 'True.'

'I didn't tell you, but Holly showed up at my house yesterday.'

Clarissa's mouth drops open and she almost sings *ohhh*, while she nods in recognition. 'So that's why you came back after no time at all in the same stinky clothes with an extra King Rat sulk face.'

I'd like to defend myself but she's pretty much bang on. Not so much with the childish name, but I bet my face looks sulkier than it did as a kid when she started calling me that.

She's been calling me King Rat on and off since we were teenagers. I went on a bit too much about the fact I thought Bennie should read the book, apparently, after my mum got me to read it. I was a bit obsessed with James Clavell books for a while. Anyway, she's been calling me that on and off ever since.

I sniff myself. Being stinky is another thing she's right about.

'Yeah. Holly was stalking my location on my phone and had obviously been sitting about all day ready to run over to Mum and Dad's as soon as I left here. I'm pretty sure she was just interested in the juicy details of what's going on to tell her mates, and not interested in me or Benedict at all.' I drop my head back and look at the tiles on the ceiling. 'Maybe that's too harsh. It just made me think Bennie was right, you know?' I look at Clarissa square on. 'What's the point in a relationship when you could be having fun instead? All the time I invested in a relationship with her, and for what?'

Clarissa shifts her expression into a sad-eyed smile. 'Yeah, he probably was right. I mean, look what happens when you do love someone.' Clarissa frowns towards Benedict still on the bed between us. 'Damned if you do, damned if you don't. Love is just a shit rollercoaster of pain. Benedict was probably saying that to you, that promise, because he knows better than anyone that long-term relationships are long-term misery. You've seen a slice of how miserable my parents made each other. And that Holly,' she rolls her eyes, 'she's enough to prove the point over and over. Your biggest problem is you're a sucker for a pretty face and a high-flyer. That and sharing your location with literally everyone we know. But, hey, what do I know? I mean, your parents seem happy enough. Maybe I've got it all wrong. Maybe Bennie's got it all wrong. It's just, the way I see it, if you love someone, they hurt you one way or another. I thought Benedict was the one person who would never hurt me. And look at him.' I look over at him, his eyes closed and still, with this almost smirk on his face that's been there basically the whole time. It's weird looking at him with his eyes closed all the time. I never looked at him like this before, not that I remember. How many people with their eyes shut does anyone stare at? Babies maybe. A lover sometimes. Not a best mate. I've never watched him sleep. Might've thrown a cushion at him when he was snoring on the sofa with a hangover, but never really looked at him. There's only the shadow of a bruise on his cheek. Other than that, he's basically a perfect Bennie with a week's worth of stubble growing in, and whenever I look at him, I keep thinking he'll sit up and laugh, maybe say "Got ya" or something. Hasn't happened yet though. Wish he would.

Clarissa continues. 'He's broken me more now than my parents could ever manage. Love is pain, no matter how you look at it.'

Her words roll around in my mind, bashing about on the sides, until it turns into a smooth and streamlined idea, the way a pebble does in the sea. As we fall back into our consolatory silence, I make up my mind for sure. Love is the enemy. Love is pain.

Chapter 11

Félicité

Ralph's feet trot to catch up with me. It gives me time to snatch a breath of the cold night air. This is a quieter part of the city and even with everything going on around the main streets all that's left here is an echo of what's happening elsewhere.

Ralph takes my hand and leads me towards a line of timber-fronted buildings. We get to his hotel, and he punches in an entry code on a keypad. The floorboards creak as we start up the stairs. With each floor we switch on time-sensitive lights. They only give us enough time to make it to the next floor as we make our way– still hand in hand–further up the winding staircase. This is all so new and yet somehow familiar. Holding a man's hand seems like something from a distant dream. Usually, the hand in mine is a miniature one belonging to Milo. Ralph's seems to encompass mine in its entirety. The hotel is much like a bigger version of Mamie's town house, only here everything is worn red velvet and ornate doorhandles. It's an old coach house dense with hundreds of years of seeing people do exactly what we're about to.

I'm led all the way to the top of the building until we arrive at a thick wooden door. With a nudge of his shoulder and the twist of a key, the door opens and we fall in after it. I take in that it's a good-size room before I'm confused by Ralph's lips again. Before letting our bodies become too entwined, I excuse myself to the bathroom.

It's not long before I'm clutching the sink, staring into the void of the plug hole wondering how this single mother has ended up in a hotel with a gorgeous semi celebrity. Because that's what he is. I looked him up when he went to get our drinks.

He has twenty-three thousand followers on Instagram – mostly women – and one of those blue ticks next to his name. This is semi madness. I have something closer to two hundred and twenty-three followers and every single one of them I've met in real life.

It doesn't matter. Why should it matter? We are two people. Two consenting adults. I need this.

When I make my way back into the room there's an awkwardness about him that wasn't there before. Maybe I was wrong, and a fling isn't his usual thing. He uses the bathroom after me and I sit on the edge of the bed, suddenly unsure where to put myself. I could still leave. I could go and just write this off as a strange evening with a handsome man. Only I feel like the last nail has gone through my hands and pinned me to the spot, waiting to see whether this is the moment that my body can be resurrected.

Ralph appears in the bathroom doorway. Like an image in a magazine, he leans on the frame, arms crossed over his firm chest;

shirtless. The clumsiness from a moment ago has dissipated and he has been replaced by his former confident self.

'You might not find beauty interesting, but I find *you* interesting.' He pushes his weight off the door frame and moves towards me. I stand and meet him head on.

'I'm sure you do,' is all I manage to say before Ralph's icy fingertips meet my jawline and skim along to the back of my neck where he manipulates me into him.

Our mouths meet once more and it's nothing like I expect. None of it is. He carefully removes my clothes and smoothly runs his tongue over my naked skin, making me shiver, and my flesh explodes with tiny mountains of goosebumps as it tries to reach out for more.

Where my moves are greedy and wild, he is calm and thoughtful, asking me what I like and what I want. He watches me, studies me as I moan against his touch like a glutton wanting more of him. Our dance flows around the room, the bed, the desk, the walls. There isn't a surface in the room or on each other's bodies that isn't now laced in fingerprints.

When finally, we are spent, we lie panting on the bed a short distance away from each other. My mind races with confusion. I've only had one other one-night stand before, and in all honesty, it was passable at best. Awkward and messy, with us both selfishly tugging the other about. This wasn't that.

This felt like the touch of someone who knew my body, and – I don't know – I'd like to believe he felt the same.

I take one last look over the contours of his body, doing my best to absorb the last dregs of the moment before I pull myself away from it. He's very muscular for someone whose job it is to eat. I suppose he has to work out to stay camera-ready.

Before I disappear from this room forever, I have one lingering question. I roll onto my stomach as he stares up at the ceiling, hands behind his head like he's almost forgotten I'm there.

There's a tattoo on the inside of his left upper arm. I haven't noticed more than one tattoo, and I've now seen this man from many angles. It's a strange one, not like anything I've seen before. It's two small hands with the little fingers locked together.

'What does this mean?' My fingers skim the black mark on the tender flesh of his inner arm.

Pressing his chin into his neck he looks at the tattoo then back at me.

'You don't do that in France?'

Removing my finger from his skin I shake my head.

'It's just something kids do in England.' He lifts his weight onto the arm then kisses the top of my head. 'It's nothing important.'

His lips linger over me, and I can feel the knots of longing beginning to tie my stomach up again. I'll ask my step-mum when I see her next. It's not something she's ever mentioned before. She usually loves bringing English culture into our lives. She always has.

'It's late.' I swallow hard, desperate for water and to wash away the feelings piling in on me. 'I should go.'

'So soon?' He adjusts his head on his tattooed arm and watches me as I snatch up my clothes and begin to dress.

'Why would I stay?' My head pops through the neck of my jumper and there's a grin spread across his face.

'Round two?'

It's tempting. So very tempting. I hesitate as my eyes graze over his firm body.

'I can't. I need to get back.' But I can already feel the oxytocin making him even more alluring than I should let it. This is what it is. Sex. Nothing more. Plus, Ralph might not know it, but I have a son to think of. I need to walk away with one spectacular memory, and one day, when my son is old enough, I might date again and have many more nights like this one. Only with someone who will stick around for more than round two. But right here, right now, in this elegant old room with its sloped floors and creaky bed, a relationship does not live.

'I'll walk you back.'

'This hotel is parallel to my Mamie's town house, just one street over. It's no distance.'

'Is it? I might be well travelled, but I have a pathetic sense of direction.'

'Her place is just over there.' I point at a blank wall as though he can see right through it and out into the rows of buildings.

'I'd have used my phone to find that out.'

It's impossible to stop my eyes from rolling, but then this is my city, my forever home to my mind. The one where my father met my stepmother and where we lived before setting off on adventures together. It's easy for me to know things, although, I've always been good at finding my way in life, no matter the country.

He slips off the bed and hunts the room for his boxer shorts and jeans. It's only polite to let him walk me, I suppose. Plus, I can't seem to force my feet to walk away from him yet. I fidget about, adjusting my clothes to give him time to catch up.

As soon as he's dressed, we creak down the stairs, this time using our phones for light on the precarious narrow steps. It's only when we are outside that Ralph engages with me again. Rubbing his hands against the cold, he asks me why I made him promise to have fun.

'Do you normally make men promise you things before sex?'

A smile lifts my face at this thought. It isn't something I usually do, or have ever done, but I can see how it could be used as a meaningful tactic to get men to agree to most things.

'No, never before. But then I'm not in the habit of sleeping with men I don't know.'

'Could've fooled me.'

'I'll attempt to take that as a compliment.'

'Sorry, that came out wrong. It *was* meant as a compliment, but now I hear it back it was–'

'Let's not dwell on how it sounded.'

Ralph's pace is almost as slow as Mamie's and the night is so bitter it could easily snow if precipitation decides to take its chance.

'So, you've never made anyone make a promise like that before?'

'No. Not like that. It just came out of me. I was looking at you, watching the sky, and, I don't know... I was worried you weren't having fun, or perhaps a one-night affair wasn't really what you wanted from me.'

I was going to tell him I always make Milo promise me to tell him whether he is having fun, and to tell his father too. He is a sensitive child and at times he will go along with things to make other people happy even if this causes him great misery. Making a similar promise with him is the closest thing, but the time to tell Ralph about my son is far past and I'm not letting him into my life any more than for tonight. I have told him the truthful answer to his question, but without the context I suppose.

'Félicité...' He hesitates, walking so slowly now he's barely taking a step. 'I don't normally see girls for more than one night, even when they beg me.' I turn to face him, placing my hands in my pockets and pursing my lips. Catching sight of my expression is enough to wipe the smug look right off his face. 'I just meant–' He visibly swallows and snatches a breath. 'Can I get your number? I think I'd like to take you for a... a real date.'

I let the muscles in my face soften and for a moment I wish everything was different. That doesn't mean a life without my son – I would never wish for that; he is my life – only that I wish things could be simple. To be able to pick and choose what's right for me without taking anyone or anything else into account would be the world's finest luxury. But sadly, not one I can abide by. If I say yes to seeing Ralph again, it would mean stepping closer to a relationship and that isn't possible right now. We don't live in the same country and I have a child who has accidently become a secret child.

'I'm sorry, Ralph. I enjoyed tonight, even more than I thought I would, but I can't give you my number.'

'I understand.' He looks down at my boots. His eyeline has dropped so much his eyes almost look closed, then they flick up to meet mine and his tone is forced and mildly jovial. 'I don't normally give out my number either.' We start walking at something closer to a normal pace again. 'If you change your mind, I'll be filming here with my camera operator tomorrow–'

'You have a camera operator?' My head whips round and a grin spreads across my face.

'Yeah, not for the whole time. Usually for two to five days for certain shots. Depends where I am and what I'm doing. Anyway, I'll be filming around the cathedral. If you'd like a repeat of tonight, meet me in front of the cathedral at eight tomorrow night. No wait, not tomorrow, I'll never be done in time. The night after? Eight?'

'Maybe.' The words leave my lips without thinking. My body wants to say yes. In fact, my body wants to walk straight back to his hotel room now and to start all over again, but luckily my head is managing to maintain some sort of control.

We arrive at Mamie's shiny maroon door, and I dig into the deep pocket of my coat for a key. When I look up again, Ralph's face is so intense in the glow of the Christmas lights still guiding us from place to place that I can't even begin to imagine what he's thinking.

He moves in to kiss me goodbye but falters millimetres from my lips. He whispers next to my mouth, 'Your beauty could never be boring.' And with that his lips press softly to mine before he turns and leaves.

With the taste of Ralph still lingering on my lips, I creep into the house, using my phone as a torch to fetch water and to tiptoe up the stairs. Being silent is an impossible task as every single step creaks and screams under my weight.

Ralph's words drift up the stairs alongside me like a ghost haunting my thoughts. "Your beauty could never be boring." I chew on my top lip. Is that really the sort of thing you say at the end of *that* kind of night? I'm no expert on these things, but it felt like more. He made it clear he wants to see me again. My lips feel raw from being kissed for hours and chewing on my lip hurts but I can barely bring myself to stop. The sensation numbs me from the crushing weight in my chest, because my ridiculous oxytocin is making me like him much too much. It's just science. Nothing more. Chemical reactions that I'll be over in the morning.

I mumble swear words in my mother tongue. Why did it have to be so good? I wanted it to be good, but that was more than I could have imagined.

As I reach the top of the stairs, I squeeze my eyes shut and push out a measured breath before continuing along the hall in the dark.

In the same way I do every night with Milo, I put my drink in my room and edge back out to check on him, only tonight I'm checking on Mamie while she sleeps instead. As I get to her door, I can see there's a light still on. Usually when I go out to see friends and come home late, the entire place is dark and she's snoring.

'Mamie?' I keep my voice low in case she is asleep. It's such a pointless thing to do, she's so deaf that even if she were awake, she wouldn't hear me coming. But it's automatic in the dead of night to keep tones low, and I really don't want to wake her or frighten her.

Nudging open the door, I squint against the lamp that's aimed at me like car headlights. That's when I realise the lamp is on its side above a pile of clothes.

Only it isn't a pile of clothes, it's Mamie.

Chapter 12

Ralph

What in the hell just happened to me?

Clicking along the cobbled streets, my head keeps shaking back and forth because I can't stop asking myself the same question.

What in the hell just happened to me?

In the past four years I've been with women in at least ten different countries. I've been having fun. I promised Bennie I would have fun and that's what I've been doing exclusively. But not anything like that. Hearing Bennie's words out of Félicité's lips shook me. I'm not shy about admitting that.

None of tonight went how I thought it would. None of it happened as it has with anyone before. I wonder if she noticed how off balance I was. She was a damn killer, and I could barely keep up with her. It feels like Félicité hit the soft point behind my knees and left me face planting to the floor. How did she do that?

How did she know what Bennie said to me that night? How the hell?

When I get to the hotel, I hover outside as a car edges along the narrow road beside me. My feet stop walking, but I can't make them go in. The sheets will smell of her, that soft vanilla scent that grew stronger around her neck, like she'd bathed in deliciously comforting crème anglaise. The scent will be there, but she won't be. For the first time in a long time, I want someone to come back to my bed and hold me. I want her. I want Félicité.

With more force than intended, my hands slap against my face to hide my eyes. Swear words flow through my veins instead of blood and fog settles over my thoughts.

I want to talk to Bennie, but I can't.

I want to talk to Félicité, but I can't.

I don't have her number and it wouldn't be kind to bang on Noëlle's door in the middle of the night just to sit and look at her granddaughter, because if I'm honest with myself, I wouldn't say a damn thing. It's too hard. I just want to be near her again.

The thing is, losing Benedict was like cutting off my ability to process the world around me. We filtered everything through each other. I didn't realise how much. We'd play games on the PlayStation and talk about everything without anything feeling like it was a big deal. Since he's been gone the word loneliness has lost all meaning because it's a constant. When being alone becomes normal and your soul has been stripped to threads it's hard to feel lonelier. But Félicité has reignited sensation where I'd become completely numb. Knowing she's out there and that I can't have her makes my skin itch. How the hell has she done this to me? Made me want to talk to her about things I don't say to anyone? Maybe it's some kind of endorphins. Has to be. She was just really good in bed, and she threw me with that damn promise. That's all it is.

After loitering outside the hotel almost long enough for someone to call a gendarme to move me along, I finally take myself inside and up the musical stairs.

Earlier, squeaking up the stairs with Félicité was funny and somehow added to the anticipation. Now I'm taunted by each lone squeal of the stairs.

I might never see her again.

I might never tell her that she said almost exactly what my best friend said to me right before he died.

Shit, Bennie, did you send her to me?

Chapter 13

Félicité

It's Mamie's favourite patisserie, Maison Vatelier. The little pink boxes always make her eyes twinkle because she knows something special is residing inside them. I'd do anything to see her eyes light up like that again.

A soft smile comes from behind the counter with a question of help, but I need time to stare into the glass. I was walking past the patisserie on my way back to Mamie's and I found myself diverted, and now, it's as though the desserts are hidden behind a cloud of my thoughts. I need to sort through all the clouds before my eyes are clear enough for me to process what's in front of me. Maybe I should leave.

'Félicité?'

I spin around in a daze at the sound of my name and am confronted by Ruby's full lips spread into a beaming smile.

'How are you?' She moves forwards to kiss my cheeks.

Ruby's looking polished, with a sumptuous mustard scarf almost swaddling her. In contrast, my hair was last brushed a day ago and I haven't slept. I'm not even sure I've replied to her, but my head has begun to bounce in acknowledgment of her presence.

'I often see Noëlle in here at the weekend,' she says, 'although I try not to be in here too much myself. But I find it hard to resist the big macaroons. Did you get home alright last night? One of the waiters told me Noëlle didn't seem too steady on her feet.'

'*Oui*, yes, no.' With Ruby speaking English and people around me chatting in French, I can't work out what language I should be speaking.

This isn't the time to crumple or lose it. I don't even know this girl, not really. Although she seems kind and Mamie likes her, she doesn't want me to explode with emotions all over her pretty scarf.

'No?'

'*Bonjour*, what would you like?' The same soft smile looks over the counter at us.

Ruby gestures me forward with her hand.

'Erm, I'll have the yule log.'

'Good choice. One of Noëlle's favourites, isn't it? She told me she was looking forward to buying some in for everyone over Christmas.'

'A whole log?' The tall girl with the soft smile behind the glass pauses and waits for a reply before I agree, and she scurries off to get the right-size box. It'll cost a fortune, but it's worth it. Mamie is worth it and much more. I can surprise her with it. When she's better.

'A traditional baguette too, and a *tarte au citron*.'

Best to have something for myself for at home when I'm alone.

My head flops down until my chin is almost pressed to my chest. I briefly close my eyes and see Mamie lying on the floor in the early hours of the morning. Now I have to return home without her.

Ruby steps forwards and places her order with another member of staff. As I move away from the gleaming glass that encases multicoloured treats like they're English crown jewels, Ruby quietly follows towards the till after asking for her pink macaroon.

'Félicité, tell me if I need to mind my own business, but are you okay? Is Noëlle okay?'

My face falls into my hands and I shake my head. My abdomen turns to stone as I try to hold back the desire to wail. I snatch my hands back from my face, holding my breath and pressing my lips together to keep everything inside my body, too afraid that even letting out air will free the torrent of feelings building inside me.

I need help and I feel completely alone, in spite of Ruby's kind query. This is one of the rare times I wish I was part of a couple and had someone to reassure and hold me. Someone to make me feel like it's not all on me.

I look into her round dark eyes and they're bulging under a frown of worry as she tightly knots her arms together over her chest.

'No,' I stammer, we're not okay.'

Chapter 14

Ralph

My eyeballs feel like sandpaper. Sleep has been as distant as my sanity for the past two nights. Both seem to be avoiding me. I've dreamed of Bennie trying to tell me something one minute, then Félicité the next.

Félicité. Oh Félicité. Every time I so much as think her name, it feels like another papercut across my chest.

Her face has imprinted itself on my mind. I keep thinking that I've changed her, that she's not really that pretty or elegant. That her hair isn't so chocolatey and soft, that her eyes aren't such a deep shade of blue, the blue that you only get on a stormy sea, so dark I thought they were brown until I saw them up close. Maybe they were brown. Maybe I've confused myself along the way. No, they were navy, I'm sure. I must be dreaming. Have to be.

Camron arrived early yesterday and will be leaving late tomorrow. It's good to have him about because at least he's someone to talk shop with. Someone to stop me thinking about people I can't talk to outside of my imagination.

He's staying in the same hotel as me to make it easier to organise shoots before he heads out to film something else for the magazine's website. Some other Christmas must-see event, I believe. I think in Paris, I'm not sure now. Or did he say it was a celeb interview? I can't concentrate. Maybe it was both.

Most of what we film and what I write is done months in advance of release, where possible of course. Most of this stuff will also come out again next year too. My article for the December issue of Future Calling is already in print, but this is keeping the online content fresh for socials, YouTube and the website. Anything to stay relevant. I'm basically clickbait and I know it. Usually, they get a gif of me licking my lips and use that to send people to the main content. It's a bit exhausting being seen in one way, but I love to travel and try new foods so I can't exactly complain about it. Online makes more money than print now and my face makes the magazine advertising money so they can print the stuff they like, too.

We discuss what's needed before we arrive on location but a lot of the shots will be about reacting to what's in front of us. Cam is a pro and we get on well. Everyone calls Camron, Cam. Cam the camera man. Sometimes just Camera. He doesn't seem bothered in the least, and he's the sort of guy who would say if he was bothered by it.

Like me, Cam is perpetually single. Unlike me, I'm sure he is married to his camera and video games. I'm married to my job – as he is married to his – but I'm also married to travel.

'Sorry, Ralph, we gotta retake that one.'

'Seriously?'

'Yeah, someone in the background tripped, staring at the camera and, well... look.'

Turning around, I scan the mayhem behind me. There in front of the pigeon-grey cathedral, a man stands wiping red wine off his jacket while a woman whose face is as red as the wine shakes her head next to him. People are laughing and others act like nothing happened.

This isn't exactly the first time we've had this problem. Usually having a few people looking over is okay for this kind of shoot. We want the audience to get an authentic view. But sometimes people go too far. Or in this case, are too funny to keep in shot. I can only imagine how the wine ended up all over him like that. It's then that I notice a younger girl behind him covered in the sticky potato and cheese mess that is tartiflette. I have no idea how it happened, and with the mood I'm in, I don't want to know.

Cam spent the afternoon getting photos and videos of the city, cutaways, some with me, some without. Now in the late afternoon and early evening it's all about me going up to the various market stalls, asking to try the food before describing it.

I walk along explaining things to the camera about the history of the food sometimes, or how it tastes, as Cam walks backwards holding his Steadicam. Sometimes I talk about local stuff to see or where to find things and enjoy them.

It's busy. We're filming mid week, knowing that the weekend will be worse, but that doesn't mean Rouen's Christmas market isn't pretty packed. It's filled with people from around the globe ready to enjoy the seasonal atmosphere. We could film when there's no one about, but firstly the places wouldn't be open to sell the food and secondly, we would then have no seasonal atmosphere to capture and put all over the internet and in the magazine.

Outside the cathedral is painfully romantic and reminds me of my night with Félicité. The sparkle of the fairy lights taunts me as I remember her coy smile as she presented her city to me, knowing how captivating it is but letting me make my own mind up. Not telling me, showing me, and letting me form my own opinions, ones that would never change her view, I'm sure. It's the same way she was about herself. She wasn't shy or bashful either clothed or naked. Félicité seemed comfortable in her own skin, and it was up to me to make up my own mind about her. As with the city, my opinion wasn't going to change the way she felt either way. Or that's how it seemed to me anyway. She was poised and confident as she screwed my brain up into a ball and threw it in the bin without even batting an eyelid.

I suck in a deep slow breath for four counts, hold for four counts, release for four counts, hold for four counts then repeat, before turning back to Cam. The calming breathing technique is something I adopted after Benedict died so I could keep my shit together. It's not something I use all that often anymore, but the lack of sleep for two nights and, Félicité... Her words, her body, have left my nerves tingling and broken, firing off signals that overwhelm my brain without warning. I don't exactly need the damn fight-or-flight response right now in a Christmas market surrounded by people in soft woollen hats, Christmas jumpers and puffer jackets, with most of them smelling of creamy chocolate or spiced wine as they look at trinkets and candies. Nothing here should make me want to run or fight. Everyone's content, everyone except me.

'Just say when you're ready, boss,' Cam's voice calls across, and his eyes adjust under his glasses to look back at the camera. I reset myself to weave amongst the people and we start all over again. But as my mouth is saying, 'This might not be the biggest Christmas market in France, but what it lacks in size it makes up for in character...', my brain is wondering whether Félicité will show up outside the cathedral tonight, and if she does, what in the hell am I going to say to her? Worse, what if she doesn't?

The take goes well. God knows how with my mind racing, but at least no one in the background did anything crazy this time. We do it another time just in case before we go on to pick a few stalls, mostly the ones with sellers who speak good English, and chat about what they're selling before Cam asks about the clock. No, the big-gold-clock just like Félicité said.

'Sally emailed me some info so that you can talk about it and the bar under it. It's a good place to chat about the atmosphere and get some of the culture and what not.' Cam hands me a carefully folded square of paper from his coat pocket. 'She emailed it to you too, I think.'

'I didn't get it.'

Sally is one of the editors for the magazine. My editor and organiser. She didn't forward this to me. She's great but sometimes forgets to CC me in on stuff.

'It's okay.' My eyes flick towards the street that leads to the clock. 'I already know what I'm going to say.'

As we follow in the footsteps that Félicité and I took two nights before, I try to conjure her voice telling me a few facts about the clock. *Le Gros-Horloge*, she called it. It's not long before Cam has me sitting at the same table where she and I sat, and regurgitating her facts about the mechanism and being the oldest working clock in Europe.

When he laughs and asks how the hell I know all this, he stops me as I open my mouth to answer. 'Don't tell me. Night one and some girl told you. Don't know why I asked.' His shoulders rise and fall in a jolly laugh before he goes to get some shots of the clock in the moody evening light.

It niggles at me. It shouldn't, but it does. Some girl. I've spent every day since Benedict's death living the way he would want and I've not been shy about it. But I don't like Félicité being piled in with all the rest. It's stupid, because it was just another one-nighter. She's just another girl. So why the hell can't I please stop thinking about her?

Tiredness and my stupid mixture of excitement and anxiety slow the last bits of filming. I make silly little mistakes, tripping over words, and we have to retake way too much. We get there in the end. I make my excuses not to go for a drink with Cam. His heavy features scrunch at me with disappointment. Normally I would. He's asked a couple of times if there is something going on with me. He's a good guy. Sadly, every time I try to think about anything else, Félicité's name and ensuing questions slosh about in my head.

By the time I'm ready to wait outside the cathedral, I'm late. Maybe too late, because she's not here. Not that I can see her between the pigeons pecking at the cobbles, and clusters of people still mulling around the stalls.

I pace along outside the imposing wooden doors of the impressive building. The rows of statues and gargoyles on the façade have seen me walk backwards and forwards half a dozen times, and now I'm standing on the steps next to the entrance of a little courtyard where there's a free Santa's grotto for kids. Santa's left now; it's getting past bedtime for his target audience.

With every passing minute, I tell myself I'll give up the wait, that this isn't fate, that it was a coincidence that resulted in exactly what I wanted: sex. But I'm still here waiting and it's now eight thirty-five.

She isn't coming.

At the pace of an *escargot*, I begin to make my way back to my hotel, squeezing past the people in the queue for the roast chestnuts, to walk in the direction of the clock. Félicité's clock. I know that's not what it's called, but that's what I'll be calling it in my head from now on. Echoing her words and facts earlier made me believe she would show. She dug her claws in so deep and we were only together a matter of hours. In part, it's the words she used, Bennie's words, but there's more than that.

Before she even came out with all that, there was something different about her. I guess most girls know who I am from my job, or find out along the way, and sort of throw themselves at me. But my date with her was almost like she was allowing me to see her. Showing me a side that she doesn't usually reveal. Other women are so needy, asking when they can see me again and surprised when I have to kindly explain the answer is never.

Even in my head I sound ridiculous. My skin crawls at the idea that I'm being needy and everything Bennie told me not to be and everything he never was. I need to channel his energy again. Protect myself.

People skirt round me as I stop just in front of the clock, my head all the way back to look up at its face. Félicité's clock, shining with its bright, golden face under the rows of Christmas lights that line the streets. A shiver runs the length of my spine.

'Hi, excuse me. Are you Ralph Williams?'

I look down to see a blonde girl with plumped-up lips and a chiselled face looking at me through wide blue eyes.

'That's me.'

'I knew it! I love your articles. I've been following you on Insta for years.'

She dips her eyes and pouts her glossed lips. She's attractive enough. This is good, I need to take my mind off Félicité, because she isn't interested in seeing me again anyway. And honestly, I deserve that. After years of not wanting to see any girl more than once, of course the one time I do want to see someone again, they don't want to see me. It's simple karma.

'Do you want to join us?'

The girl indicates a brunette sitting at the same table Félicité and I sat at before. She has done her make-up and hair in the same way as the blonde. They could almost be sisters, but I bet they're not. They're more like clones, trying to look how magazines like mine tell them to look and act.

It's gone beyond boring. Félicité isn't like that. She is real, tangible. There is a slight kink to her nose and her skin is pale. She doesn't look the same as anyone else I've met. She has no need to paint her body and hide it or pretend to be someone else. Something about hiding behind trying to be someone else feels like I'm being tapped on the shoulder. Like Benedict is behind me, asking me if I'm doing that with him. If I've been doing that for the past four years, hiding in his shadow and pretending to be him because that's easier, almost like he's still with me walking me through life.

I smile at the blonde girl. 'It's really nice to meet you, but I actually have somewhere I need to be. Have a lovely night.'

And with that, I turn around and start to walk in the direction of Noëlle's town house.

Chapter 15

Félicité

Of course the boulangerie is shut today. It's probably been shut for at least an hour. I don't know why I even thought it might be open.

My hands scrub my face, trying to wake myself up and make sense of the world again. Where's the nearest place to get some bread? I walk in a dizzying circle like a dog settling for sleep. I'd love some sleep. I can't sleep. Food needed. It takes a moment to find my bearings. I know these alleyways, come on, think.

The streetlights and the Christmas decorations shouting from every shop front, even when the shops are closed, are overwhelming. It's all too cheery. Everything's blurry and smeared as though I've rubbed my eyes with oil. There's a Carrefour a street over, that should still be open.

'Félicité?'

In my daze, there's Ralph gazing down at me.

'What are you doing here?' It sounds like I'm accusing him of being alive when he shouldn't be. It's not polite. My brain vomited words before I had time to think them through. His face collapses like a dejected puppy, but I don't have the energy to do anything about it.

'I was looking for you.'

'I'm sorry, Ralph, I am. But I need to buy some bread.'

I begin to walk, realise I'm going the wrong way and turn to go back on myself, only to bump against Ralph's chest.

'Get away from me.' My voice is shrill and I push him back.

'What the hell?' He takes a few steps back and I see a few people stopping. A woman in a red coat, maybe only in her early twenties, steps forward and asks if I need help. I reassure her, but I can feel the tears collecting in my eyes.

I turn back to Ralph. 'I'm sorry, it's–' I cut myself off. I can't bring words to my lips.

'Has something happened? Is it Noëlle? It is, isn't it?' Ralph takes a cautious step towards me and his hand presses over his lips like he's holding back any more questions.

No matter how hard I swallow, the tears won't subside. My head rapidly bobs up and down like a buoy caught on the waves and being dragged out to sea, as tears stream down my cheeks. I've been holding it in. Holding it together. Calling people, sorting things.

Without another sensible thought, I press my forehead against Ralph's chest and sob. I don't know this man. Not really. I've seen him in his entirety, but I know nothing of his life, his dreams, his past, his future. Yet here I am, pressing myself to him once more, now in a completely opposed but oddly equally intimate act.

Ruby was so kind to me yesterday. Another stranger, she stayed with me and took me back to Mamie's house before she had to get to work. I was grateful for her time and patience while I sorted myself out, before I had to be alone in the town house. It wasn't until after she had gone that I realised she had paid for the whole extremely expensive yule log. I need to make sure I get some money to her for it.

Ralph's fingers weave into my hair and he holds me tight.

'Come on, let's get you some bread.' His voice melts into my ear.

Something about his practicality reflecting my own makes me laugh in spite of my pain.

'That way.' I point over his shoulder and wipe my cheek with my fingers. Removing his hands from me, he digs into his pockets and pulls out a packet of tissues, passing me one. We begin to walk together towards the Carrefour. He stays close to me, as close as he could be without actually touching me. We aren't a couple, and he owes me nothing, but having him here is the same comfort as a loyal dog, there just in case.

'What happened? Is she...' Ralph's voice trails off.

'No. No. Hospital.'

'Good. I mean–. You know what I mean.' There's a pause, 'You know what I mean, right?'

I nod my head, but this conversation is too much for me right now.

Nothing more is said until we are in the shop. Ralph scoops up a basket and turns to me, 'What do you need?'

He carries the basket for me and shadows me around the shop as I put bread, wine and fresh tomatoes in the basket. I can't think what else to add.

'I think that's it.' I gaze at the three items.

Ralph's eyebrows knit together as he looks down into the almost empty basket. His nose twitches then his eyes dart about as he begins to fill it with more items, some croissants, cheese and a host of vegetables, cream, and finally a large Milka chocolate bar. He then marches to the counter to pay.

'Let me take my things out.' I grasp for the basket, but he tugs it away from me.

'No,' he pulls it out of my reach.

If I go for it, I run the risk of knocking it into the old man paying in front of us. 'I can pay for myself.'

'No one said otherwise. I know you can. But I'm getting this. You can get the next one.'

'There won't be a next one.'

Ralph doesn't reply, but I also stop arguing because I haven't eaten properly for forty-eight hours now and I'm too tired to argue the point.

Ralph walks me all the way back to Mamie's. I don't invite him in, but he just comes in with the shopping bags. He follows me all the way into the house and begins opening cupboards in the kitchen. He rattles around finding saucepans and chopping boards, plates and olive oil. He does everything I need without a word and without me asking.

I curl up on the dining room chair opposite the space where Mamie always sits. I close my eyes, but that's worse because then I'm back to seeing her in a helpless heap on the floor.

'No allergies, right?'

My eyes open at the muffled sound of Ralph's voice. His head's in a cupboard. When I don't reply he pops it out to look at me.

'No. No allergies.'

Ralph is still in his coat and scarf. As he pushes at his sleeves, it's like he has noticed this too, and he divests himself of the coat and scarf. That's when my eyebrows lift at the sight of his vivid blue jumper with a cartoon reindeer on it.

'It's for work.' His cheeks turn a similar colour to the reindeer's nose before he goes back to what he was doing.

'I didn't say anything.'

'Didn't have to.'

Instead of thinking about what's happened here in the last two days, or even Ralph's surprising jumper, I message Henri again. Milo has been doing better. He's managed to keep down some toast for a day or so now and is watching some TV. It seems Henri was right; it was a twenty-four-hour thing and nothing more. Henri is now sure that Milo is just playing up to it so he can live on bread and watch whatever TV he wants. Which is a huge relief.

Henri has said the right things in regards to Mamie, and asked if I needed anything. I politely declined knowing that even if I said yes, he would be more in the way than actually helpful.

My brother, Pierre, is coming back from South Africa, but he won't arrive for another two days. It's hard to get a last-minute flight just before Christmas. My cousins all have jobs and commitments, so won't be here right away. Mamie's not dead. She's only in hospital. *Only.* My mother, Carole, said she'll try to change her flight, but I hope she doesn't. Urgh. Papa is working in Africa too at the moment, and I couldn't get hold of him or Lizzie, my stepmother. Mamie and my papa have always got on well. I think she gets on better with him than she does her own daughter. He isn't due back in France for another week, but at least he'll be here with Lizzie then.

I place my phone back on the table in front of me and watch as Ralph unwinds a hand blender and looks about for a socket to plug it into.

Without thinking, I speak in my native tongue. 'Why are you doing this?'

'*Désolé, je ne comprends pas.*' His reply – Sorry, I don't understand – in perfect French triggers a laugh to splutter out of my lips.

'Said in perfect French.'

'Thanks. I can do the same in German, Italian, Spanish and Japanese. What did you say before I impressed you with my linguistic prowess?'

The smile lingers on my face and in my bones, settling back into my question.

'I asked why you're doing all this for me. I know you said you wanted to see me again, but even that I can't understand. I had you pegged as the sort of guy who likes to keep his distance.'

'What made you think that?' Ralph turns back to the pot and stirs the vegetables in the pan of bubbling water, before splashing in some cream. The room begins to fill with a rich onion smell. Ralph doesn't look back at me while he waits for his answer.

'The way you were looking at Ruby and grinning at how forward I was. I'm not sure why, I'm just sure I'm right. You confirmed it for me anyway. You said something about not seeing women more than once. No, you said girls. I know because I hate that.'

'Yeah, I guess I did say that. You were right about me all along then.' Ralph switches on the hand blender which forces the conversation to stop. The screaming of the mechanism takes over as he presses down into the pot and purées the vegetables.

The noise stops, but we don't pick up our conversation. Instead, I turn back to my phone and reply to the new barrage of messages that have arrived and spend another five minutes trying to get through them all. I let him get away with not answering my question. I guess I don't know if I want to know the answer or not. It's nice just to let someone look after me for a change.

'Here.' Ralph places a bowl of steaming soup in front of me. It's a mixture of onions, carrots and garlic among other items. 'It's comfort food. If you want something cooked, I mean a proper meal, I'm happy to make something else, or go to the market and–'

'This looks delicious. Thank you. In all honesty, I'm grateful to eat anything.'

My phone buzzes and Henri's name flashes onto the screen. Ralph is hovering over me, and can easily see it. He turns away and goes back to get the wine and two glasses, then returns for the baguette, knife and board.

He drags back Mamie's chair and sits in it before popping the cork off the bottle and glugging a small amount of wine into each short glass. That's my favourite sound, the glugging of wine. It's usually linked to happy times and memories. Not today.

Before taking a sip, or picking up his spoon to eat the soup he has served out for himself, he watches me sip at the piping hot soup. It's seasoned to perfection and the flavour has just the right amount of sweet and savoury. The vegetables are in complete harmony. I suppose you don't get to be a food critic unless you know your way around a kitchen yourself.

An involuntary sigh vibrates in my lungs, and it's only then that I see Ralph's muscles relax. He picks up some bread from the board he's put between us and dunks it straight into his bowl. Before putting it to his lips he says, 'Can you tell me what happened with Noëlle now?'

Chapter 16

Félicité

Guilt ripples over my skin. I should have walked her into the house. I shouldn't have been with Ralph that night. The last time I felt guilt like this I was a teenager travelling with Papa, Lizzie and Pierre across Africa. We spent July and August travelling and working with small schools. We were in a small village and there was a boy I liked. I wandered away with him. I was determined that Pierre was not to come with us. I'd screwed my fists into balls and narrowed my eyes until he left us alone. Pierre and I had been told to stick together, but I wanted to get to know Kofi, with his coffee-coloured skin and inviting eyes. When I got back, Pierre was in so much trouble for leaving me, and apparently everyone had been looking for us. Pierre was so distressed he ended up hurting himself. To this day and until I die my skin will wash with the angry red of regret each time I think about that time. I didn't even speak to Kofi again. We had one stolen kiss and that was that.

Finishing one mouthful of creamy soup, then another, I process what Ralph has asked. I don't want to let a stranger into my life but I also really need someone to talk to, and I'm irrationally drawn to him. His eyes are softer than they were last night. They'd been sharp with desire, almost angular. Now they seem somehow rounder than before.

I try to say simple words and keep my emotions under my ribcage. Put simply, my mamie had a fall and hit her head. She caught it on the nightstand, knocking over her lamp and pulling her night clothes off the bed. It seems likely that she drifted in and out of sleep, or perhaps consciousness, until I arrived home. Mamie was disorientated and seemed pleased to see me, as though she hadn't seen me earlier in the day. She didn't seem to understand the situation and wasn't able to tell me herself what had happened. I had to deduce it all and piece it together.

I called the emergency services and did all the normal things that you do when an incident occurs. It was only when a doctor came to see her in the hospital with her medical notes that it was explained to me that she would need a blood test to see if she'd been taking her medication. I had no idea about any medication that she might be taking. Apparently, she's been prescribed tablets for dementia for over three years. They caught it early and taking medication can slow the onset, so the doctor told me, but that's no use if she can't remember to take it. Or worse, if she forgets she's taken it and takes too much. The results were that there were traces of the medication in her blood, but not at the level the doctors would expect.

Seeing Mamie frail in bed with a cut on her papery white skin, barely knowing where she was, felt like the Eiffel tower had fallen on my head. Nothing made sense. Nothing makes sense. I'm no fool; we all age, and I know she isn't going to live forever. I'm perfectly aware that she's an old lady and that this isn't exactly early-onset Alzheimer's. But knowing something is very different to seeing your rock crumbling there in front of you.

I do my best to calmly say all of this to Ralph. Every time there's a chance more tears will burrow their way out of my tear ducts, I thrust food down my gullet. Aggressive chewing is now the only thing I have control over.

Ralph only interrupts to ask sensible, thought-out questions, such as, do I know when she'll be home?

'No. I think she'll be back tomorrow. I'm not sure. It was too much to take in.' I push my empty bowl away from me, wishing I could push thoughts from my mind instead. None of this was meant to happen this way. This week was meant to be filled with little trips to town and maybe a trip to the cinema. Relaxing together and catching up.

'Are you alone? I mean, I know you are right now, but is anyone coming to be with you?'

There's something about the way Ralph's eyebrow raises and the slight flick of his eyes towards my phone that gives me the impression this question is a little loaded, like he wants to know the answer for more reasons than my comfort, but perhaps also for his own.

'I stood you up.' The words cut out of me and sit starkly in the air between us. With everything that's happened, I'd completely forgotten about the time or the day, let alone that today he was hopeful to see me again.

A smile glances over his lips. 'I forgive you.'

'Lucky me.'

My sarcastic tone and the twist of my lips into a smile raises a small snort of laughter from him, which in turn makes me almost beam against my pain. 'My brother should be here tomorrow. He lives with Ruby, the maitre d' from the restaurant.'

'I got the impression she was single.' His eyebrows furrow and he scoops up our dinnerware.

'She is, I think.' There's a niggle. A pang of something that makes me add, 'Why? Bored of me already?'

Ralph chuckles at my childish jibe as he rinses out the bowls in the sink, but he doesn't rise to my question.

A message flashes on my phone from Henri. He wants to know where I keep the garlic press. I quickly type a reply and hit send. Ralph carefully places the bowls to drain. It's not like me to sit back and let someone else do everything, although this is the one house where it can happen a little more than usual. Not so much in recent years of course, more when I was a child.

Memories of sitting at this very table with Mamie and Grand-père discussing the most recent strike action and putting the world to rights pour over me. All as Mamie slow-cooked something or other, often wild boar rillettes, filling the house with the smell of garlic and gamey flavours. That was a Christmas tradition. Usually with Pierre to my left always playing devil's advocate and saying the opposite of anything anyone else had to say. It was all fun, all loud voices and love. Now those times are memories, and this December doesn't even feel close to those times. It's as if this house is made of paper now, slowly disappearing into a void of Christmas cards and decorations.

I stand and nod towards the living room. 'Come and sit on the sofa.'

We move to the adjacent room. I carry my wine glass and Ralph carries his. I do my best to stifle a yawn as I sit down, then Ralph joins in and yawns behind his glass too.

Looking into the dark red of the wine reminds me of the dried blood over Mamie's head and a shiver pulses through my body.

'What is it?' Ralph's squinting at me over his glass now, his angular jaw tense. How can he read me so well?

I take a slow breath before answering. 'It's the colour of the wine. It made me think of the dried blood on Mamie's face. Oh no, I haven't sorted her room. I need to clean it up in case she can come home in the morning. I should've done it yesterday, but I haven't been thinking straight and half my time has been spent replying to messages from my family.' My head falls back and a groan echoes from my chest into my gullet. 'I hope she'll be out of hospital soon. I want the house ready and for things to be normal again. They're only keeping her in for observation, in case she's much worse than we realise, not because she's hurt. Usually, they would send her to a convalescent home, but as she'll be coming home with me there's no point moving her around so much. They seemed confident it would be tomorrow.'

I lean forward to place my glass down on the coffee table, but Ralph catches my wrist with his free hand.

'You need to rest. You're in shock. You've had a lot to take in. Rest now, and I'll help you clean up later.'

'Why are you here, Ralph?' I snatch my arm out of his grasp. 'If you think that by staying you'll get some rerun of the other night, I can assure you that won't happen.'

His eyes flick over my face as the muscles of his jaw create harsh lines over his face.

'We don't know each other, but if that's really what you think, if that's *really* the impression I've given you, then I should leave now.'

Ralph carefully places his wine glass on the table next to mine. He takes one last look into my eyes but I'm unable to speak. I'm more knotted up than the Christmas lights and I feel strangled by the mess. I want to be held and reassured and I'm sure it's only that I want it from Ralph because he is here, and no other reason.

'Goodnight, Félicité. Please send my best wishes to Noëlle.'

He presses his hands into his knees and stands. I let him get to the door before the thought of being alone is too much for me. I'm never alone. I'm lucky if Milo lets me go to the toilet uninterrupted. It's what I'm used to. I've never lived alone, I've never functioned without thinking about someone else. One of the reasons I couldn't sleep last night, or the one before, was because the house was full of absence, of creaks and moans.

'I'm sorry. Wait... I do want you to stay.'

Chapter 17

Félicité

Ralph returns to me without a negative word, although I'm sure the reindeer on his jumper is giving me a dissatisfied look.

He sits down next to me with his elbows resting on his knees and his chin on his hands. The lower half of his face is covered by his fingers as though holding back unsaid words. I want to say sorry for snapping, but I seem to have lost the ability to talk.

'What's with the naked tree?'

My eyes follow his gaze into the corner of the narrow room. There stands Mamie's petit tree, ready and waiting for the decorations to lace its wobbly branches and delicate needles.

'We would normally....' The word I want escapes my tired mind and I wave my arms in front of me miming placing tinsel.

'Decorate?' Ralph correctly offers.

'Decorate. We decorate together. Actually, she watches as I hang everything and she will go over the stories for each little item.'

'Sounds like a lovely tradition.'

'It is. It used to be all ready for us, me, my brother and cousins. Mamie and Grand-père would still fill the house with stories, though. Sometimes picking out one ornament and telling its tale, or recounting a Christmas from when our parents were young. But these things, they change.' I stare blankly at the branches and wonder what will happen over the following days. Will she recreate this scene with me? Will this be one of the last times before she doesn't have any more stories to tell? 'And you, Ralph, what are your traditions from home?'

An absent smile spreads across his face and he sucks air in through his teeth as he pulls his weight back into the sofa and sinks into Mamie's thick orange cushions with frayed edges.

'To be honest I'm not big on Christmas. I usually spend the day with my parents in Devon. We take their dog, Tilly, for a walk next to the sea in the morning before opening the presents.'

'And when you were a child?'

Ralph's eyeline drops to his hands in his lap. The smile remains but it's not as natural as it was. He opens and shuts his mouth before looking up at me with a distant smile.

'Used to go out on Christmas Eve-Eve with my mate Benedict.'

'I don't know this "Eve-Eve"?'

Ralph chuckles before explaining it's the night before Christmas Eve. Apparently, it's become a norm in England to use this term for the date.

'And do you still go out on Christmas Eve-Eve?'

'Every year, I still go out every year.' Ralph's voice comes out soft and raspy.

'You must be very good friends.'

A hum of distant acknowledgement sounds behind Ralph's lips before his hands slap down onto his legs. He shifts his weight and turns his torso to face me. 'Are you usually here for the big day? Didn't you tell me before you're only in for a week or so?'

The big day. Here in France, it's not the biggest of days. When I was growing up it was more about New Year's than Noël in many ways. And the sixth of January with *la Fête des Rois*, and who would find the figure in the galette and be crowned the king? Milo loves that tradition too. But for the last seven years, Noël – Christmas – has all been for Milo. Nothing else. My papa and Lizzie visit. Papa bakes us fresh *pains au chocolate* that he prepares the night before. We all dip them into the thick dark liquid of rich hot chocolate before Milo can't wait a moment longer to get his hands on the goodies under the tree. If I tell Ralph that now, I'd be telling him about Milo.

I swallow in a dry throat weighing up my options. My son is no secret, but I don't know this man well enough to let him know about the most precious person in my life. I never even intended to see him more than once.

'We have a small family Christmas, usually, back in Carnac. My papa bakes *pains au chocolat*. We have other traditions here though. It is more important to be crowned king on *la Fête des Rois* than Christmas Day.'

'Ah yes, I know about that one because it involves food. I know most traditions that involve food. The galette is a frangipane tart, right? With puff pastry.' My head bobs in appreciation of his knowledge as he continues. 'Then there's the *fève*. It used to be a bean but now it's a figure or something. Am I right?'

'Is all your French connected to food? We could speak my language as long as we talk about dinner. Oh, and of course to tell me you don't understand me.'

Ralph's laugh fills the air. Talking to him is comforting. Easy. Being around him is easy. Perhaps it's the removal of expectation. When something is a *date*, it feels pressured. We have no such aspirations and so no fear of the future or the what if. We can just be comfortable with each other. We have already seen each other naked and tasted each other's skin on the tips of our tongues. There's nothing left to hide behind. It's refreshing.

'I want to hear more about your traditions. Any chance you could show me some of these decorations? Tell me some of the stories?'

I move off the sofa and kneel down in front of the Christmas tree. Some needles have already begun to lace the floor. I must remember to hoover them up before Mamie is home. I want the place to look perfect for her.

In the meantime though, Ralph distracts me with questions about old baubles. We laugh together over our wine at stories of my childhood and my parents' childhoods. Stories of mishaps or travels that brought each decoration into the house.

As time drifts past us, it's Ralph who looks at his watch and announces that the hour is late. I know it's late, I just don't really want to be alone. Ralph has been the perfect escape from everything in my head.

He looks over at me. He's still on the sofa and I'm now on a chair next to the tree. His expression is sombre and serious as he says, 'I can stay if you'd like.'

Without thinking, my head is nodding at the thought of him here with me.

He says, 'I'll get us some water and we can sort out Noëlle's room before we sleep.'

Before we sleep. I wonder if he used those words to show me his intentions are honourable. I guess I'll find out.

Chapter 18

Ralph

This woman has my stomach in knots in a way I can't explain. I know I should leave. I should run. Love equates to pain. The evidence is right there in front of me. She is in pain because Noëlle, a woman she clearly worships, is unwell. There's no way I can cut out those I love already – my mum, my dad, Benedict's little sister Clarissa – but I don't have to add more people and more pain to this journey through life. Why am I even thinking of love? I've only just met this girl. I don't love her. I just have some building infatuation because she's confused me.

I look at the gold face of my watch to see it's almost eleven. No more excuses, no more stories. It's time to go.

'Wow, I can't believe the time.' Looking up from my watch I see her looking at me. She's all alone and her navy eyes look mournful. All I've done is glance at my wrist. 'I can stay if you'd like.'

What the hell am I doing and why does being around this woman always leave that question lingering in my mind? What the hell am I doing?

At this rate I'll be down on one knee begging to stay. Don't joke about that, not even in the confines of thought. I made a promise four years ago and I have every intention of keeping it.

Félicité's head bounces with agreement and her eyes glisten with the warm glow from the overhead light. I have to stay. I can be a good friend to someone. It's still within my realms of capability, even if most of the people I call friends likely call me an acquaintance. Maybe not Cam. We spend enough time together to be mates. Unless we're just work colleagues.

'I'll get us some water and we can sort out Noëlle's room before we sleep.' And with that I head towards the kitchen to gather up my thoughts.

This place can't have more than two bedrooms, or maybe three. If it's three, I'll grab the spare because keeping my hands off her would be hard and I don't want to take advantage of a vulnerable woman. I don't need more hanging on my conscience for the rest of my life.

I follow her, trying not to stare at her bum as we make our way up the winding staircase. Instead, I grip the wooden banister, shiny and smooth from wear, and blankly look at the photos lining the walls.

I wonder if she's been at the hospital all day long. She might be in the same clothes from two days ago. I can't be sure. I remember the cream jeans and how nicely they show off her legs. Focus. At least I'm not in line with them as we get to the landing.

'This is her room. *Merde*, the lamp's still on.' Félicité switches on the overhead light and marches in to turn off the lamp. The whole room is neat and tidy. The timber frames are painted a coffee brown and the walls are pale green. Noëlle's floral bedding is half on the floor and covered in blood.

'Didn't you come in here last night?'

The question stops her in her tracks.

'No, I... I couldn't bring myself to come up here. I slept downstairs.'

Félicité begins to tug at the sheets, trying to strip the bed.

'Stop. Félicité, stop.' I place my hands on her arms and I can feel the tension in her body relax a little at my touch. 'I'll put these in to wash. I've stayed in enough Airbnbs that I'm sure I can work it all out. You go and have a shower.'

'There isn't a shower. It's broken. There's only a bath.'

'Then have a bath. You need to look after yourself so you can look after Noëlle. Trust me. If you're falling apart then she'll have no one to lean on.'

Félicité puts down the covers and turns to face me.

'Thank you.' Her voice catches in her throat and her eyes shimmer in the lamp light.

She reaches up and cups my face with her hand. There's an urge to shift my mouth towards it and kiss her palm. Instead, I smile and tell her to start running the bath.

Only when she leaves the room do I consider the fact I have no idea what I'm doing. It's not that I can't strip a bed, I'm not completely useless, but I should organise as much as I can for her and I don't know where anything is kept. I guess I'll work it out one step at a time.

As I gather everything that has blood on it and take it down the stairs towards the kitchen, my mind settles on Bennie. When we were kids, I mean, really young, maybe seven or eight, he would invite me over to his nan's. I was a kid, so I didn't ask questions that didn't involve Lego, superheroes or football. I didn't really give two shits about much else. That's the nature of being a child,

I guess. His nan was brilliant. She let us have sweets and play outside near the street. My mum would've gone up the wall if she had known.

We liked it because we would look for bugs or wander around the streets to see who was about. It was only when we got older that I found out why he was always at his nan's and not much at home when I was invited over. His parents would argue. Not how mine would argue now and then, but in a way that seemed to stem from pure hate. I didn't go to his house until I was at least eleven, maybe older. He had stayed over at mine tons by then, and I'd of course been to his nan's loads.

It's not that I hadn't met his parents. I had. One or the other would pick him up from my house and they always seemed pretty normal. I never cottoned on that they were never together when they picked him up. Sometimes his little sister, Clarissa, would be with them. That first time I stayed there, they were on their best behaviour, yet they still used Benedict as a go-between. Clarissa was pretty much ignored. And quiet. Which should've been a sign too. Normally she wouldn't stop chatting given half the chance. When she was at their nan's she would drive us up the wall talking and getting in the way. When we stayed at their house she kept out of the way.

I remember that Bennie's mum would often be in the living room with a glass of wine while his father was in the study. I soon learned that they would talk shit about the other one to Bennie, like *don't listen to your mother,* and *your father's a lazy fool, never be like him.* Then there would be the standard insults of *you're being like your dad.* They both used him to vent, and with all the hurtful words they'd say about each other, it's amazing Bennie was sane. Clarissa always had it easy. If she stayed quiet, she was ignored.

Bennie was a good kid. Better than they deserved. Clarissa was as well. He'd have done anything to make his mum and dad happy. That was his painful memory of love and relationships. Mine is watching them and losing him. My parents seem happy enough, but if they lost me, then where would they be? I know Mum said that if I died, she would kill herself. Bennie's mum made a big scene at the funeral, but didn't really care. That's not fair, maybe she did. Seemed superficial to me though. His nan on the other hand, she was like my mum, I guess. She didn't commit suicide, but she died two days after his funeral. She'd been quietly sobbing into her cotton hanky and I don't think she even spoke to anyone except me. Not even her son, Benedict's dad. She died of a broken heart, I'm sure. It's a real thing. Emotional pain can cause serious stress and damage to the heart. I read an article about it once and know that's what did her in.

Now, as I put Noëlle's bloodied bedsheets on to wash, I need to remember all the hurt, because something about Félicité is catching me out. She's attractive, yeah, but I see attractive girls all the time. There's more to her. She's open. Honest. Cutting. Challenging. I guess in that way she's kind of like Bennie. They're nothing alike really, but there's something there.

I traipse up the stairs and past the family photos again. It's easy to pick Félicité out, even as a kid with her brother and cousins. She's got a way about her that's elegant yet feral. Not a normal combination. Like she'll be holding herself with perfectly put-together poise while her legs are covered in mud. She's unique. I weave up the narrow staircase and away from photos that leave me feeling even more impressed by her.

Back in Noëlle's room, there isn't too much blood anywhere else; it had been absorbed by things I've now put in the wash. There're no clean sheets in any of the cupboards in her room and it's starting to feel peculiar, poking about in someone's wardrobe without asking. It might be the best idea to ask where to find such things.

'Félicité?'

I walk along tracing the line of beams with my fingers. I have no idea where she is. She's in the bath, but where the hell's the bathroom? There's a small toilet downstairs that I used earlier but the only sink was in the kitchen.

'Félicité?' My voice seems so loud in the empty house.

'In here.' I move to follow the sound of her voice.

'Are you in here?' My knuckles carefully rap on the door.

'Come in.'

Come in? I had no intention of intruding on her bath. Now she's said it though, I swallow hard and glance at the doorknob, a shining copper that reflects my face back at me, only warped out of shape.

'I was just wondering where the bed linen is.'

'Oh, it's in the airing cupboard. I'll be out in a moment.'

I should've gone in while I had the chance.

Chapter 19

Félicité

It's only a shallow, practical bath. I'm not in the mood for relaxation with bubbles and candles. I just want clean. Mamie has a jug to wash her hair. I have no idea how she manages this place. It's not the sort of place to grow old in. But then, I suppose if you do something every day, it's just what you do. It's neither hard nor easy. It's habit.

With a towel twisted on my head and one clinging to my body I walk to the door and let Ralph in. There he is in the corridor, presented to me as the door swings away from him. His eyes are as round as Christmas baubles and his mouth is hanging open a little. I'm not sure what he was expecting to see. Either way, I ignore his expression and bring him over to the airing cupboard, picking out sheets almost identical to the ones that were on Mamie's bed.

He leaves in the direction of her room, and I leave for my own, up the next flight of stairs. I get straight into my nightwear. I've only brought simple clothes. I only own simple clothes.

I put on a navy cashmere pyjama set that Mamie gifted me last Christmas. Once dressed, I make my way to Mamie's room to find Ralph. I peek in before he hears or sees me and watch as he smooths out the fabric of the covers. He's done a much better job than I would have.

'Thank you.'

His whole body clenches at the sound of my voice, before he releases and laughs. 'You really made me jump.'

'I noticed.' I prop myself up on the door frame and he moves towards me. At first, I think he might kiss me, but then he stops.

It was stupid to think he might. Instead, he enquires about a toothbrush and sleeping arrangements.

'Mamie always used to have spares.' I turn away, back towards the bathroom and he follows me like a kite on a string. When I find a toothbrush and place it in his hand, he lingers and looks at me from under his neat eyebrows.

'And sleeping arrangements?'

I lick my lips because I don't know how to form my words. I don't want him to sleep in Mamie's room without her permission.

'There's my room or the sofa. The other spare bedroom doesn't have a bed in it. It used to, but M– It's a long story. My room has a double bed. I don't really want to offer Mamie's room...' My palms nip with sweat because I nearly told him that Milo broke the bed by jumping on it.

'I wouldn't take it. I've spent too much time making it look nice for her now.'

This makes me smile. He really has made it look welcoming again.

'If you don't mind sharing my bed...'

'That's fine with me.' Ralph inhales as though he's going to say something else, but then firmly shuts his mouth, only to open it again moments later to say he should brush his teeth.

'Okay, well, I'll be in the room upstairs,' I point towards the curving flight of stairs. An arbitrary movement before turning and leaving him.

As I climb the stairs myself, a gremlin gurgles and bites in my stomach. I'm exhausted emotionally and physically drained. I need a cuddle, but I can't ask Ralph for that. It's bad enough he's staying because he feels sorry for me. This throws all of my strong single mother attitude right out of the window.

Once I'm in my room, the spare room, I snuggle under the covers. The room itself is plain white with black beams but the cover has a pattern of kittens in red-and-green Christmas hats. Mamie purchased it a few years ago for me to use each December. I remember the first time I saw it and how it made me laugh, the way she knew it would. It's quirky, like her. Like her whole house. That was when Milo was a baby; he loves the cats now too.

The door creaks open and Ralph edges in. He presses his lips together in a tight-lipped smile before saying, 'Hey.'

'Hi.'

'Is it okay that I feel more awkward now than I did the other day?' Ralph gently closes the door with both hands as though he's trying to do it quietly so as not to disturb anyone.

'It's alright if you want to leave.' I sit up tall and confident in the bed. He shouldn't feel he has to stay, and I shouldn't have made him feel that he should. 'You've been very kind to me, and my mamie. You don't owe me anything.'

'I know. I'm happy to stay.'

Ralph pulls off his reindeer jumper, followed by his T-shirt. He unbuttons his jeans, and when he's down to only his sharp-white boxers he says, 'Budge up. I thought you said it was okay to share.'

I'm still bolt upright. I slide myself down and burrow under the covers once more, before he joins me, lying on his side to face me.

'I like the duvet cover.' Ralph wrenches his neck to look over it again before coming back to grin at me.

'It was bought to make me smile. Which it does.'

'Noëlle seems like a really lovely lady, from what you translate anyway. I think I'm a pretty good judge of character even if I don't speak the same language as someone.'

'Oh, yes? Well, I suppose you are here with me.' I shoot him a furtive look, trying to hide my thoughts.

A soft, deeply genuine smile creases the corners of his eyes. 'Yes. I am.'

I wiggle down further in the bed to avoid his intense face, and ask a question I know I shouldn't as soon as it escapes me. 'Why don't you have a girlfriend? Or am I being fooled, and you have a wife back in England?'

Based on his social media, I'm quite sure he doesn't. In fact, there's no mention of a girlfriend at all, not that I've had much time to study it. Only when I was waiting to see Mamie. I needed the distraction.

'I made a promise to always be single. I haven't been in a relationship for exactly four years.'

I don't want to tell him that it's longer for me. Although I'm sure it's only the relationship part he has been missing out on, unlike me.

'That's a bizarre promise. Who did you make this promise to? Yourself?'

'Myself... A friend.'

'A friend?' My head pops back out of the cover in surprise, 'What sort of friend would ask you to make a promise like that? They can't like you very much to dominate your life in such a way. It's yours to decide, not anyone else's. Unless perhaps you are desperate to be liked by them, or you want their approval.' I pause as my brain searches for why on earth anyone would make this sort of deal for someone else. 'I don't see you as a man who would make a promise like that. I don't see it. You're using this friend as some – what do the English say? – escaped goat, no scapegoat. Who hurt you so much you would make a promise like this?'

Ralph rolls onto his back and stares up at the ceiling, bringing his arms out from under the cover to fold them on top. This perfectly showcases the shape of his arms and the sharp line of his jaw. He draws in a deep breath then seems to hold it before slowly releasing and holding it again. I can feel my eyebrows beginning to press down over my eyes.

'Are you alright?' My hand slides onto the curve of his arm, near his tattoo. The action makes him twist his head to look at me.

'Yeah. I'm fine. There's just no evidence that a relationship will bring me any happiness in the long run. I've been happy without them.' In the dim light of the bedside lamp, his grey eyes look like Santa's coals. 'What about you?'

'Much the same.' I grin, hoping this will distract him. 'I haven't had a relationship in about five years – not exactly five as you say – but thereabouts.'

Ralph's eyebrows shoot up in surprise, but he doesn't make a comment.

A ferocious yawn leaves me covering my face with the duvet. As I reappear, I divert from the topic. 'I should get some sleep.

Thank you for everything, Ralph. I hope I'll be able to repay you for your kindness.'

I stretch forward to kiss his cheek but he turns to face me and catches the side of my lips. Our mouths snatch back to hover only millimetres away from each other. All the lust and feelings from the other night pulse through me. We were good together, but I know that this isn't the time to slip into something with a man who has openly said there is no future. If it happens again, and after all his kindness today, I know I won't want to let go of him.

Ralph's hands brush across my waist and rest on my lower back. 'You should get some rest,' he murmurs.

But instead of agreeing, our lips collide and melt together. His arms wrap around me, and he pulls me on top of him in a passionate embrace.

I don't want to like him this much.

A strange sound makes me pull away, but I can't think what it is. A strange humming like a bee.

'Is that your phone?' Ralph's eyes dart across my face.

'*Merde.*' I propel myself off him and hunt for my phone. It is vibrating on the floor.

'*Bonjour.*'

I don't recognise the voice on the other end of the line, or the number. The voice starts to explain their reason for calling and within moments I hang up.

'Who was it?' Ralph is there by my side, mirroring my confused expression.

'It was the hospital,' I swallow, even though my throat is as dry as a crisp, 'about Mamie.'

Part Two

Chapter 20

Félicité

One Year Later

'Maman, can we go to Fnac and look at games?' The way Milo says *Maman* sounds like the pin-pon moan of a French fire engine. His wide amber eyes peer up at me from under his woolly Spider-man hat.

'Not tonight, *mon grand*. We need to do some shopping that isn't for you.' Milo hops along the cobbles next to me. He seldom holds my hand anymore. He enjoys the freedom of existing just outside of my reach.

'How did your mathematics quiz go today?' We round the corner to be confronted by the rows of white market chalets in the cathedral square and the Christmas trees neatly trimmed in berry reds and glittering golds.

'How do they get the star on the top of the big trees? Is it with a big ladder?' Milo points up at one of the far trees.

'You answer my questions and I'll answer yours.'

We bank the corner onto the main high street, into the sickly-sweet smell of roasting chestnuts and away from the main market, with its zesty aroma of mulled wine.

'I passed with ninety-four per cent. Now your turn.'

'Probably a ladder. Perhaps an aerial platform.'

'Why?'

'Because that's what ladders are for.'

'Why?'

'Must we play this game?'

'Yes. Why?'

This is a game I never lose at. He tries to catch me out, but I will always find an answer to "why" until he tires of it.

'Because people aren't always tall enough for the things they want to do.'

'Why?'

'Because evolution didn't think we all needed to be tall. Instead, it thought we should make ladders.'

'Why?'

'Ralph?'

'Why did you say "Ralph"?'

I stop dead in the street making someone huff as they quickly weave round me.

It's him. Ralph. I'm sure of it.

He's looking up at *Le Gros-Horloge*, the clock, right where we had our first drink together a year ago.

We haven't seen each other since I was called back to the hospital. Part of me hoped we would, but another part hoped we would not, and we didn't. There's no room in my life for any man other than my son, not yet anyway, and Ralph was very clear that he had no room for a partner either.

'Maman, why did you say Ralph? Ralph isn't an answer. Why have you stopped?'

'I can't remember what shop we need to look in.'

I begin to edge backwards, but it's too late. Ralph tilts his head down and he's looking right at me.

He's walking towards me.

Striding in fact.

A warm smile spreads over his lips, and I have nowhere to hide from this fling from the past. *Please don't say anything in front of Milo.*

'Félicité.' He moves towards me and kisses my cheeks.

'Ralph.'

'Is that why you said "Ralph"?' Milo's loud voice booms out to my right.

Ralph looks down in surprise, as though he hadn't even noticed Milo up until now. Perhaps he hadn't realised we were walking together.

'Yes. Ralph, this is Milo. Milo, this is Ralph.'

'*Bonjour,* Milo. *Ça va?*'

'I am well. Are you English? You speaked English.'

'Spoke. It's spoke, not "speaked", *mon grand.*' I slip my arm round him and rest my hand on his shoulder. The street is busy with people going to and from the market, and in and out of shops, and we have stopped right in the way of everyone like a boulder jutting out of a lake.

'Spoke English,' Milo repeats to correct himself.

'Yeah, I'm English.' Ralph chuckles and rubs his bare hands together against the cold. 'Your English is very good, Milo.'

'Thank you. I am the best in my class. Maman taught me when I was a baby so I could have two languages.'

'Your maman must be very clever.' Ralph's still beaming down at my son, but I'm quite sure he hasn't put two and two together yet. He seems oblivious.

Ralph's attention turns back on me, 'What are you up to now? Can I see you tonight?'

'Why are you here?' I don't mean to sound abrupt, but seeing him has brought up everything I've pushed down for a year.

'To see you.' His voice is steady. 'Sorry, I can see I'm intruding on your time with your...' He pauses and looks quickly from Milo to me. We have the same-shaped face, similar eyes. Although, Milo has his father's nose and full top lip. '...your nephew?'

'Nephew?' Milo sneers. 'What nephew? Maman, who is your nephew?' He slips back into French for the last part.

'Ralph... Milo is my son.'

'Your son?' Ralph's eyes widen. 'You never said you had a son.' His weight shifts from one foot to the next as a group of teens squeeze past him, given little choice or room with the tide of people coming the other way. His arms cross over his chest, tucking his hands under his armpits.

'You never asked.' I don't like the tone of his voice, the accusation, so I meet it with my own. Then I switch into a breezy smile. 'Anyway, Milo and I have some gifts to buy, don't we, Milo? It was nice to see you again, Ralph. Merry Christmas.'

In one swift movement I clasp Milo's hand and we merge into the flow of people and head towards C&A where I saw some nice scarves and gloves in the window a few days ago.

'Who was that man?' Milo chimes up at me, almost skipping to keep up with my pace.

'Someone I met in La Belle Cuisine last year with Mamie. I taught him some things about the golden clock.'

I silently add that Ralph taught me some things about time. How it warps and bends when you keep thinking about someone. I'm sure not for him, not for Ralph. He moved on to the next job and the next adventure, so I gather from his social media. I admit that I have watched his video about Rouen more than once. All my words about the clock poured from his lips like he knew them by heart. Like he had stolen a snippet of me and played it back for the camera. I'm still unsure whether to feel flattered or used.

So much has happened in the past year. It's been non-stop, and everything has fallen on my shoulders. Every moment has been saturated, yet it's been as slow as walking through toasted marshmallows, and just as painful when I wonder about what could've been.

Milo and I moved to Rouen, into Mamie's home, so we could look after her. She was adamant she was fine. The hospital called late that night with Ralph, asking me to come back to say goodbye to her, that she had slipped into a coma and they thought she might not come round. They were wrong. She fought back and was out of hospital in a week.

We didn't get to celebrate her eighty-fifth birthday the way we all hoped. Everyone still visited her around her birthday, but the planned gathering was cancelled. That's why we intend to try again this year to make up for it.

Henri brought Milo to Rouen, instead of me going back to Carnac, and we stayed with Mamie over Christmas until I had to return to Carnac for work. I got to see the real picture of how she was. Some days she was fine but on others she would wake up and be surprised that we were there. It was heartbreaking, and I knew that it was down to me to do something. We've always been so close. She is with Pierre too, and my cousins, but that isn't the case with Carole. My mamie will always love her, take her in, be kind to her, but it's always hard to love a narcissist.

It was around Easter time that we moved back to Rouen. I quit my job and started teaching English online from home. I also mark exam papers too. Anything I can to keep us all afloat.

'Do you think Mamie would like this one for her birthday?' Milo tugs at a red scarf.

'Nice to hear you practising your English.' I smile down at him.

'Can I take my hat off? My head is hot.'

I give him the okay to tug the red and blue hat off his head and thrust it into the deep pockets of his winter coat.

Milo was devastated to leave his friends in Carnac, but he loves his great-mamie enough to have supported every decision we've had to make, and I swear having Milo around has helped her no end. He sees her as *his* mamie, instead of great-mamie, and even simply calls her Mamie. I couldn't be prouder of the way he is with her. He gets her playing board games and reminds her of things she needs to do. Even the doctors said that she's at very least no worse, which I guess is the best we can hope for.

Next week Mamie will be eighty-six. She usually goes with me to do the food shopping and takes us to La Belle Cuisine every week too. I asked after Ruby when we first came back, but apparently she's moved away, to Corfu of all places. Shame; it would've been nice to have a friendly face nearby. She was so kind to me when I fell apart in the patisserie last year.

As it is, most of my school friends are spread out through France, so I'm no nearer to them by moving back to Rouen. All except Bernadette, of course. She's helped me no end, even picking Milo up from school twice a week for me so I can teach more lessons from home.

The thing is, every time it's been too much, every time there was only me to wash the clothes, iron, pick up Milo, sort out Mamie's medication, pick her up off the floor... every time I feel alone, I think of Ralph. I don't need a hero or to be saved. I've been independent from birth. But I can't deny how much I enjoyed having the support of an equal, even if it was just for one night. It was nice to feel looked after and loved. That doesn't mean I believe he loves me, only that as time has passed, I have let myself imagine as much. I have let myself imagine what it would be like to have him here with me. There was something about our connection that has stayed with me and followed me like the Christmas star. I haven't been able to escape the idea of him.

My finger skims the maroon fabric of the scarf held out in Milo's little hands. It feels soft and cosy to the touch, and it has a gold thread running through it. Festive and fun.

'She will love it,' I say.

Milo's cheeks bulge as he grins. He has lost his first teeth and there's a gap in his bottom and top teeth.

We continue round the shops until Milo decides we should go to the market for tartiflette. I'm more than happy not to make dinner and instead to enjoy the warmth of gooey, cheesy potatoes and lardons. Mamie is staying with Pierre tonight. It's a short walk away, but as she said, *it's nice to have a change of scene. It's a bit like a holiday.*

As we walk back down the high street in the direction of the cathedral, Milo chats to me about Marvel characters and a game he made up at school to do with them. As we get nearer to the golden clock, my palms begin to sweat and I can't help but scan the people going past me.

Ralph is still there under the clock, now drinking what is likely to be a coffee. He hasn't seen us. There's a good chance he will as we walk past him. Perhaps not. Perhaps we can blend in. The crowds are thinning out now as the shops are starting to close.

'Look, Maman, it's your friend. What was his name?'

'Ralph.'

'Ralph.' I look down at Milo who is tilting his head at this unknown man, chewing his name over in his mouth and his mind. 'Ralph,' he mutters, before repeating it again. Only this time he stretches open his mouth as wide as it'll go and shouts it out towards him.

Milo has obliterated our chance of sneaking past, as now Ralph, and everyone else, is looking at Milo.

Ralph straightens up and puts on his best presenter smile. I may have watched a few more of his YouTube videos over the past year when I was bored, so the smile seems even more familiar to me. There's no joy, mirth or anything much behind the smile. It's automatic, and he's displaying it for Milo as he bounds towards the table. Apparently, Milo sees Ralph as *his* new friend now. I should've seen this coming.

'You are here still. Are you hungry?' There's barely a breath in Milo's words as he hovers over Ralph's round table. 'We are going to the... *marché.*' I get a sideways glance in question.

'Market,' I confirm.

'Yes, we are going to the market and we will eat dinner. Will you come?' Ralph opens his mouth to answer, but instead of waiting for it, Milo looks up at me, 'Can Ralph come?'

I lick my lips, taking a moment to look Ralph over. 'That's up to Ralph.'

'Am I welcome?' Ralph tilts his head at me. He has dropped the smile he was presenting for Milo and is now completely unreadable.

'Sure.' My shoulder automatically rises and fall in a shrug, but this rips me in two.

On one hand, I've never dated. After my one and a half nights with Ralph, I made the decision to try again and give dating a go. That changed when we had to move house and settle in, meaning it just hasn't happened. Between looking after Milo and Mamie, I've had even less time than ever. On the other hand, yes, I do want to spend time with Ralph. I do want to know why he came all this way to see me. There's no denying I would love to relive our night of passion many times over, but that isn't possible with Milo here. That doesn't stop the intrigue though.

'Are you hungry?' Milo enquires, gently bouncing on his heels, his little gloved hands gripping Ralph's table.

Perhaps Milo misses having a male influence. He's been like this with Pierre since he's been back too. Desperate to talk to him or to tell him things. He wants to play with him and continually seeks his approval.

'Yeah, I am hungry actually.' Ralph pushes his chair back and taps his hands over his pockets to check he has everything. 'So where are we going?'

Chapter 21

Ralph

Six Months Earlier

I've kept my promise to Bennie alive... But things have been different since Christmas. Women who would normally spark my interest have seemed so generic. Dull.

When Félicité vanished from Noëlle's town house, asking me to lock the door on the way out and post the key back through, I was left with a pounding pulse and a disappointment in my chest and... lower areas. It was a good thing probably. I didn't want her to think I was taking advantage, but she's intoxicating. Something about the curve of her mouth and her cashmere-soft skin makes me want to bite her. To hurt her and hold her all at once. It feels like that's what she's done to me; taken a chunk out of me with sharp teeth, right after the perfect Hollywood kiss.

I didn't want to be reeled in, and even though I would deny it to anyone who asked, I know that she brought me way too close to breaking my promise to Benedict.

It was good on every front that she left.

Good that I didn't let myself be around her more.

Good that I stuck myself hard into work and smiling for the camera.

I don't want to break my promise to Bennie, and break myself for someone else.

Never again.

This week I'm doing some filming here in Devon, not far from Mum and Dad's, which has given me the perfect opportunity to see them. Mum keeps saying I've changed, but she can't put her finger on what it is about me.

'Are you depressed?' She looks at me over her thin, teal-framed glasses.

I'm sitting on their kitchen counter the way I would when I was a kid. Obviously, it's a different counter. It used to be red and now it's black, but the action is the same. Mum hates me doing it, but I still do. She stopped telling me she hates it years ago, maybe after Bennie died, because she knows it won't change anything. In spite of her dislike, I think she puts up with it because it's part of me and she doesn't want to put me off popping in when I can. To be honest, I think she'd hate it if I stopped doing it, now. She just doesn't want to admit it.

'It is coming up to five years without Benedict. Is that what's upsetting you?'

At first, I shrug off her question, hopping back down from the counter. It's easy to put all my problems under the umbrella of missing Bennie. Everything always leads back to that clawing, vicious pain.

Eventually she stands in front of me, stopping me pacing about the tiled floor. There's a pause as she dusts nothing off the shoulder of my T-shirt.

'Is it about that silly promise you made before he died? Look, your dad told me about it years ago, and honestly, this isn't what Benedict would have wanted for you. I'm quite sure it isn't what he meant. He was very mixed up about relationships, but had he been given more time on this earth, he would have worked it out. And you needn't blame yourself for his death, because ultimately, that's what it comes down to, doesn't it? You punishing yourself and not letting yourself be happy because you feel like it's all your fault, or because you think it's unfair somehow that you lived. It's all nonsense. Think how Benedict would feel if it were the other way around.'

'Please don't.' I grit my teeth and begin my cycle of breathing to calm myself. Every nerve in my body is beginning to fire and anxiety is creeping in like the ghost of Christmas past. I guess that's exactly what Bennie is now.

'How many times do we all have to say it? It wasn't your fault, my love. None of it was.'

'Please, Mum–'

'No, I need you to hear me, because I can't see you miserable any longer and I want grandchildren one day, do you hear me? You would be a brilliant father too. You're so good with all your cousin's children. You're just cutting off your nose to spite your face.'

'Margret.' My dad gasps as he enters the room. 'Leave the poor boy alone.'

Mum's eyes become as reflective as a mirror under her glasses, reflecting the stark white kitchen spotlights at me.

'I want him to know he is allowed happiness. Someone has to say it. We all knew Benedict and, by Jove, this isn't the life he would've wanted for our Ralph. Never. Benedict looked out for you, and yes, sometimes he pushed you out of your comfort zone – good and bad – but this punishment has to end–'

'I've got to go.' I slide past my dad and hear them both call after me in pleading tones, as though it's me who's gone too far.

I grasp for my keys on the hook and press them so tightly between my fingers that they could easily draw blood.

It's best to take myself away from the house.

Away from them.

As far away from Mum's words as I can get.

I know exactly where to go and who I need to talk to. There's only one person who could remotely understand my feelings right now.

Chapter 22

Félicité

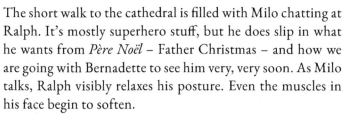

The short walk to the cathedral is filled with Milo chatting at Ralph. It's mostly superhero stuff, but he does slip in what he wants from *Père Noël* – Father Christmas – and how we are going with Bernadette to see him very, very soon. As Milo talks, Ralph visibly relaxes his posture. Even the muscles in his face begin to soften.

Both of them look over at me during this one-sided conversation and smile. They're getting on. It's like I've slipped into a bizarre dream where everything has come together nicely and I have everything mapped out. I remind myself that this is the man who has promised himself never to have a relationship. I have a child to think of, who might seem happy enough right now, but who might have a different idea about things should he no longer be the proverbial man of the house.

As we move towards the market, the archways of brilliant white lights linking the little chalets form the most impressive glittering view, a view enhanced and framed by the Gothic cathedral behind, bathed in warm golden lights to highlight its detailed stonework of figures, creatures and arches.

I'll never tire of this sight. It summarises Christmas. I may live here now, but I don't want to take it for granted. It helps to see it through Milo's enthusiasm. His zest for life is contagious. That's what it is to be six, though, I suppose.

When I wasn't much older than Milo, my father met Lizzie and worked with her to teach English across the world, and we began to learn about the world as a whole, rather than only our tiny corner of it. This has since inspired both Pierre and myself to do the same. We had a new stepmother and they uprooted us in the most extreme sort of way. We arrived in Japan, a place nothing like our home in France, and we began to eat with chopsticks and settle into a new life. Every moment was wondrous and terrifying. I wanted to hate Lizzie, but she loved me more than my mother, Carole. She made us all laugh and whisked us off into the magic of planet Earth. It was impossible not to love her.

As we pass under the blanket of lights, Milo throws his head back, his mouth hanging open. Christmas carols chime around us like a comforting embrace.

I glance at the beautiful things on offer, from handmade jewellery to handcrafted chocolate treats. Ralph isn't watching the lights or glancing at the heaps of saucisson on offer at his elbow as we walk; he's watching Milo. A hint of a smile plays on his face, almost like a laugh is trapped in his stormy grey eyes.

'Have you seen the market before, Milo?' Ralph chuckles before crossing his arms over his chest as he carries on admiring him.

'Yes.' Milo stops walking and snaps his head back into place. To him, this is a ridiculous question. He has walked past it most days since the end of November when it appeared. Milo sounds completely bewildered and even glances at me for some reassurance or answers. 'We live here. Have you seen here before?'

There's a look on Ralph's face like he is on the brink of bursting with laughter, as he presses his lips together in a restrained smile.

Ralph slowly nods. 'Yeah, I have seen it before. Last year. I didn't know you lived here though.' His eyes flick to meet mine.

'We moved here at Easter to help Noëlle.' I cut into their conversation as we turn right to join the queue for food. The smell of bacon and melted cheese is mouth-watering.

Noëlle had already had the paperwork drawn up to gift me the house, her mental state had been checked and deemed well enough. Every detail was already in place, ready to transfer the town house to me not long after she came out of hospital.

Turning to look up at Ralph once more, I open my mouth to speak but close it again when I catch the look on his face. His lips are pressed together, making them thinner than before, as though they have disappeared into his thoughts. It is the same with his eyes. His brows are lowered and his grey-blue eyes look dark in their shadow. It's his turn to open his mouth to speak.

'How–'

'Maman, look! Georges is over there. Can I go and see him?'

'Yes, but come straight back after.'

Milo trots over to his little friend to say hello. Georges and his parents are only a few metres from us, looking at stacks of dry cured meats.

'I can't believe you didn't tell me you had a kid.' Ralph's voice is low, but I can hear him well enough.

'And did you tell me your life story in our one and a half nights together?'

'No, but I didn't lie either. I just can't stand when people hide who they really are.'

'My son is none of your business. I did not lie about him. I kept him safe from a man I don't know.' I stare up at him blankly. His eyebrows have lifted, and there might be some hurt in there, but he quickly shakes his head and softens his sharp features again.

'You're right. I suppose it's different. Why would you have told me.' He momentarily pauses, looking from side to side. 'I'm hoping you're not married though.'

'No,' I snort and turn back to watch Milo as he snatches up free samples of saucisson with his friend.

'Father in the picture?'

'Why are you here, Ralph?'

I twist to look at him again as he flings his head up to the stars and mutters the word, 'Shit', through gritted teeth. 'I don't know, Félicité.' He drops his head and looks at me, perfectly presentable with his gelled hair and smooth skin. It's only his eyes that look messed up, like he's searching for the answer in me, flicking between my eyes. 'Because I knew you'd be here. You told me last year that you come here every year for Noëlle's birthday. I needed to see you, to talk to you, because of something you said, and–'

Ralph gets cut off by Milo bounding back, just in time too, as we are next in line to be served.

'Good timing, *mon grand*.' I ruffle his straight black hair, so much like mine, only softer and floppier when it isn't spiked up. 'You should put your hat back on.'

The couple in front of us move to one side to pay and we are faced with two enormous hot plates, one of them with tartiflette and another with a chicken dish. I can never remember what it's called because I'm only here for the tartiflette. The other is rich and red, and I'm sure delicious too, but we always have the same thing.

'Are we all having the same?' I dart my eyes from Ralph to Milo and they both nod. 'Three large tartiflettes.' I turn back to them. 'Drink?'

'Minute Maid, please, Maman.' Milo's eyes are bulging as the stallholder unwraps another huge circle of cheese to add into the tartiflette mixture, pushing it all about with equally impressive spatulas until it slowly turns to goo.

'Me too, please.'

I raise an eyebrow at Ralph's response, recalling his reaction to me last year ordering one for myself. I say nothing but vow to bring it up later.

While ordering the drinks, I chat to the server, and he also chats away with Milo too. When the overly stuffed plastic tubs and drinks are on a tray for me, I try to balance it to get my purse out, but before I can do anything Ralph passes a few notes across the counter and waits for his change.

The server's red face beams as he looks right at Ralph and says, '*Vous avez une jolie famille, monsieur. Bon appétit!*'

I open my mouth to correct the man, but he's already turned his attention to the next customer.

Milo chuckles to himself and remarks to me in French on the server's comment.

Ralph's voice sounds at my shoulder. 'What did that man just say to me?'

I expel the air in my lungs, not really wanting to tell him, but I know it shouldn't matter.

'He told you that you have a beautiful family.'

A new chuckle follows behind me as we move into the marquee. We head to the side that's filled with benches, many of which are taken. As some people stand to leave, we shuffle into their space.

The walls have plastic pictures of alpine scenes, the snow-covered peaks continuing the festive feel. Tinsel lines every space and berry-coloured bows pinch at the loops and corners. The forecast said snow for tonight, but I'm not sure I believe it. It's bitter enough, but I'm not so sure.

We tuck into the potatoes, cheese and salty lardons. It's luxurious comfort food, perfect for warming us through on this chilly evening. I absorb myself with the rich taste and the creamy texture so that I don't jump on *la grande roue* – the ferris wheel – of wondering why Ralph is here. What did I tell him? What did I say that made him come all this way to see me again?

'Milo,' Ralph begins, 'can you guess my favourite French word?'

Milo's mouth is full of chunky potatoes, so instead of answering, he rapidly shakes his head back and forth.

'Reblochon.'

'Reblochon?' Milo can't help himself; he repeats the words through a full mouth. Then he swallows, and says, 'The cheese?'

'Yeah.'

'That's in this?' Milo stabs his spork down at his little plastic tub.

'Yeah.' Ralph's eyes are creasing at the corners as he stabs at his food just like Milo did.

'But, why?'

'Dunno really. I just like the way it sounds. When I first read it, I hated the way it sounded, because I was saying it wrong.'

'I know why!' Milo loves to be a know-it-all with his English. I was determined to give him two languages. Why not when I can speak two myself? It's such an advantage. 'It is because in English a C and H make a CH sound, and in French a C and H make SH.'

'Yep. Something about that word in a French accent is just fun to say.'

Milo then shares the words he finds fun to say and Ralph laughs along with him as they discuss these very important matters.

They're getting on too well. My mouth falls dry, forcing me to gulp back my juice. It curdles with the cheese and makes me sweat.

I don't want Milo to start getting attached to someone he won't see again. After my one-and-a-bit nights with Ralph, I've spent a year with him in the back of my mind and I don't need Milo asking if or when we will see Ralph again, because he *just has to tell him something* or he *thought Ralph was so much fun*.

'Maman, remember you promised to take me to *la grande roue* tonight. What's *la grande roue* in English?'

'Ferris wheel.' I sip at the last of my drink.

'That sounds like fun.' Ralph pushes his empty carton away. 'Can I come?' He gives me a furtive glance and folds his lips in.

Milo answers for me, telling him, yes, and gushes about how much fun it is. Although, according to Milo, not as much fun as the big fair that was in Rouen in October. That was apparently the best thing ever. He tells Ralph in detail about the rides and games that lined the river those months ago. Ralph beams at him and says how amazing it sounds, and how maybe next year he'll bring his cousin and their kids. He's sure Milo would get on great with them because they're great kids, just like him.

I can feel my skin tingling with an itch. "Next year"? At this rate I'll never find out why Ralph is here, let alone why he would intend to be back again next year too. And what should I do or say if he says he came here because he wants to see more of me?

Because right now the hairs on the back of my neck lift when I think about it.

Chapter 23

Félicité

Here we are, the three of us, standing in the square where Joan of Arc was burned alive. As we watch *le grande roue* slowly circle, my brain feels like it's being burned alive with scorching questions that I'm trying to ignore.

Damn Ralph for being so sweet and charming and getting on so well with Milo. And now, contrary to my prediction, fine flakes of snow are beginning to fall. At least the snow's not settling.

'Maman, look, it's Georges again. Georges!' Milo waves as he calls his friend. 'Maman, can I go on *le roue* with Georges, if his parents say it's okay?'

Georges and his mum and dad – whose names I should know but can't remember – meander over to us. We chat for a moment, and I explain that Ralph is a friend from England but he doesn't speak French. Luckily, they don't ask further questions as the boys start repeatedly asking whether or not they can go on the ride together.

'It's fine with us.' Georges' mum smiles at me with her neat mouth and slanted teeth.

Glancing at all the expectant faces around me, I go ahead and agree.

We walk up to the booth at the foot of the ferris wheel, and this time I pay. Georges' parents get on first, the kids take the next gondola, then Ralph and I settle into one. We are alone on a romantic Christmas fairground ride that slowly ascends to display the eighteenth-century buildings in the square and views across the roofs of the city. As soon as we are seated, I return to the conversation we started almost an hour ago.

'Well, why are you here? Are you stalking me?'

He looks hurt. I can't imagine why a man who claims never to want a relationship could possibly be hurt when he seems to be in pursuit of something he claims not to want.

'Last year, you said something to me, and it messed with my head. Big time.'

I twist to face him head-on as best I can to make sure he can see my expression. To look him in his eyes and show him my confusion without the need for words. If I use words, they'll come out all wrong. I can feel the ball of confusion making me defensive. I have to protect myself because a face like his can lure people to their death... willingly.

Ralph opens and closes his mouth before saying, 'You forced me to promise you some stuff, before we... had our night together.'

It takes me a moment to recall it. It wasn't as cold as it is tonight. He'd been hovering near the museum and something made me want to be sure.

'I did. To have fun... Although I did not force you to do anything.' I lower one of my eyebrows to convey enough inference that he quickly catches my meaning.

'No, you didn't. That's not how I meant it. I just meant... you asked me to promise you "to have fun. If it's not fun, we tell each other".' Ralph pauses, sucking on his lips as he tugs the cuffs of his coat. Then he shuts his eyes and holds his breath before letting it slowly out through his teeth and holding it again. When his words do come, I have to lean closer towards him to hear, and we are in a small space as it is. 'Five years ago, I made my best friend the same promise.'

'You slept with your best friend?'

Ralph blinks his eyes open. The glittering city lights reflect in his damp eyes, but my flippant question has changed his oddly sombre words into a laugh. Nothing chesty or loud, but enough to lift his cutting cheekbones and wrinkle the corners of his eyes.

'No, no. But he made me promise to have fun. Have fun with girls and don't get tied down. That sort of fun. Only be there if it's fun and move on when it isn't.' The smile I gave him slips from his eyes as he falls back to the past. All that's left is sadness traced on the lines of his pointy cupid's bow. 'He walked away from me that night and I never got to say goodbye because some...' There's a catch in his voice. '...some low-life shit wanted to prove himself.'

Ralph's fingers curl in on themselves and he aggressively sniffs, twisting his face as he does.

'What was his name, your friend?'

Ralph sniffs a little again and I'm starting to wonder if it is to thrust back tears or emotions that have been circling him for five long years.

'Benedict. Benedict Morris.'

'And why did Benedict ask you to make this promise?'

'Honestly? I think he was sick and tired of watching people he cared for getting hurt. He was protecting me.'

I nod for a moment even though this makes little sense to me. I look out at the warmth of the city as it slowly edges further away from us. 'What happened to him?'

Ralph watches his fingers as they stretch and flex, contracting them as he speaks. 'Some runt punched him in the face. That was all it took. One punch. Bennie fell back and hit his head on the kerb. Spent the next month in a coma before the machine was turned off.'

'I'm sorry for your loss.'

One side of Ralph's mouth lifts into a minuscule half smile. 'Thanks.' He pulls his shoulder back, as though trying to gain strength again. 'The thing is, four years later and this confident, beautiful French girl demands the same promise of me. And I don't know what the hell to make of it. But there's no way I'm going to back off and not find out. Then, well, I don't know about you, but our one night wasn't like my normal one nights. My nights are usually pretty good, but with you...' His voice trails off as he bites his smiling bottom lip. I can feel the smug blush grazing my cheeks.

'I haven't had as many one nights as you, so perhaps I'm not the best to say.'

A momentary smile, not breaking through to a laugh, touches the muscles in his face. Then it falls slightly. His eyes adjust and he begins to glaze over, staring out into the world and not at me.

'I really am sorry for you and for Benedict.'

'Me too. I wasn't there for him when I should've been.' He snatches a breath, 'I've stayed true to the promise I made, up until now, but I've spent the last year thinking about you, wondering if he sent you to me, and told you to force me into the same promise. Or whether you were right; I was putting all this shit on myself, and it was nothing to do with him at all. You might not remember but you said that too. Although you didn't have the full context then. So, yeah, you repeated his words *and* I liked you. Then I find you again today and you have this kid and even *that* doesn't put me off. If anything, I respect you even more because you were protecting him, and he seems like a cool little dude. Smart too. You must be proud of him.'

'I am. And you're right. I do need to protect him. He is my priority. So, I need to ask... what do you want from me?'

My heart is pounding and even though it's snowing harder around our little bubble in the sky, I feel like I'm sweating in my coat, like suddenly I'm melting next to a cosy fire. My fingers free a hank of hair that's tucked itself under my thin woollen scarf, and I loosen it as best I can.

'A date? I mean, your son has set you up on a date with me whether you like it or not.' Ralph gestures at our surroundings. It couldn't be more romantic, other than our strange conversation.

Flakes of snow fall as we hover above my city like we are one of the clouds. I look out across it all; we're almost at the top of the wheel again now, our second time round before they let us off. We're almost at the point of seeing it all.

Only the snow is clouding the view, and however pretty it is, I'm not sure I can see clearly enough. My lips and face are numb and yet there's a film of sweat around my neck. Milo has set Ralph and me up on a beautiful and romantic date even if it wasn't on purpose. Everything I have thought about this man for the past year has been wrong. Our brief meetings were a snapshot, the close-up corners of a detailed oil painting, one that I could never have anticipated.

I look up at him and see the vulnerability in his face.

'Is that the truth? That you made this promise and for some reason I am the one to break this spell Benedict's death placed on you?'

'Yeah, I mean, yeah. I... You're the only woman who has lingered in my mind. Christ, I'm impressed when I remember someone's name.'

'How charming.'

'I'm just trying to be honest. This isn't exactly easy for me. I'm starting to think this was a crazy idea. I guess I knew that the whole time but I had to see you again. I pushed all ideas of happiness aside in the name of fun. Then there was you and then, well, let's say I've had time to think, I guess. Or rethink. You got under my skin.'

'You don't sound sure–'

'No, I'm not sure.' He cuts me off with wide searching eyes like a fox being chased by a pack of hounds, because the look is different when hunters become prey. And this is different. Ralph's voice is sharp and clear, but his hands are taut in their movements as he talks. His eyes cut through me like scalpels. 'How can I be sure? I met you a year ago and I've had a year of building you up in my head. This confident, caring, hot French girl–'

'Woman.' It's impossible not to correct this and it causes a laugh to splutter out of him before he continues with his wild hands and eyes.

'Yeah, woman, exactly. You know your own mind. You manage to be down the line but have this soft edge with your family. Then there's the promise, that damn promise I made to a friend I swore I'd never break and it's there on your lips being spat in my face.' I lift an eyebrow at this statement and he shrugs before softening himself a little. 'Not literally, obviously.' His shoulders become round, and his eyeline lowers along with his voice. 'It's like I've had this insane dream and you're at the centre of it. If I don't see what the hell this is, or could be, or get you to tell me to fuck right off, at least, then... Then I'll be stuck wondering *what if.* And I already spend half my damn time doing that with Benedict. *What if I'd gone with him? What if he'd stayed with me?* I can't take another *what if.*'

Ralph is crumpled and broken in front of me. I'm not sure I have the strength to put him together. Like him, I don't want a *what if* lingering. Life is too short for regrets, and as we age, we can slowly fill ourselves with them if we're not careful.

Tentatively I nod. I agree.

Snow swirls around us, but I'm throbbing with warmth, except for the tip of my nose and tips of my fingers that are numb under my leather gloves.

'I've thought of you too,' I admit. 'And too many times.'

The ride is coming to an end.

I stretch to look down and see the boys getting out to meet Georges's parents waiting for them. We'll soon be there too. I need to make up my mind.

'Tomorrow. Dinner.'

'What time? Where?' The urgency and relief muddle in his voice.

'Nine.' Milo will be sleeping and so will Mamie. I can ask Pierre to check on them, but I'm sure they'll be fine. The ride comes to a stop, ready for us to depart. 'Here. I'll meet you here.'

Chapter 24

Ralph

Nothing should be left up to chance.

That's one of my many mottos since losing Benedict. It's impossible of course. Each day we step out the door into a world of chance, a world of unknown actions from everyone else we encounter. But, when I have the choice to make decisions of my own, I do. I plan and prepare when it's important to me. Today is no exception.

I don't meet Félicité where she said. Instead, I casually wait not too far from Noëlle's door.

Of course, I'm aware this means I'm running the risk of being a stalker, or being seen as one. It doesn't matter. I've risked everything on seeing this woman again. Shame runs its icy fingers over my skin, but my cheeks still blaze hot at the thought of what's happened over the past six months. I still can't believe I'm here. That I'm doing this.

I glance down at my watch. Eight forty-three. Surely she wouldn't have left already. Maybe this was a mistake. Maybe she's leaving from Pierre's house instead. I have no idea where that is. Did she say it was nearby? I can't remember. If she's not walking out of that door in five minutes, I'll jog to the square where I said I'd see her.

My breath clouds the air around my face. It looks much like the fog that's settled in my mind.

Please let this be the right choice.

Please don't let this be me running away.

It's not. I know that. I think so anyway.

Part of me thinks I need to explain the past six months to Félicité, but the other part needs to see what this really is, outside of what I've built up in my mind. I've spent too long thinking about this, about her, working through all the stuff in my head and then knotting it back together again.

I look back down at the round face of my watch and the seconds slipping by. I think it's time to run. A small squeak alerts me to the door I've been staring at; and there she is, her chocolate hair falling over her scarf, and her full bottom lip touched with gloss that catches the light from the decorations. Félicité sees me and tilts her head as she crosses the road towards me, skipping over the slush left over from the snow.

'I thought we said the ferris wheel?'

She stands so close to me I can smell the fresh spritz of an elegant perfume. Looking up at me, arms folded over her coat and a confused crease between her brows, she waits for me to answer. It takes me a moment longer than it should, because I can't help but feel a pinch of nerves every time I'm near her. It's like I'm hovering at the top of a fairground ride right before bring thrust over the edge. I'm just waiting, knowingly ready to fall.

'I didn't want to leave it to chance.' My voice comes out huskier than normal because I haven't spoken much all day.

A smile brightens her face and she says, '*Il ne faut rien laisser au hasard*. It is a saying that means, nothing has been left to chance. I was only just now thinking this phrase.'

Chapter 25

Félicité

Nothing is to be left to chance.

And so, nothing is.

Not this time. I can't come home to disaster again.

Pierre is waiting at the house and like the good brother that he is, I'm under strict instructions not to come back unless I want to. He will happily sleep in my bed until morning. I've assured him that won't be the case, but I suppose we shall see.

A year ago, when Ralph and I went out for our drink, there was no pressure. There was only excitement and electricity in the air. This is some strange retake as we walk the same way towards the cathedral, under the heat of the white Christmas lights that dig into the dark sky. Only now we have expectations to weigh us down.

'We don't really know each other.' The words slip past my lips without thought.

'How much do you ever know anyone?' Ralph's voice is flat and as cold as the snow that's beginning to flake again. 'Where do you want to eat?'

'I'm not really hungry.' It's true. I was ready to eat an hour ago, but I've passed hunger. Instead, the swell of anticipation grows in my belly.

'Me neither.' Ralph shrugs as we walk along, arms not quite touching. 'Ask me something. Anything. That way you'll know me better.'

My teeth nip in my cheeks as I mentally chew on this. But fundamentally, there's one question that is sitting heavier than the others in my mind.

'Are you really here to see me because of some poorly chosen promise I asked you to make? I didn't hear Benedict whisper in my ear. And I'm not sure I believe in such fate.'

His forceful exhalation creates a plume of vapour that flows around his face as he walks. I stare up at him as we meander along the street. His eyes are focused forwards and his posture is pulled straight and tall.

'It did throw me, tip me over the edge as it were, but no. That's not the only reason. Alone it wouldn't have been enough to make me come back after a year. I might have been freaked out about it at random points, but it wouldn't have been enough to push me so far off course. A lot has happened this year–' Ralph cuts off as the people walking in front of us abruptly stop and turn around. We awkwardly move around them as we arrive at the plethora of white that is the market, and the snow that's settling on the peaks of the chalets. 'Mulled wine?'

'Sure.' It'll be nice to warm me through, and even though I'm sure all the alcohol is cooked off, I can imagine it'll be enough to calm the adrenaline that's making my chest tickle.

We move towards the nearest place that sells the sickly-sweet warm wine. They have plastic reusable cups with Rouen written on them and pictures of nutcracker soldiers. We have to pay extra for these cups, but I know Milo likes to collect them each year, so I don't mind, and I'm happy to reuse them if we go back for another. I've brought my shoulder pack with the big silver buckle on it. I put a few spare clothes bits in there, just in case they are needed. There's plenty of space to slip in the cups for Milo.

Outside the mulled wine chalet, there are tall barrels as tables for people to stand around with drinks. Just as ours are poured, one becomes available, and we move away from the orange glowing lights showcasing the mulled wine, and edge into the periphery of the lights.

'Can we start again?' I suggest. 'Let's get to know each other more naturally, if there is such a thing.'

'I'd like that.'

I begin by telling Ralph about Milo, about everything from his love of maths to his relationship with Henri. From there I explain everything that's happened over the last year with Noëlle, and how, all things considered, she's doing well now we are with her.

We have another wine and I ask him more about Benedict. Not how he died, but how he lived.

Ralph tells me about Benedict's zest for life. That they had been working in a health food place together and studied nutrition and fitness together, Benedict in the light of science and Ralph in the light of lifestyle. Although that wasn't what Ralph did for his degree; it was more as a side interest. Every story Ralph shares about Benedict leaves him with a smile that fades to sad eyes.

'I recently found out that his mum used to abuse him, more than I realised.' Ralph studies his cup, avoiding my gaze and my tilting head. 'When we were kids, he had these funny red marks on his wrists and the back of his neck. He told me they were birthmarks and I had no reason to doubt him. They were literally always there. Didn't think much about the fact that they faded away when we grew up. Stupid really, because I do remember the marks. I think sometimes we see what we want to see, you know.'

Sadly, I do know. 'My brother used to self-harm when we were younger. He did a good job of hiding it, and I was all too willing to believe his excuses. No one *wants* to see pain in the people they care for.'

'Exactly.' Ralph's eyes lock onto mine. 'I found out that his mum would drag him about by his wrists, digging her nails in, I think. Back of his neck too. I'm sorry about your brother. That must've been really hard.'

'Thanks. It was. It is. How did you find out about Benedict?'

His eyes drop back to his cup and he attempts to drink up the droplets of wine that are left in the bottom.

'His sister. His sister told me. I knew they were seriously shit parents, that much was obvious. I can't believe he didn't tell me, you know? I thought we told each other everything. I've tried to replay conversations in my head to see if I wasn't listening right. But memories slip further away and I don't know what was said anymore.'

'I'm sorry he didn't tell you. Sorry he had to go through it at all. I can never understand these parents who hurt their children.'

'Thanks. I wish I'd known when we were kids. He stayed over at ours a lot, but if I'd known I'd have begged my parents to let him move in, I swear.' He drags his eyes back up to mine. 'What happened with Pierre?'

'Well, I suppose my parents were a bit more clued up than me. When my stepmother saw the marks, she and my father got some professional help involved. I think a lot of it came down to school pressure and Carole disappearing to the South. I think he wanted to control something. In this case, to control his own pain. He said as much to me once, after a bottle of wine a few years ago. When he cut himself, he was in charge. He decided how much it hurt, how deep it would go. No one else was inflicting it on him.'

Ralph's eyebrows lift and he licks his lips before saying, 'Wow. Oddly, that makes a lot of sense.'

'These things so often do.'

'Who's Carole?'

'Oh, she's my mother.' I wince as a reflex at telling him this, and suddenly have the desire to change the topic. 'Ralph... this conversation has turned very depressing.'

It's hard for me to recall Pierre like that. Guilt creeps in like a shadow. I'm proud of how far he has come since those times, but I don't feel it is my story to share too much. Even though Pierre bears scars and is open about the past, I don't like to bring it along into the future.

I glance to the side and catch sight of someone eating a Nutella-filled *gaufre* piled with banana slices. 'Let's get some *gaufres* – waffles, I mean.'

Ralph laughs, and presses his face into his hands. 'I'm sorry. I don't have many friends and I'm still processing all this. And anyway,' Ralph's right hand drops to point at me like a gun, 'I've told you, the only language I can pretty much always speak, is food. So yeah, a *gaufre* sounds damn amazing.'

We walk together like moths to the bright lights of the waffle chalet. There's a basket of fresh fruit on the counter and the smell of sweet batter being cooked warms the cold night air.

'What toppings you going for?' Ralph eyes the fruit then the powdered sugar over the shoulders of the couple ahead of us.

'That is a silly question.'

'Nutella, right?'

'No.' I screw up my face and fold my arms over my chest.

In response his square chin recoils towards his neck.

'Nutella and strawberries.' Relaxing my face, I let it fall into a grin as he begins to shake off his surprise and replace it with a gentle laugh.

We order the waffles and watch as they're freshly made, the viscous batter poured into the mould before they're left to cook.

Ralph tells me about his next foodie adventure, which isn't until January as he has taken some time off. 'Italy next for two weeks at the end of January.'

His life is exactly what I would want; adventure and travel. Something that stopped when Milo filled my belly with this delightful but heavy weight. It doesn't matter that he is out in the world, his mass is something I will always carry with me. Milo is the biggest part of me now. When Henri left, I became his everything. That was not Milo's fault, but it is what it is now.

The lady behind the counter passes us the *gaufres* on thin white cardboard plates the same size and shape as the large rectangular waffles.

We attempt to eat them while walking side by side. Strands of chocolate drizzle across my chin, I can feel them. I take one look at Ralph and he's just as bad. We look at each other and our shoulders bounce and our full mouths become even fuller, but now with suppressed laughter. Laughter that doesn't have the space to escape our lips.

When I do manage to swallow, my mouth is still sticky with warm Nutella, so I indicate with my head for Ralph to follow me. We move to the left side of the cathedral where there's a small courtyard. At the moment, it's also home to Santa's grotto and a flame-red letterbox made out of tinsel, with the words "Père Noël" in lights on the front and a bright star above the slot to post letters for good measure. There are benches here too, and since Santa has gone, it's quiet. Sometimes this area attracts small crowds of youths, but not as often when the markets and Père Noël are about. So, we are in luck.

We chat and laugh and consume the taste of Christmas in the way of Nutella on waffles with thinly sliced strawberries layered on top. We continue to laugh at the mess we are making and talk about trips to see Father Christmas when we were children and discover we both wanted, but didn't get, an ant farm. This bizarre choice makes me feel closer to Ralph, linked to him in a strange past desire.

There is something here. I felt it too, of course, last year. Some strange gravity I couldn't explain. He stayed with me on my shoulder for twelve months, just as I apparently stayed with him.

When we have finished eating, I collect up our rubbish and walk to the nearby bin and back before slumping down on the bench next to him.

'I should get back soon. It's getting late.'

'I thought you said Pierre was there.'

'He is but–'

'You have chocolate on your lip still.'

My tongue darts over my top lip then my bottom lip, before scrubbing at it with my thumb. 'I thought I'd got it all with the napkin. Did I get it?'

Ralph shakes his head. A shadow from a nearby tree is over his face making him hard to read.

'Here,' his thumb glances my lip.

'Did you get it?'

His head shakes back and forth. 'Uh, uh.' Ralph leans forwards and his tongue glances my lip before it parts mine and explores me more. I press into him desperate for more.

I don't believe in love at first sight. It's a ridiculous romantic notion. But this started with attraction and was soon undeniably different. I have no way of explaining how or why we connected ourselves so quickly, but there *is* a connection; and I never want to let it go.

Chapter 26

Félicité

I wake up to my phone vibrating on the bedside table next to my head. My body pulls me bolt upright before my hands reach to answer it, all without engaging my conscious mind.

'*Bonjour.*'

'Félicité?' The voice in my ear is excruciatingly loud and shrill. 'Félicité, are you there? I can see your ear.'

I pull the phone from my head, and there she is, my mother, Carole, perfectly made up with her signature light-red lip and the small gold earrings that she always wears. They're Chanel and likely cost double the deposit on the place we rented in Carnac.

'Carole? Why are you calling?'

A groan next to me sends my heart racing with panic, only to remember that Pierre and I stayed up talking last night and he couldn't be bothered to walk home after. I let him sleep on the floor next to me with the promise he would not snore.

I have told him about Ralph, more officially this time. He thinks I should invite Ralph to Mamie's birthday meal. We are seeing each other again tonight and Pierre has said he will invite Milo and Mamie around to his flat for a sleep over so I don't have to worry about being home at all. I don't think he likes staying there when he doesn't have anyone renting the spare room. He likes to find excuses to be out. Pierre has always been one to prefer rooms that are filled with the sound of others rather than silence. I'm sure it's really the reason why he was happy enough to sleep next to me last night instead of walking the five-minute distance home at one in the morning.

'We are arriving this afternoon. Pierre didn't answer his phone. Tell him to get his place ready. You know he is always a mess.'

Pierre drags himself up from the floor and waves as I turn the camera towards him.

'Get home and tidy up. We'll be with you this afternoon.' Carole's eyes roll so far back I'm sure she can see her tailbone.

'Why are you early?' Pierre demands as he slots his right fist into his eye socket and rubs.

'What a beautiful warm welcome.' Pierre doesn't rise to her statement; instead he patiently waits for her to answer the original question. 'Must I have a reason?'

'Yes,' we chime in unison.

She doesn't like this. We snigger like we did when we were teens, and she looks down her nose into the phone.

'We will see you soon. *Au revoir.*'

There's a lot of watching her press the screen before she disconnects.

'For someone who prides herself on being effortlessly elegant, that woman really needs to learn how to hang up a call.' Pierre is laughing before I've even finished my sentence.

'Why does she have to be early?' He slumps back on the floor, and I tuck myself back into the Christmas-cat bedding. 'You going to introduce her to Ralph?'

'*Putain!* No!' My hands slap to my eyes to cover them. I didn't mean to call my brother a whore, but the thought of them meeting is too awful to consider.

Pierre chuckles so hard, I can almost feel the tears squeezing from the corners of his eyes. 'Do you remember when she met Henri, how she asked him about his upbringing? How nothing he said was good enough?'

'Yes. She treats him like a god since he left me and her only grandchild. She's sick.'

'Yes, that's Carole for you. When is Henri coming to see Milo now you live here? Is it this week or next?'

'He arrives in time for Mamie's birthday celebration and leaves a few days before Christmas. You're lucky I didn't ask for him to stay with you.'

My hands fold themselves back under the covers and squeeze tightly closed at the thought of Henri coming to Rouen and charming everyone. With the addition of this new complication, if Ralph does meet everyone and lives to tell the tale, we'll be together for life.

Milo's bouncy feet pound past the door and bang down the stairs to the TV in the living room, where he will put on cartoons. He'd sit there all day if I let him.

'Guess I best go and tidy my house... apparently.' Pierre stands and collects together his bedding from the floor. 'Did Dad tell you he wants to come visit for Mamie's birthday too?'

'Yes. She'll love seeing him, but Mother on the other hand–'

'She is going to kill us for not telling her sooner. Mother would do anything to avoid being in a room with him and Lizzie. She might avoid us for years after this.'

'Good.'

There's a pause and I have the urge to hide under the covers for the next week. I wonder whether I could do that at the flat Ralph is renting. I'd enjoy hiding out with him while Milo gets spoilt by his father for a week.

Pierre says, 'Maybe I could move out for the week as Carole will be there.'

'*Merde*! You said you would have a sleep over tonight, with Mamie and Milo, so I could see Ralph and figure out what's going on there. Now what am I going to do?' I sit bolt upright and clutch one of the kittens on the duvet as I stare up at my brother's wincing face.

'I could stay here again,' he says, 'or you can go back to mine. Or stay out all night and tell Carole you're having a catch-up with Bernadette at her house.'

There's no hesitation; I don't even need to think about my response. 'I'd rather lie than have to wake up at yours with Carole breathing down my neck.'

Chapter 27

Félicité

Pierre leaves quickly, without coffee or breakfast. His place is usually quite clean, but I'm not sure it's Carole-clean. Now Carole has done what she always does – made it all about her. He has to bend to her will or spend the whole time with her bending his ear.

Mamie, Milo and I sit at the table with bowls of hot chocolate and *pains au chocolat* to dip into them. Milo has managed to pull himself away from the TV for the occasion.

'Mamie told me that you were out with a man last night. Who was the man?'

My scowl throws itself at Mamie, but only momentarily. She must have forgotten I had said not to tell Milo that I was out with a man. It's my fault for talking to her about it. I'm not used to hiding things from her and I love to hear her opinions. She didn't remember meeting Ralph last year. She can tell me whole tales from my childhood but details from yesterday can be a little bit more loose in nature.

'Yes. Ralph. You met Ralph.' Milo nods enthusiastically, clearly happy he has actually met the man in question. 'Well, last year when I was visiting Mamie, he helped me to walk her home when she wasn't steady on her feet.'

'I don't recall that.' Mamie looks affronted at the assertion she isn't great on her feet at almost eighty-six years old.

Milo is wonderfully gentle with her. He outshines me at every turn. 'It's okay. I can tell you that Ralph seems cool. You'll probably remember him when you see him.'

I'm quite sure he knows this is very unlikely, but he also knows the chances are this conversation will have slipped her mind by then too. But now, in this moment, she's happy with his verdict and continues to sip her hot chocolate. In turn, Milo is happy that he has both helped his Mamie and knows who I was out with last night.

'I'm going out again tonight, with Bernadette.' I don't really want to tell this lie. I'd have rather said nothing much at all, but Carole's imminent appearance has pushed me into a dark corner. Now it's no longer a fun night at Uncle Pierre's, it's more about spending time avoiding the cloud that will look down on us all for the coming week. 'Uncle Pierre will be staying here and your Mamie-Carole is coming to stay at his house.'

For most children the mention of a grandparent is an exciting moment, but Milo manages only a mild ripple of feigned enthusiasm, because she often gets him a magazine. It's usually one about the planet or wildlife which he enjoys. But she doesn't engage with him, so he no longer does much with her either. If I had said his Grand-père was coming to stay, he would have been giddy.

Mamie says, 'Carole is coming to visit. That'll be nice. Have you told your Grand-père?'

This is new.

This is something I don't really want to deal with.

Milo looks at me then back at her. By the look on his face, he thinks she means *his* Grand-père, but she was looking right at me not at him. She meant *my* Grand-père. I'm quite sure she's not talking about my dad. She means her deceased husband. I skip over the trauma or the questions from Milo. I have no idea whether that's the right thing to do. Is there a right thing to do? Milo can carry on assuming she means his Grand-père.

'No, Mamie, I haven't.'

She bobs her head and rips off a corner of her *pain au chocolat* before dipping it carefully into the thick dark liquid in her bowl.

I know things won't get better for her. In fact, I think she does so well, all things considered. She wakes up and puts herself together without a stitch of help unless she's having a particularly wobbly day. And I'm still firmly of the belief that having Milo about has made her younger. It's helped bring back some more clarity and has possibly helped to keep it there for that bit longer. My heart clamps tightly in my chest at the thought of losing her. I'm practical about it. I know she can't live forever. None of us can. That doesn't make the thought any less excruciating.

Before Milo can ask any questions on the subject, I tell him to eat up his breakfast because we're already running late. It's enough to distract him and enough to keep us going, one morning at a time.

As soon as Carole arrives, I'm impressed. She actually manages to combine being offended and being blasé about the fact no one really wants to see her or her partner, Jean-Claude. Jean-Claude is nice enough. Mostly he is as pointless as a toy with no batteries. That's why she likes him. He does as he's told, and he dotes on her. She left us so she could be the child again and never work or clean, or anything much. It sounds rather dull to me.

My mother is attractive, with a well-maintained slim frame, hair as tidy as Audrey Hepburn's cropped hair and just as dark. She's nowhere near as pretty, but she has seductive almond eyes and a youthful complexion, all of which she likes to use to her advantage. She is under the belief that everyone admires her in one way or another. Her words are as sweet as candy canes and her face is that of an angel. Or at least, I'm sure that's what she believes.

The afternoon went a little like this: Carol arrived to see Mamie first. She came in and remarked that our Christmas tree was too small, the house didn't look as though it had been dusted and we should all go out for dinner. I swiftly told her I was busy, in fact we all had plans and she hadn't been included in any of them. Maybe she could squeeze into anyone's but mine. She pressed her hand to her chest and her mouth turned down, before she shrugged the whole thing off and announced she already had plans anyway.

Good. Let her believe she is the one calling the whole thing off. I have no desire to argue with her today, or any day for that matter. Life is much too short. I've considered cutting her out of our life, but so far, her arriving and leaving has had no effect on us, on Milo and me. We know who our real family is and it doesn't include her. Cutting her out could cause drama and arguments. As it is, I only have to put up with her now and then. It's a relatively easy bad habit to maintain.

As soon as Mother leaves to undertake her invented plans, I get ready for my fictitious plans with Bernadette and arrive at my plans with Ralph.

Chapter 28

Félicité

I have Ralph's mobile number now. After kissing for more than twenty minutes last night and nearly, so nearly, going back with him to the flat he has rented, we exchanged numbers before he walked me home.

I send him a message to make sure he will *not* surprise me at the door tonight. He agrees, and even suggests I come to his for takeaway. This is perfect, because I do not want to run the risk of seeing Carole in the very cold night air.

For some unknown reason, I feel more relaxed about tonight. A calm excitement sits low in my torso, the same as if I were about to go on a holiday to somewhere I've been before that I enjoyed. I already know it'll be good and there's some comfort that comes along with the knowing.

Ralph told me last night that he's rented the flat for two weeks. It's not too far from Place du Vieux-Marché, and the big wheel where we had an accidental first date, thanks to Milo.

I send Ralph a message to let him know I'm on my way.

As soon as I arrive at the building, he's there, swinging open the door before I can look for a buzzer.

We kiss cheeks before I follow him up tatty stone stairs. I know appearances are often deceptive in these buildings though and as he says, 'Come in,' with a relaxed and welcoming sweep of his arm, I know I'm right. But rather than focusing on the forest-green chairs with matching curtains, it's the food that catches my eye.

'What's all this?'

There are two tables in the open-plan living room, a round dining table, and a low wooden coffee table between the TV and a sage sofa with forest-green cushions. Both tables are laden with food. Not takeaway as we discussed; instead there's every possible cheese, specialist cured meat, traditional bread, handmade chocolates from the market and all manner of nibbles... everything imaginable. It looks like a Christmas party for ten or more people.

'I got a little carried away. I hope you don't mind, I took photos for Instagram and videos for YouTube to use. That's not why I got all this food, but it made sense to make a feature out of it. Plus, I find it hard not to share my excitement for food even when I'm not working. Do you like it?' Ralph's words flood the air and whirl round like snowflakes in a blizzard.

I think my stunned reaction has made him nervous. Maybe I'm wrong, but he's wringing his hands and looking from the food to me, waiting for something more to be said or perhaps to happen.

'Do you always do this for women when you're in charge of dinner?'

'The last time I made a meal for a woman I was dating she broke up with me, and that was a long time ago.'

'I'll take that as no.'

'No.' Ralph walks along between the tables and picks up a brie and squeezes it gently before smelling it and passing it to me to do the same. 'It started with picking cheeses and not knowing what you preferred, and it went from there. Champagne? Cider?'

I pass the cheese back and tilt my head at the choice of drinks. 'Quite the difference.'

'Well, I thought champagne because it's a date, but we're in Normandy and you lot are known for your apples, so cider felt like a safe option. And I know you love an apple Minute Maid.'

A laugh of agreement glides from my lips as Ralph moves to the next room but stays in sight. He pulls open the fridge door and holds two bottles up to me.

'Champagne. Why not?'

My answer makes him glow and he begins to search the box kitchen for some glasses. Its decor is glossy and black, making it look even smaller than it is.

'Are you sure you haven't organised a strange surprise Christmas party?'

I scan the food. There seems to be three types of meat rillettes and four pâtés as well as all the saucisson, cheese and everything else. It's almost as much as my stepmother Lizzie would provide for one of her Christmas gatherings – although she adds her English touches like Christmas crackers, something I think my father will never understand the point of, and her favourite festive song, "Last Christmas", on repeat. Wham is still her favourite band of all time, so she has told me many times. She also prefers to serve biscuit crackers rather than baguette, because she moans that all the bread gives her indigestion. We French have no such issues.

A pop sounds from just past my shoulder as Ralph opens the champagne bottle without making a mess. 'Tell me one of these is goose.' I wave a finger over the shredded meat of the rillettes.

Ralph produces two half-filled glasses of champagne, one of which he passes to me before using the other to point to one of the rillettes and confirming, 'That one.'

'Good. Goose is my favourite.'

'To me it's the most Christmassy too. It seems very Dickens to have some kind of goose at Christmas time. Do you read English literature? Or just French?'

'"Even though there are books of which the backs and covers are by far the best parts, I still read them..."'

Ralph tilts his head and a small crease forms above his nose.

'It's a quote from Dickens, "there are books of which the backs and covers are by far the best parts"... It's from *Oliver Twist*.' I roll my eyes enough to rival Carole, and Ralph starts to laugh.

'Haven't read it. I've only read *A Christmas Carol*.' He raises his glass. 'Chin-chin.'

We clink glasses and sip at the streams of bubbles, then Ralph pulls out a chair for me and invites me to eat my weight in Christmas treats.

Chapter 29

Ralph

I eat for a living. My hobby is to keep fit so I can keep eating for a living, but it's only now, sitting here with Félicité, that I realise it's been a long time since I've sat down with anyone one-to-one to quietly enjoy the food in front of us. Food that I have served. I've had dinner with my parents, but that's all I can think of. To experience a meal with a person and not a camera seems alien. I have to avoid the temptation to narrate my thoughts about each bite. When I slip and say something out loud in my food-critic voice, Félicité doesn't make me feel stupid. We laugh it off together and chat about her thoughts on the food too.

She tells me about Milo's favourite cheese, one that's a bit strong even for me. I never thought I would fall for a woman with a child. Or any woman. My palms turn clammy and I drink deeper from the flute than I mean to, because I don't want to break my promise to Bennie, but then I know that I do want to break it. That's a tough one to admit to anyone, and something I've only been able to admit to myself in a silent room for a matter of weeks. I used to always have relationships. I liked the stability. Then I latched on to the stability of what Bennie wanted. Meeting Félicité threw me off balance. I had to see her again after a whole year to see if I'd blown it out of proportion. I hadn't. There's something about her that is as addictive as eating all the Christmas chocolates in one sitting. I know I shouldn't let myself get close to someone, but I just can't seem to help myself.

Stop.

Take each moment as it comes.

Don't fall in love. Not yet. For a thousand reasons not yet. Milo, Bennie, Noëlle... they're all good reasons to step back.

Change the subject.

'Have you always taught English? And why English? You're French.'

'Yes. I've taught French too here and there, but English is more popular. My stepmother is English and she and my papa took us with them travelling and teaching. Then with Henri, Milo's dad, we travelled too. We would teach in Africa, Japan... Anywhere that would have us or needed us.'

Félicité studies the crust of bread in her dainty hands as she swipes it with camembert over and over even though it's already spread.

She visibly snaps out of it and pulls her shoulders up and gives me a mild smile.

'Henri left us because he missed travelling. As though I had no interest in it anymore. *C'est la vie*. We are better just the two of us.' Félicité takes a decisive bite of her bread. She's so strong. Resilient.

'Would you travel with Milo? If you could?'

Félicité chews methodically before swallowing. Her nose wrinkles with thought.

'It's not something I've had the luxury of thinking about. Mamie needs us. She has no one else. We could put her in a home, and maybe we will have to, but I don't want to. She is capable and so are we. Milo adores her. I adore her. It's not an option.'

'You miss it though, I can tell.'

As I pop a slice of nutty cured meat into my mouth, I have the urge to describe the sweet and smoky flavours. I repress the urge just in time.

'I like exploring the world, learning new languages and meeting people. Finding out what their Christmas traditions are, or if they have any, and if they don't, what do they celebrate? I want that for Milo one day. To see more than just France. That's not to say France isn't beautiful. What's not to like? Just look at all this.' Félicité picks up her glass and tilts it towards the table. 'But I want him to understand that there is more to the world, to get his country in perspective and to form opinions based on more than just one nation's ideas.'

Félicité pauses with her glass in her hand. I pick up the bottle and top her up.

'You seem to be passionate about travel for someone who's determined to stay. If you don't mind me asking, how old was Milo when Henri went off to travel again?'

'Six months old.' She says this with such a calm demeanour that I know it must have cut her badly. It likely left her bleeding out for a while. It's probably the real reason she hasn't had a relationship since Henri. It must be impossible to trust anyone after that. And here I am, with my own shitty mess to confuse us both. Guilt nips at my heels.

'Wow.' I snatch a breath. 'I can't understand how he could leave you both like that. I mean, before I made my promise to

Benedict, I sort of assumed I'd have kids one day, and no way if I had one could I just walk away, even if they weren't planned.'

'Duly noted.' She smiles without mirth. Perhaps she took my comments as a dig. I hope not.

Félicité gently shakes her head making her glossy hair brush over her shoulders before she takes a measured breath and releases it through her teeth. She is stunning in an elegant and natural way. The flat has a small plastic tree in the corner kitted out with very white lights. It makes her skin look translucent and glowing, like she should be on top of the tree in a tinsel dress instead of the star that is on it now.

'I wasn't trying to be insensitive.'

'Thank you, for saying that. It's fine. I just– I just find it hard. I trusted Henri and we made a decision together to keep Milo, but he walked away. He sees him twice a year to be the fun dad. Sometimes three times. But that's it. I wouldn't change Milo for the world, but I miss the freedom of adventure, and a small part of me can't help but resent Henri. That's not to say I'm not pleased he left. I am. Better to find out sooner rather than later that he wasn't worth my time. We are better off.'

I admire her words, but I'm starting to get sucked into her beauty. The glass and a half of champagne is lowering my ability to be the gentleman. The slight clef of her chin, the line of her cheeks and the blush of her lips... As discretely as I can manage, I wipe my sweaty palms on my jeans, and say, 'I agree. If he had stayed, you wouldn't be here with me, eating all of Rouen's cheese.'

'And charcuterie,' she adds, with a lift of her glass.

We share a laugh together, not throwing our heads back and roaring, but a relaxed one. When it's over, we're left staring into each other's eyes.

'You're actually making me like Christmas again, at least a little bit anyway. Seeing it through Milo's eyes the other day really helped. Same with my cousin's kids I guess. It takes me away from, you know. Kids are so innocent. They're not burdened with expectations and problems in the same way adults are. They brim with hopes and dreams.'

She shifts closer into me. I wonder whether she's as aware as I am of how close we are. The only sounds come from outside as a moped roars past and the TV in the flat above us burbles away.

Félicité's lips part and her head tilts before she asks the killer question.

'Do you still stick to Benedict's promise, or are you here because you want to change?'

Chapter 30

Félicité

I think perhaps I have somehow stepped outside of myself, because asking Ralph if he still sticks to Benedict's promise was bolder than I intended. Hearing him talk about Milo and Christmas; it got be worried about the forming of bonds. I don't want Milo getting attached to people who might let them down.

'Don't answer that,' bursts out of my mouth at twice the speed of my original question. I grip the table, and shuffle my chair forwards. Ralph's hand curls over my fingers.

'I can't answer it anyway. I don't have an answer.' He's leaning towards me and his voice and eyeline have both dropped. 'Something I do know is, for the first time since Bennie died, I like someone enough to see her more than once. In fact, I like you enough that I came back to France to find you. I don't know why.'

'Thank you very much.' I raise a sceptical eyebrow and provocatively tilt my head.

'I didn't mean it like that. I mean... I don't know how I can feel so strongly about someone I barely know. But you've been wedged under my skin and now I'm reluctant to have you removed.'

'You've made me sound like a growth or an infected splinter.'

Ralph swings his head and laughs as his fingers pull mine from the edge of the table to hold my hand. 'I'm shit at this.'

'I think you're demonstrating how long it's been since you've cared for another person.'

His chin lifts and his eyes lock on mine.

Without another word, he raises his other hand to slide along my jawline. Still wordless, we look at each other. There's a calm and sumptuous peace between us.

Ralph leans forwards to kiss me. I don't resist. I have no desire to. Would it be a bad idea to fall too far with this man? Of course. He has more issues than anyone I've ever met, and I have a child and elderly grandmother to think of. That doesn't mean I can't enjoy what's in front of me. It's like any delicious treat; it's best to think of the calories tomorrow at the gym.

We begin to absorb each other, in much the same way we did that very first time we were together. Only now we have many rooms to fill and weave between. Pulling curtains closed, we tug away our clothing.

It's only when we fall down on the forest-green bedding that something seems to shift. We're already naked, having shed our clothes somewhere not far from the table where we unwrapped each other. Now though, we're lying on our sides breathing each other in.

Ralph turns onto his back, and I slide myself on top of him. We press our lips so firmly together it borders on painful. My chin is already raw from the light stubble on his chin.

Everything has slowed down to an almost standstill, like we have all the time in the world and there's only us. Our foreheads press together, and I open my eyes to admire every detail of his flint-grey irises, with flecks of blue and green that can only be seen in intimacy, there only for me.

Our bodies writhe and grip tightly together. The air escapes our lungs and heats the air around us, and then we relax and fall away to the bed with staggered breaths and hurried pulses as we try to catch back the air that we stole from one another.

'I didn't think it could be better than that first time.' Ralph's chest heaves by my side. 'But it turns out, I was wrong.'

I roll back towards him and take in another lingering kiss. He wraps an arm around me.

'Part of me hoped it would be dreadful.' I cover my eyes with one hand at the admission. Sadly, it couldn't have been further from that.

'It'd make it easier, right?' Ralph laughs. 'I hoped the same stupid thing. What a pair.' Ralph squeezes me closer and kisses the top of my head. 'I just don't understand how I feel like I know you, and I know nothing. No really. I know, tell me the best moment of your life, and the worse.'

'Now? Can I have a glass of water first?'

'Nope. Tell me.'

The first part is the easiest. 'Milo is the best moment. Not giving birth. Birth is not a good moment. Holding him, feeding him. Looking at his face. Now can I have a drink?'

'Worst, then drink.'

I lick my lips and begin to run through all the painful moments my mind throws up. Losing my grand-père, and my

Uncle Marcel, Henri leaving me all alone. All of these fractured my heart in a measurable way, in a way that can never be repaired. But the truth is something else.

'You don't have to tell me if you don't want to. I won't really stop you getting a drink.'

'No, you have told me yours, about Benedict. But mine is very different. It's, well, it is–' I stumble over my words. 'The moment that comes to mind first, before all the other pains of life, is the day I realised my mother could never love me the way a mother should. It was before she even walked away from us. All young children copy and want to be like those they admire. I put on some of her lipstick from her handbag. She told me that it was hers, and not mine. Which, yes, I know, that part is fair. I shouldn't have taken it. But she followed this with why. The answer was, I wasn't ever going to be pretty enough, my nose was too crooked, not straight like hers, and my hair was never tidy enough. I played in the dirt too much. I would never be good enough. No one ever could be. It sounds silly now. But it was the look on her face and the tone of her voice.' I sit up, separating myself from Ralph like the sharp removal of a plaster. 'Time to get a drink.'

Without adding clothing to my body, I slip away to the bathroom to give me enough time to catch my breath. Everything in here is green too, sage and forest-green towels and tiles. Perhaps the owner of this place is as particular as Carole. Although, her whole place is a white box I'm not allowed to enter with Milo, in case he gets chocolates fingers anywhere.

I've never shared that childhood experience – however briefly I may have just done so – with anyone. Not out of any particular reason, only no one has ever really asked, and it's not a moment I like to think about. Ralph has been vulnerable with me, and it felt only fair to give him the same.

When I come back into the room, I slip straight under the covers, not from embarrassment, life is too short for such worries, but because walking around naked in December, even with heating, can be a cold affair.

Ralph sits up and points to the water on the bedside cabinet. I prop myself up and reach for the glass before gulping the cool liquid.

'It was meant to be fun, or bonding, or something. I think I'm better when I don't try too hard.' Ralph's voice is soft over my shoulder.

Replacing my glass, I lie back down, facing him. '*C'est pas grave.* It's nothing to be sad over, nothing to worry about. You have shared so much with me. So much sadness. It must have been your worst of all times.'

'It's a tie actually. It's the loss and knowing the shite that did it to him is out there living his life like nothing happened. I couldn't protect Bennie and I couldn't give him justice either. Basically, failed as a friend, didn't I?'

Ralph moves deeper under the covers. Instinctively, I wrap my leg over his and soft hairs tickle my calf.

'They couldn't find who did it?'

'The bloke looked generic and drunk people don't make good witnesses. I don't know who he was. Just some kid looking to prove himself.'

'I can't understand people.'

'Me neither.'

'You have to tell me your best memory now,' I say. 'The one that always makes you smile. The best moment of your life.'

Ralph pouts his lips and exhales, rolling onto his back under my legs. Only the lamp behind him lights the room. I roll onto my tummy and look down at his face, at the square cut of his jaw with its fine layer of stubble. His expression is focused as if he's been asked the meaning of life or to explain some new theoretical science.

'Well?'

'My best moment hasn't happened yet.'

This response stumps me. I cock my head at him and he refocuses to look at me. His hand stretches up to my cheek, and his thumb carefully skims along my skin. 'Or maybe it has and I just don't know it yet. Maybe it's something we can only really know when we're old, you know? When you can look back and can see how it all panned out. Then maybe you can say, that day changed everything. That day changed my life.'

Something about the tone of his voice, the serious edge, accelerates my pulse. I want to ask if he means us, or whether I'm reading something that isn't there. But as my mouth opens, he contracts his body into mine and his lips latch onto me, forcing me to gasp into his mouth. He rolls on top of me and delightfully takes more than the words from my mouth.

Chapter 31

Félicité

Time changes everything. Memories move, warp and get re-written as time passes by. I knew my night with Ralph last year was good. I've thought about it many times in the dark hours of lonely nights. But my memory of Ralph hadn't done him justice. I suppose I could no longer believe it was as good as my senses recalled. That perhaps I'd exaggerated it in my mind, that it was never as delicious as I believed it to be. Letting myself believe he felt so divine made it more unbearable that he would always be outside of my reach. Then last night happened and made my memories shatter and sprinkle like broken glass, because it was everything, and much more, than the first time.

Perhaps it's because we have thrown feelings into the concoction now. Perhaps that has made it even more intense like a dying flame being given air and gasoline to thrive.

Carefully I roll away from Ralph's warm embrace. Stretching out, I pull my watch off the bedside cabinet to check the time. My alarm hasn't gone, so it must be early. Ralph's still peacefully snoozing next to me. His lips are gently parted and his hair, normally without fault, is a jolly mess. I have every urge to lift the heavy duvet and admire the rest of him, knowing we both fell asleep with nothing on, pressed against each other. I bite back the urge. It wouldn't be fair to wake him, considering how late it was by the time we did sleep.

A vibration sounds next to his head from his bedside cabinet, then moments later, it goes again. Maybe that's what woke me so early. I have found since having Milo that I'm a much lighter sleeper, attuned to waking up at any sound in case he's calling out for me in the night. Something that rarely happens nowadays, but the instinct doesn't fade so easily. Milo, he was the conversation Ralph and I avoided, the one we didn't want to have.

Last night we were living in a bubble as true as a politician's word. We both know it will end but we are steering clear of the thought, or the words. This can't be real – the idea of whisking Milo off and going on an adventure with Ralph to Italy, Greece, Australia, India... anywhere. To have a little family. Swiftly I squeeze my eyes shut to suppress emotions from bleeding out of me. That isn't our ending. Our ending is exactly that, to end. We are like a phoenix, something not of this world and designed with every intention of burning in the flames. Hopefully we will at least be born again as friends.

The moment before he threw himself at me resonates in my mind. Did he mean me, when he was talking just before about something that could be his best memory? Does he want me to be the best memory that he will look back on when he's old? I can't think about it. I can't let myself think about it.

Ralph's phone vibrates again, almost dancing itself around the silver lamp. It might be important, or it could be just an active group chat. He looks too peaceful to wake up for nothing. Surely if it were that important, the person would call, not message.

Watching him, I catch sight of his tattoo on his unfurled left arm. It makes sense to me now, of course. It's his reminder of Benedict. He told me so last night. It's his permanent reminder of the promise he made all those years ago.

Inhaling one last look at the defined lines I can see peeping out from the cover, I decide to leave him to sleep. I take myself off to the bathroom to freshen up and to find my overnight bag with my clothes. There's a nightie in there, but it never made it out of the bag.

When I arrive back in the room, Ralph is leaning on one elbow frowning down at his phone. He's still topless, but now has jogging or pyjama bottoms on. I've never seen him look casual before. Everything he's worn has been smart – shirts, jumpers and tidy jeans – other than perhaps the Christmas jumper last year. Although even that wasn't strictly casual, more that it was playful.

As he realises my presence, he releases a broad grin and we exchange morning pleasantries. Before I can ask whether everything's okay, he discards the phone and propels himself off the bed, marching towards me for a kiss. His fingers wrap around the back of my neck. It's a brief and gentle moment, but a shiver of memory floods my skin.

'Coffee?'

I gladly accept. As he walks past me, my fingers gravitate to my lips. There was something comfortable about his silky kiss; it made us seem like much more of a couple than almost strangers. It felt easy and comforting. Ralph doesn't feel like a stranger at all. Each time we've seen each other it's been so intense, so real, like picking a fresh orange and biting into the citrus only for it to bite right back with its tang. Each time we've spent time together roots have grown into something... Into friendship, or maybe one day something else. Maybe.

I follow Ralph into the mess we left last night. Luckily, he had the foresight to put some things back in the fridge. It feels strange to have someone else thinking of these practical things. For so long it has just been me worrying whether the perishables have made it into the fridge or whether plates have been washed.

As Ralph moves around the kitchen, making coffee in the narrow space, we exchange conversation about that beautiful part of life which is nothing in particular, although it's hard not to be distracted by the lines of his muscles as he moves, as he's yet to put a shirt on.

We are in the in-between that's neither here nor there, the mortar that holds together the bricks of life. The conversations that are so easily forgotten and yet bind us all together in normality. For me, this easy grown-up conversation with a man is refreshing, because it's a rarity, and something I've missed. It's also delightfully easy with Ralph. We bounce ideas around about politics, food, education and work while he serves me a fresh mug of coffee. We could sit like this at the table for hours, I'm sure.

That is until I ask, 'Who was on the phone? You looked concerned.'

Ralph makes a short noise in the back of his throat before holding his coffee to his lips without drinking.

'You could say that. It was Clarissa, Benedict's sister. She's... She's having a hard time lately. I'm the only person she can talk to, I guess.'

'I'm sorry to hear that.'

Ralph nods before leaning his elbows onto the table to cup the drink in his hands, still not taking a sip, as though he has forgotten why he lifted the mug all the way to his face.

'We've spent a lot of time together over the past six months, between work. She's been doing better, feeling better I mean, so she decided to come off her antidepressant medication. It's a big step. I'm proud of her... But all the texts today seem a bit off. I've told her to call the doctor. She said she would. She's probably fine.'

'I know how important it is to do these things slowly. They say these medications are not addictive, but they are. Perhaps not in the usual sense, but the body and mind get used to things. Pierre went on some for only, maybe, seven months and he found them hard to get away from. How long has she been on them?'

'Maybe four, almost five years. Since Bennie died.'

My eyebrows jump up. I hate all pharmaceuticals. I could have my eyes clawed out by a feral cat and not take a painkiller. Here in France, we like to take more of a holistic and natural approach when we can. Or perhaps it's my family. I'm not sure. What I do know is, I remember talking to a woman many years ago, a scientist, who told me placebos outdo most antidepressants in tests. But that doesn't make money. It's not as sexy as a drug that claims it fixes lives, when, in my experience, it can ruin them. Of course, not everyone is the same, and I would never judge anyone for making a decision for their life that suits them. Only that I am more cautious about these things. It's big business the world over to upsell prescription drugs.

After Clarissa lost her brother at such a young age and so tragically, she probably needed something. I just wonder whether she was offered proper grief support first, or only the easy and money-making route of drugs.

'What's with the face?' Ralph nods towards me like he has been reading my thoughts.

'Nothing. Well, no, not nothing. I'm remembering how antidepressants were for Pierre. There were a lot of side effects and he struggled to move on from the lift they'd been giving him. He took up running to help him feel better. He ran until there was almost nothing left of him. He became sinewy and thin. I'm not sure whether it was to distract himself from what was going on in his mind as it recovered, or whether he was addicted to the small high of endorphins.'

'It is hard. These drugs fix a chemical imbalance, don't they? So, I guess when you stop, the imbalance is still there.' Ralph takes a sip of the drink he's been holding under his nose before replacing the mug on the table.

I can't help but shake my head as I pick up my drink too and sip the bitter black coffee.

'What? Am I so wrong?' Ralph is laughing, but his face is telling a different story. Lines have formed between his brows. His leg hitches up to rest his foot on the chair and he hugs it in, as though he is trying to hide behind it.

'Sorry,' I say, 'it's just that was a marketing campaign in the nineties. I'm surprised anyone still believes all the propaganda. Look it up. As with most medications, the companies have no idea *why* they work, they just *do*. They often seemingly fix one problem only to cause another. I've met a lot of people around this strange world, and some of them only want to spread lies for money.'

'Just a little bit negative.'

'Mmm. Or perhaps reflective of experience.' I twist an eyebrow in Ralph's direction. 'What I find most interesting is how different countries talk about different subjects. Governments and organisations lie and tell the truth about different things in every culture. Some propaganda goes global of course, and is deeply set, but some things stay regional. Lizzie, my step mother, grew up with the fear of nuclear war in England and my mother, Carole, always said she would never go into a shop's changing room for fear of being sold into slavery as a youth. They're the same age, from countries as close as cousins and yet these were the standard fears for people of their generations in their countries.'

'Blimey. In all your travels you've got to have some good stories too though? Surely? Not everything is fear and propaganda.'

'True. I've met inspirational people pushing for change. I once met a small group campaigning against one of the most well-known chocolate manufacturers for stealing and contaminating water from indigenous people, and another time I met a woman working undercover to expose oil companies. The bravery of those people goes unnoticed and yet they deserve awards.'

'Most of that story still sounds pretty gloomy, you realise? And that undercover one, surely she wouldn't tell you that if she was? How could she trust you?'

'Are you suggesting I'm not trustworthy?'

'No, just–'

'She was French, and she needed some help. So, I helped her. I've always fancied myself as an activist. In itself, it's a very long story and it all started with a tampon.'

Ralph begins to relax as he considers my past, perhaps, instead of his own.

'Your passion is infectious. Pretty sure you are an activist, you know. Think you could make the world a better place if you wanted to, as well.' He gives me a cheeky smile that's so boyish it almost reminds me of Milo.

Meeting people who have a thousand new stories from around the world was always a highlight for me. Travelling is the best way to gain a small perspective on this massive planet. Without it, we are just staring at the wall of a cell filled with the media messages and constructs of our own government with no way out.

A content sigh shudders from my chest. Not because of the flaws in the world – that would be too much to change to even let myself worry about – it's because it's early in the day, and here I am, having a grown-up conversation with someone who isn't my grandmother. Not that I don't enjoy an early-morning chat with Mamie, in fact, it's often the highlight of my morning. She's always better in the mornings. Sometimes, as the day goes on, she can become more forgetful or even moody on bad days. But this is a new and exciting conversation, an exchange of thoughts and ideas that could challenge and change the world. World politics and ideas are almost the language of love for me. I can see myself waking every morning to Ralph with fresh ideas and conversation, pooling knowledge and working out how to make this world a better place for future generations.

'I think I need to explore more when I travel. Talk to more people who aren't just foodies.' Ralph snatches a breath. 'You know there's a documentary about a French girl exposing oil companies. I wonder whether it's the same girl?' Ralph's eyes widen at the idea. 'Maybe you're in it. Maybe she had a hidden camera.'

'God, I hope not!' I settle into my own thoughts for a moment, thoughts of Ralph and travel and Milo seeing the world the way I did as a child, and suddenly the words fall from my lips: 'Ralph, would you like to come to Mamie's birthday meal?'

Ralph's phone buzzes with more messages. Clarissa's name is on the screen. Regret fills my lungs the way water pours into a bathtub. I've let myself get wrapped up in a beautiful night followed by the joy of grown-up conversation, instead of the usual schoolwork and afterschool clubs.

Ralph pushes the phone away with a small wince before looking up at me. The corners of his steely eyes wrinkle into a smile. 'I'd love to.'

Chapter 32

Ralph

Six Months Earlier

Clarissa's arms envelop me and squeeze me like I'm one of those stress balls, her fingers kneading my triceps.

'It's been too long, King Rat.'

'Please don't call me that, Clarissa.' If I had any air left in my lungs from her bear hug, I'd sigh.

Clarissa lives with two dogs, three cats and no people. She works as a dog walker and helps at a kennels too. She used to be wild and social, a lot like Benedict, until he died.

She was there that night, when it happened. It was her voice I heard screeching like a broken coyote into the night. She'd just arrived at the club with her friends. The timing was pure coincidence. People were around him, some trying to help, some onlookers pointing and vomiting. The scum that punched him had already made a run for it and everyone about was too drunk to remember who it could have been, or even why it happened.

'I'm about to take the dogs out. Want to come?' Clarissa cranes her head to look up at me because she's tiny and too close to me to see me without putting a crick in her neck.

'Sounds good.'

She weaves between the animals jumping over each other to get their leads and little bags for poo. 'Have you come from your parents'?'

'Yeah.'

'That good, huh?'

I don't really want to recount it to Clarissa. Seems unfair. Mum banging on that it's coming up to five years without Bennie, even though that's months away, and almost chasing me out of the house because she wants grandkids... no.

When Benedict was in hospital after hitting his head, Clarissa never wanted to leave him. Neither did I. We would do shifts. You'd think his mum and dad would be the same. They did the big drama over him being in a coma, but after a week they only popped in now and then to check. That's how it felt. It wasn't long after that, that I couldn't blag any more time off work. They'd all been good about it because they knew Benedict too, and knew he was like a brother to me, but there's only so much time off anyone will allow, even unpaid.

I quit my job to sit there so Clarissa didn't have to be the only one.

You'd have thought she and I would get close, and in some ways we did, but it was more like those male and female figurines in those old decorative weather houses, or two ghosts passing in the night. Sometimes if we were at the hospital at the same time, we would silently hold hands.

I felt responsible for her. I *feel* responsible for her. Only now I have a job that prevents me from honouring the amount of time I know Benedict would want me to spend watching over her.

Benedict always looked out for his sister, I guess we both had at times. But when he became Sleeping Beauty, there was only me to check on her, which I've made sure to do whenever I can. I feel kind of like I've adopted Clarissa since Bennie died. It's what he would have wanted. He never said that's what he would want if he died. That wasn't the sort of thing we ever talked about. It's not the sort of thing most twenty-somethings talk about. That doesn't stop me from knowing it's what he would want.

We leave Clarissa's thatched terrace cottage to be tugged along by the dogs. Eventually we get into the fields and with no one about, she lets them off the lead. They're good dogs, Flopsy and Cottontail they're called. Both mixed breeds who don't look anything like the names suggest. But Clarissa used to call Benedict Bennie-Bunny sometimes, so I'm guessing it's to do with that. Although, I've never asked, so I might be wrong.

So far, our catch-up has consisted of talking about work, her mocking my YouTube videos and telling me she still can't believe people would pay me to eat food, and the fact that she found plastic in her fish dinner the other night at the chippie.

It's only when Clarissa asks for the third time about my parents that I cave.

'Mum's nagging me that she wants me to forget my promise to Bennie and have kids instead.'

Clarissa presses her lips into a firm line. She looks just like him. Same-shaped mouth and the same sturdy look he could hit me with sometimes. She's got the girl version of his hooded eyes.

'She's right. Maybe not the kids part. I think that one is up to you, but the promise... I don't think this is what he meant. He didn't know he would be brain-dead five minutes after saying it. You need to start thinking for yourself not second-guessing what Bennie would do when he isn't here to correct you.'

'This is coming from *you*?' I snort in her direction.

'I think I'm more qualified than your mum on the subject. And yeah, *from me.*'

Flopsy runs over to us with a huge crooked stick dangling from her drooling mouth.

'Drop,' Clarissa commands, and is quickly obeyed.

Flopsy bounces from side to side. She looks a lot like a whippet or something. Pale coat and slim.

'When was the last time you had a relationship?' I tightly fold my arms and turn to face Clarissa head on. My whole body is so tense that my T-shirt feels too tight around my chest. It's evening but it's June and sweat is beginning to form on my top lip. I quickly lick it away. I can't show weakness. I'm sick of everyone knowing what's best for me.

'Don't do that,' Clarissa snaps. 'Trying to turn it back on me and get that shitty posture like you're squaring up. At least I've tried. I'm not stupid enough to be forcing myself to be miserable for fuck's sake. You, on the other hand, went from Mr Relationship to Mr I-hate-love literally overnight. I wasn't big on them before Benedict passed. And it's more than that, anyway. You live your life like you're trying to *be* him because he isn't here to live it for himself.'

Clarissa's words feel like it was me who was punched in the face, not Bennie. She's never said anything like this before. She's always been understanding. Or maybe quiet. There was camaraderie. Or so I thought.

'Oh.' There's nothing more I can say. Nothing more I can bring myself to say.

I guess I could tell her about my possible feelings for Félicité, but I feel kind of stupid now. If I say it, it's like I'm trying to prove something and that would be ridiculous. It would sound pathetic. Plus, I haven't seen the girl for six months. She's basically slipped into the realms of myth and legend. She's a distant figure I can use to measure every other girl against and say, *Well, she isn't as good as Félicité, isn't as funny as Félicité, isn't as caring as Félicité*. It's a great way to keep even further away from people, and I know this is exactly what Clarissa will gleefully point out, because I've somehow managed to piss her off even more than I have my mum.

'"Oh?" Is that it? I was expecting you to get all defensive.' Clarissa picks up a ball that Cottontail has dropped by her feet and tosses it into the distance for the setter cross to bring back.

'Nope. No point.'

I want to remind her that she was the one who pointed out to me that love is pain. They say that time heals all pain. Maybe for some people it does, but for others blood creeps into their dreams from the open wounds in their hearts, along with the screams of their friends. It's a constant reminder that loving someone, anyone, can cause permanent damage to the heart, until it becomes distorted beyond recognition.

I keep my mouth shut. It doesn't matter what everyone around me thinks, or whether Clarissa has changed her opinion about relationships or love. Most people don't realise the promise is about more than Benedict's dying wish to me. The more people I love, the more I'm opening up the door for pain to come flooding in. I thought that Clarissa was the one person who understood that, who understood that there's no way I can handle that amount of loss again. Maybe I *am* trying to be a bit more like Bennie. He was smart enough to protect himself from having too many feelings.

'Can I just remind you,' Clarissa says, 'that Benedict wasn't devoid of love? He loved you and me, and he didn't shut everyone out the way you have. He had loads of friends and adored them all. How many friends do you have now? I mean *real* friends? Ones you actually see and haven't pushed out of your life and you don't just see because of work? You fill your life with one-night stands and acquaintances from your foodie travels. I–' An alarm on Clarissa's phone sounds. The one that sounded from not long after Bennie died until now, the one for her antidepressants. 'Damn, I forgot to bring my pills. Come on, I need to get back to the house.'

Chapter 33

Ralph

Five Months Earlier

After months of doing everything I can to not be back in my apartment, I can no longer avoid it. There was the two weeks I spent at Mum and Dad's, and a fair amount of that was with Clarissa talking about the past and Bennie. Sometimes the future too. Then I went to Germany to do the Grimm trail and see what eateries were good along the way. Got to do that for a couple of weeks for a freelance job as well as a magazine feature.

Now I'm here. Back in the stale air of my white box. The hall looks like Miss Havisham's place with spider webs lacing the corners. My suitcase wheels wobble behind me as I walk down the hall. I dump the suitcase, and all is quiet. Everyone else in the building must be out at work because there's no sound from anywhere.

I slip off my shoes, place them on the rack next to the trainers that I never wear but might one day. I walk through into the open space that's the kitchen-living room and click the kettle on. I pull down one of my four white mugs and wander away to sit on the couch, letting the kettle boil to itself.

This place has become more and more devoid of life.

It hasn't, actually, I'm just letting myself notice it. I guess I knew that before, but I didn't care. Life, or more, the life force of others, was too overwhelming in my space. Solitude and brief social interactions have been my life. I have very few things, apart from nice clothes. I have a lot of good quality stuff for work. Aspirational stuff to get people asking what I'm wearing a lot of the time. Half of which was gifted to me, as I'm apparently some kind of influencer. Helps with my appeal and that's important, because my job is my life. It keeps me out of this empty white box.

I wonder what Félicité's doing now, and what happened to Noëlle. I've spent a bunch of time trying to find them online but without a last name it's basically impossible. It was just one night, sort of two. One and a half. She's probably forgotten I even exist. I wish I could forget she existed. I tried. Then last month Clarissa tells me I'm ruining my life, I'm trying too hard to be Bennie, and now I don't know what I'm doing.

It was Benedict who helped me to see I needed to have fun, to relax, and I promised him I would do that. Then it was Clarissa who pointed out that all love leads to is pain, one way or the other. But now...

Now she's telling me that I need relationships in my life. Any relationships. I have her, Mum and Dad... my camera operator and I get along well enough too. One of my editors is chatty. It's a depressing list.

I want to talk to Bennie. He would ask the right questions to get stuff out of me. I didn't see that until I missed it. After A levels, when I didn't know what I was doing, he shrugged and said, 'What did you enjoy the most? Can that be a job? Is that a job you'd enjoy?' Which led me to do media, which is paying off now, I guess. Not how I planned, but nothing ever is, I guess.

For five minutes I stand up, sit down, pace, put the kettle back on only for it to click off unnoticed and I end up in my bedroom.

I can't speak to Bennie, so I do the closest thing I can. I pull open my wardrobe and tug down a heavy cardboard box. It's been quite some time since I've opened it. There's a dead spider curled up on top that floats away as I place the box on my untouched bed. Then I edge down the next box and place it beside the first one on the bed.

Scooting next to them, I carefully open one of the boxes and find all the familiar items inside.

When Benedict died, I had to let his parents into the flat. Clarissa and I went with them. She didn't want them to go through his stuff, but I couldn't tell them no. I just kept thinking how my mum would feel if Bennie didn't let her in for my stuff, so I couldn't stop them. It wasn't my place to decide, it wasn't my stuff, and they are – were – his next of kin after all.

They gathered up anything of value, his PlayStation and laptop, a couple of bits here and there, but then his mum said I could do what I wanted with the rest. Then they left and I haven't spoken to them again since. Not once. They haven't checked in on me. I always message or see Clarissa around Benedict's birthday and the anniversary of his death just over Christmas, but never them.

Clarissa didn't want much. She had photos of her own. She took a hoodie that Bennie used to wear when he was hanging, but that's about it. No, she took his sunglasses too, they were pretty iconic Bennie. Square and reflective so you couldn't see his eyes in the sun.

Everything else I boxed up and kept. I think everyone thought I would charity shop or bin a lot of it, but I couldn't. Two large dusty boxes of stuff, plus another of clothes that I haven't opened for about three years. Last time I did, they smelled so potently of his heavy-handed CK spray, like musty pineapple, that it took a week of deep breathing to recover.

In the first box I open, there are schoolbooks. Unlike me, when he moved out of his parents' house, he took everything he wanted to keep with him, whereas my old bedroom at Mum and Dad's still has junk of mine hiding under the bed, and some of my toys live in their loft for no apparent reason. Not like I've expressed an interest in playing with my old Pokémon cards for the past twenty years, let alone my action figures.

There're some fiction books in the box, including *King Rat*, that I got him, some advanced chemistry books, and some random workbooks from high school. I pull the workbooks out. I usually skip past them, going for the photos and the notes off his old pinboard. They all have that old library smell, the smell of paper and the soft glue in the spines.

My fingers skim over the worn paper covers – blue, green, red –with his name on the front, written in his miniscule scratchings. He should've been a doctor with writing like that. A smile twitches on my face because that was a joke that he made himself.

I pick a book at random, the blue one, an old English book from GCSEs. It's some kind of notebook. I flick through the pages and something catches. There's a piece of paper in there that's been folded and glued in along one edge to keep it in place. I unravel it to see the title of what looks like a poem.

Set title: Life: a poem for spring

The lamb goes
unloved. Its mother hasn't loved before.
She doesn't

know how. It's just another
chore. Instead she bites
at the back of its neck. The lamb isn't
recognised, she thinks it's a cuckoo.
It isn't.
It can be loved by someone
else. The mutton takes it in,
and feeds it to stop it being
thin. Because where there's life
then love can be too. Even if someone
is cruel to you.

The teacher's green pen has left a tick and a comment, "Nice attempt at enjambment. I'd like to see more of this, Benedict. An interesting take for the given title."

'Enjambment?' I turn this new word over on my tongue. Maybe I have heard it before; we were in the same English class for GCSEs so it's more than possible it's one of the many things I've forgotten I knew.

Wriggling on the bed, I slap my hands to my pockets. I must've left my phone in the other room, so I can't look up the word unless I go and get the phone. No point. I read the poem again. Then again. Then once more.

Did I write a poem for spring? I don't remember that either.

Carefully, I peel the poem from the ageing glue with a satisfying *krrr* sound as it pulls away. The only trace of it left in his book is a shiny line like a slug's been on the page. I close the book and lie back to read the poem again. Bennie wouldn't mind. If it had been left to anyone else, the notebook would've been put in the recycling.

The poem is mostly about how life can be cruel, that bit I get, but the part I'm stuck on is: "Because where there's life then love can be too."

It's skipping in my head like a stone on water.

First, Clarissa's changing her mind from what she said almost five years ago. Now she's telling me to rethink my life and make connections instead of thinking that love is pain – and Benedict's telling me life can have love too. His poem does anyway.

I exhale and close my eyes, letting my head relax on my pillow. This is one of the best parts of being back in the apartment. My memory foam pillow engulfs me just the right amount. I'd take it everywhere if it didn't cost me too much in space.

Félicité's dark-blue eyes wait for me behind my eyelids. She plays on my mind for no obvious reason at all.

I know why Benedict sits on top of my thoughts, Clarissa too. Their shared history and words swirl over my head like the beginning clouds of a tornado. Maybe it was Félicité's words about having fun that make her feel like unfinished business to me. Although, I know it's more than that.

I think maybe her asking me to make that promise woke me up, or something. That's the only way I can possibly describe it or understand it. But it was like Félicité ripped off some flimsy bandage I'd been using to hold myself together and in doing so all the blood drained from my head, leaving me open to see her for more than just another person to pass a night with.

I was able to see her confidence and her vulnerability, the spark in those eyes of hers and the look of intrigue she gave me when she touched my skin, my tattoo. She hadn't wanted me to leave her when she was at her lowest. I wish I'd never left her.

She's probably with someone else now. She's moved on and hasn't looked back at the random English guy she met last Christmas. She knocked me so far off my game she probably thought I was useless. My body contracts at the memory of us. Nothing about that night felt useless. It felt more like fireworks bursting from my chest that I didn't even know lived inside of me.

Maybe I do want to see her again. But I don't even know where she is, or where she lives. All I know is that she goes to Rouen to visit her mamie every year for her birthday. Assuming Noëlle is still around, then I guess I know where Félicité will be in December.

I'm not sure I'm ready to give up my promise to Bennie, but then, he said I had to have fun, and here in this poem he says where there's life there can be love. So maybe he believed in love too. All I know is, since that night with Félicité, nothing has seemed like fun.

Chapter 34

Ralph

Present Day

After Félicité has gone, I'm left replying to a thousand messages from Clarissa. I take myself off to the bedroom and flop down on the sheets. They smell like Félicité. Just how I remember her, sweet vanilla like crème anglaise. Lying on my front, I press my face into her pillow, taking in deep lungfuls of her scent.

"Because where there's life then love can be too." Benedict's poem. I am alive and I can have life and love. It sounds in my head when my brain goes quiet.

My phone vibrates, and it's Clarissa *again*.

When are you coming back? I need to see you.

Me: **I think we both need space after what happened. I'll be back before Christmas.**

Clarissa: **I need help and I don't know who to speak to. After everything I told you, everything that happened and you left. You can't keep ignoring me, it's fucked up.**

This is making me feel like dirt.

I want to look after her, but I know that right now, that's just not the right thing to do. After seeing her, what was it, must have been six months ago, and her telling me that what I was doing wasn't for Bennie, but about trying to be him or something, we started to talk more. Turns out we both needed more support. Maybe Mum was a little right too, with the anniversary of Bennie's death coming up to five years – it's like taking off the plaster that's been holding me together. I think there's something about the milestone, something that makes me want to run from everything I know, because it'll soon be five years since we last laughed together. Five years since he pushed me to better myself or to shake things off and smile instead of getting bogged down. We wanted to travel together. Instead, I've been doing it alone and not taking any of it in. Not properly. I got lucky. I got a break when I needed something. It was when I no longer cared enough to be nervous; I saw an opportunity and I went for it. Just the way Benedict would have. Then I hear what Félicité describes about taking in cultures and getting to know people from all walks of life... that's how it would've been with Benedict. He would've started the right conversations and created adventures. Unlike me. Alone I float from place to place, existing and reporting on the taste of food, but not the taste of life.

At every turn Félicité is opening my eyes to what my life could be.

With the way things have been sliding sideways, I need to do what Clarissa keeps telling me; I need to think for myself. I text Clarissa again.

I'm not ignoring you. We'll talk when I'm back, yeah? Face to face is better. I'll come round and see you. Stay safe xx

I want to tell her about Félicité. I want to tell Benedict about Félicité. Telling either of them is impossible right now. Instead, I push my phone to one side and let myself fall into the dream of her, her vanilla scent and the small dimple in her chin. She woke up and she was straight in with strong coffee and stronger conversation. I want this to be our strange story. Falling in love even though we seriously didn't mean to. One day this could be something we look back on.

"Because where there's life then love can be too."

The idea overwhelms me, like it did last night, although Félicité isn't here to distract me from my feelings and replace them with lust. My hands scrub over my face. I need to get up and shave.

Falling for her is sucking all the air from my lungs. I hold my airless lungs for four counts, as I know to do. When I try to breath in, it's like I'm drowning myself on purpose with my greed for crème anglaise.

Chapter 35

Félicité

Ralph will be meeting my entire family.

This thought is enough to make me sweat in my cashmere gloves as I walk home. Ralph offered to walk me back, but I don't want to introduce him to anyone too early on, and without preparation. For me more than for him. Bumping into Carole right now is not an option.

As I arrive at the house and slip my key into the door, it flies open and is almost pulled off its hinges.

'*Merde,* it's you.' Pierre screws up his face at me and rushes away from the door before I have time to respond.

'Good morning to you too.'

'Mamie is gone.'

With only one foot over the threshold, I stop dead and the sweat I had been feeling runs cold and sticky.

'Gone? Gone where?'

'I don't know.'

'What do you mean you don't know?'

'I don't know!' Pierre begins swearing as I beg him to tell me when she went missing. He has no idea.

'Milo's still asleep?'

'Yeah.' Pierre exhales and paces the room.

'You're sure? You've checked?'

'I mean– No, I didn't check, he just isn't up yet.'

'Check on Milo now. I'm going to look for Mamie.'

'I don't need to check.'

'Yes, you do. What if she's taken Milo with her? Told him they were going for a walk? Just check, will you? Text me as soon as you have.'

I'm out of the door and running down the street. My brain is scrambled eggs churning around, doing its best to spit out an answer as to the whys and wherefores being ladled into the mix.

My eyes dart from dog walkers to alleyways between timber-frame houses like Mamie's. I question a passerby, but they haven't seen her. They don't know her. They've been looking at their feet and listening to their music; they haven't seen or heard a thing in years, I'm sure.

I move along because there's only one place I can guess where she might be, but I could be wrong. Please don't be wrong. She's never gone out without telling anyone before, not in the whole time I've lived with her. I tell her where I'm going, and she tells me where she is going. Sometimes I write it down for her just in case she forgets.

My pace quickens to a jog, fast enough to get somewhere quicker but not so fast that I might miss a vital clue as to her whereabouts. My phone buzzes. It's Pierre; Milo is asleep in bed. Or he was. Now he is up and wondering why his uncle has woken him for no apparent reason, just to tell him everything is okay.

I ask each passing person, and there aren't that many at this hour, whether they've seen a lady in her eighties, curled grey hair, smart, maybe glasses, maybe not... It's hard, I have no idea what she's wearing or what people would notice. Do people notice quiet elderly ladies walking alone? Or are they invisible to the naked eye? For so many, older people are like the sun's rays. They are everywhere, but only noticed when you are forced to look directly at them. That's how it feels right now. Like she's invisible. A ghost.

I send a snappy message to Pierre asking whether her coat is gone and her shoes.

Quickly, he confirms they are; that's at least a start. Another message from him: it's her fancy coat that's gone, the one with the fur trim round the neck that she saves for best.

Soon, I've reached the Christmas market. It's all closed up; each chalet is like a lonely wrapped gift waiting to be opened on Christmas morning.

I head to the cathedral and open the heavy dark wooden entry door that's set inside the enormous doors in the facade that would be impossible to open unless you were a giant.

The air in the nave seems thinner and colder than outside. Tapered white candles burn here and there, in memory of lost loved ones. I just hope I haven't lost mine.

Although it's not the biggest cathedral in France, it's one of the tallest and widest, and each sound echoes from place to place. The space is filling with people for the morning service. My feet echo over the other muffled sounds in the Cathedral as I swiftly dart here and there.

It's only when I think I'm about to tug every last hair from my head that I see her. In one of the pews right at the front. I stop in my tracks, and the squeak of my boots on the floor causes some people passing me to screw up their faces at the sound.

I know it's her. It's her grey, curled hair and her black fur-trimmed coat. She doesn't turn around to look at me. Her head is lowered, possibly in prayer. She's so still. Too still.

The weight of the blood throbbing in my throat is enough to feel like I'm being strangled. She's safe. Mamie is safe. I let the words roll around my mind, but they're hard to believe. Mamie fits in perfectly with the immortalised figures around her, carved in stone, from the Viking Duke Rollo to Richard the Lionheart, all perfectly still.

Sucking the stale air of the cathedral deep into my lungs, in through my nose and out through my mouth, to steady my nerves, I walk calmly over to her. As I get close enough to touch her, I hear a little sniff and it's enough for me to want to cry with relief. Emotion swells up, making me lightheaded.

I place myself down by her side, and the wood of the pew creaks under the movement.

Indeed, she does have her coat and shoes on, but she's in a floor-length cotton nightgown. She must have got out of bed and come straight here.

'Hello, Mamie.'

'Hello, *ma petite chou*. Are you here for the service?'

'No, Mamie. Are you?'

'Oh yes, we come every week.'

We don't.

We come every year at Christmas to listen to the carol singers. I do know that she used to come every week when she was a girl.

'Is this why you left the house?'

A frown burrows into her skin, wrinkling her face more than it already is.

'No, I–' She hesitates. 'Marcel was staying. I saw him sleeping and I wanted to get him a special breakfast. He never comes to visit anymore. I was so pleased to see him.'

My Uncle Marcel passed away years ago, crushed in an accident at work. He was only young, in his forties, and no amount of compensation helps with the loss of a child that I'm sure Mamie feels every day. Pierre does look quite a bit like him, the same slightly crooked nose and sallow skin. People have commented on as much in the past about their looks, but they don't look alike enough to mistake one for the other, and besides, Mamie knows he is gone. I've never seen anyone look as dead as she did at Uncle Marcel's funeral. She could hardly speak, and when she did, it was the smallest voice in the world. We all loved Uncle Marcel, but Pierre is not him.

I should tell her, I know I should, but it feels too dreadful to correct her when she might just forget this conversation anyway. She might forget that she forgot, and remember the truth of the matter on her own, without it becoming a dreadful slice of seemingly new information. My toes clench in my boots because I hate this. I want her to be her, I want to shake her and tell her how frightened I was and that she needs to snap out of it.

'Did you get the breakfast for him?'

Mamie looks at me, shaking her head. 'Where were you this morning, Carole?'

'Carole? Mamie, it's Félicité.' It's hard to keep my voice steady; a wobble kicks its way out no matter how hard I try.

'Oh yes, I knew that, *ma petite chou.*'

'Shall we go home? We can get some nice breakfast. Pierre's waiting for us.'

'Do you not want to stay for the service?'

People are filing in around us and I'm sure we only have about five more minutes to escape. My phone begins to blare out in my pocket leaving people casting me pointed looks.

'Come on, Pierre's calling. I think he wants to see you. Let's get some breakfast. I bet you're hungry.'

'Mmm, I suppose there's a hole to fill.'

I slip my arm in hers. Once it had been sturdy, something I could hang off as a girl. Now it's wiry and frail. More so than a child's arm or even a tissue.

We walk back past people who look but say nothing. A rock sits heavily in my throat and however much my eyes sting, I know I mustn't blink. I tilt my chin up and do my best to portray perfect confidence as I lead my grandmother from the cathedral and out into the slush that's been left by the snow, melted by hundreds of trudging boots including my own.

'Are you still seeing that Ralph fellow? He was a nice chap.'

I splutter a laugh through my gathering tears and drop my head like she's broken my neck with her sudden clarity. The woman I adore asking me a sensible question in amongst the madness.

'Yes, I am. Would it be alright for him to come to your birthday meal?'

Her pointy nails grab at my arm through my coat. 'Oh yes. I think it would be nice to have a handsome man to look at for my birthday. Not to mention your mother will have a thing or two to say, I'm sure.'

We are chatting as though she's not in her nightie and everything is perfectly normal. Carefully we meander along the cobbled streets and back to the safety of the town house. Back to something a little less known. A new, slightly more warped reality where I'm going to have to start to hide keys.

Chapter 36

Félicité

Mamie has been herself, with the usual sprinkling of confusion, since she wandered off in the early hours of the morning a couple of days ago. I've tried to be normal about everything, because I think it was seeing my mum that shook everything up a little too much for her. Carole unsettles things and causes confusion at the best of times.

Tonight, I have a different sort of engagement, one with my son, Bernadette and her daughter, Luna, who is a year older than Milo. Romain, Bernadette's son, didn't want to come with us today, because, apparently, he is now officially too old to see Père Noël, which is exactly what we are doing tonight.

'Maman, why doesn't Romain want to ask Père Noël for anything?'

'Maybe he has everything he needs.'

'He could ask for something for someone else.'

'Is that what you're going to do?'

Milo gives this some thought as he scuffs his shoe over one of the smooth cobbles in front of the cathedral where we're waiting for Bernadette and Luna.

'Maybe.'

'Look, here they are.'

Milo lights up like a Christmas decoration at the sight of Luna bounding towards him. They wrap each other up in an almost aggressive embrace. Milo lifts Luna, who is a good few inches taller than him, right off her feet. They start buzzing with conversation about what they'll be asking Père Noël for, as Bernadette and I offer each other a swift glancing kiss from cheek to cheek. She smells of pink grapefruit body spray, as she always does. It's a pretty smell and if I closed my eyes, I could find her with ease.

'How is Noëlle?' Bernadette pulls off her floppy white bobble hat and scrubs her fingers through her cropped curly hair before replacing it back on her head.

I shrug in response. I'm not sure what to say. She knows about the dreadful episode, so there's no need to explain. We follow on behind the children towards the grotto. It's there in the courtyard where Ralph and I kissed a matter of days ago on a bench.

'I've hidden her key. I worry though. What if there was a fire and she couldn't get out? Normally the key is right there on the hook.'

'Yes, yes, of course. But what else is there to do? Does Milo know where the key is?'

'Yeah, you know he is so good about it all.'

'Mama,' Luna calls over her shoulder, flicking back her flowing black hair, 'There's a queue.'

'It's not serious, get to the back.'

Luna tugs at Milo and they skip past the fence that encases the courtyard and the grotto.

'The queue isn't long. Shall we get hot chocolate afterwards?' I say this loud enough to catch the ears of the children, who cheer and jump. It's so lovely to see their delight that I can't resist adding, 'And if Père Noël says you've been really good, maybe we'll have a trip to Glup's.' Mentioning the sweet shop of my childhood means even more squealing.

'Really?' Bernadette lifts an eyebrow. 'Are you sure? Glup's before bed with all that sugar?'

'You do know that all the science says that's a myth about sugar. A small amount apparently calms the nerves. It's the chemical colours you should be worrying about.'

Bernadette laughs, her rose lipstick exaggerating her broad smile. 'Trust you to know such facts.'

There are only a few families ahead of us. The people at the front do their best to encourage their screaming toddler forward to the frothy-bearded Père Noël in his velvet suit. In the end they have to give up and move along, holding the little girl cocooned in her playsuit like she's a dolly.

Bernadette complains about her supermarket job. She works early shifts to make sure she is at home with the children every evening.

'I've been working there for five years, and this kid has been working there five minutes and won't leave things to be. I can't understand her. You're so lucky to work for yourself.'

'As with all of life, there's good and bad. I miss working at the school and talking to the other teachers over lunch. Although I do like to be able to chat with my mamie between classes, or take her out for lunch when I can. In that, I'm very lucky.'

'We're next!' Milo whooshes around, his nose glowing red from the cold and his eyes golden in the lights of the grotto.

It's all kitted out with silver-wrapped presents and big bows stuck on the painted red walls alongside the odd ice-skating boot, a plastic tree in one corner and a silver candelabra in the other. The man himself isn't as is so often portrayed. Of course, he is as the English say, suited and booted, in his long red coat with soft white trim and gold detailing. Not to mention the hat to match. But slightly younger eyes than expected rest behind the thin gold-framed glasses, and he has no giant round belly. He sits on a dainty wooden armchair and patiently listens to children of all ages as they stand by his side and ask for their Christmas wishes to come true. All of this entertainment is free, and it's here throughout the lead-up to Christmas, along with the market.

If I didn't know better, I would think Milo was desperate for the toilet, the way he's jiggling about and hopping from one foot to the next, but I know it's the excitement of getting his turn in the grotto.

The people in front take a few photos and then it's our turn.

I grab Milo's shoulder. 'Let Luna go first.'

Even though Milo winces like someone has stepped on his foot, he obliges and watches with round eyes under his thick Spider-man woolly hat as Luna expertly lists all the things she would like for Christmas: a doll from her favourite TV show, a new bike instead of her brother's old one and a Furby, because her Papa had one when he was young and she would like one too. Bernadette takes a photo of Luna's gappy smile before it's Milo's turn to take the stage.

Milo doesn't blurt everything out the way I expect him to, the way he has in other grottoes in other years. He does something I couldn't have expected. He edges close, and closer still to the Père Noël, before glancing over his shoulder towards us. The man in his cotton-wool beard leans in to make sure he'll be able to hear what Milo has to tell him. I already know what he's going to ask for. He'd like a new bike too, and the latest Spider-man toy car.

'I would like three things this year please, Père Noël.' Milo's trying to not be heard, his voice is almost a whisper, but I'm his mother and I can hear him and read his lips just about well enough.

Although I do edge a little closer to be sure as Luna booms, 'Speak up, Milo. Père Noël is over one hundred years old. He won't be able to hear you.'

Milo clears his throat, although that doesn't increase the volume too much more. 'I would please like my Mamie-Noëlle to be well again, so that Maman doesn't worry, and I want Maman to have a friend as good as Naomi is to Papa, and a Spider-man bike, please.'

The man in the wooden chair looks from Milo to me then back again. Next to me I can hear Bernadette open and close her mouth with a noise like she's going to speak but changes her mind, and Luna is staring up at me.

Père Noël says he will try his best, but the things Milo has asked for aren't the sort of things he can help with. Elves are better at making wooden toys instead of making friends.

I can only imagine my face matches the walls of the grotto and Père Noël's suit.

After photos are taken, Milo bounds away beaming, without so much as a mention of his wishes for me and Mamie. Instead, he begs to go to Glup's right away. We strike a balance and agree on hot chocolate from the market first, as it's right in front of us and Glup's is further along the high street.

We decide to slowly walk along with our drinks to make our way towards the big clock and, in turn, the sweet shop. The children stay two steps ahead of us, talking over each other about something that happened at school involving a teacher telling off an older student in the playground.

'Do you think Milo said that because he saw you with Ralph?' Bernadette has always been straight to the point. Which apparently is one of the things the person at her work doesn't think is appropriate. She is also a very soft and kind person; she just happens to ask questions close to the bone.

'I have no idea. He's never said anything like that before, so... maybe? But we weren't obvious. Even now, I have no clue what we are. In more ways we are nothing.'

'Just two people enjoying each other.'

'Exactly.'

Although this is true, there's a string pulling at me, one that wants more from Ralph than that. It's a string that I know I need to take scissors to, but each time I try, my willpower falls blunt.

'I've asked him to come to Mamie's birthday. With Milo's wish to Père Noël, perhaps it's a bad idea. I wouldn't want him to get his hopes up.'

'You know, you can't always protect him from everything. His own father left when he was a baby and he survived. You might need to give yourself permission to be happy sometimes too.'

'I do.' I can hear the shrill defensiveness in my voice, so do my best to sip my cocoa to avoid Bernadette's gaze.

'Really? And when would that be? You look after everyone else but put yourself last. A happy parent is a good parent.'

'Who says I'm not happy?' This time I meet her head on. Her plastic cup is rimmed with pink lipstick and hovers about a centimetre from her lips as we meander through people.

'That's not what I meant. You have so much to deal with, I think it's good you are having some fun for a change. Just remember, children are resilient. You can put Milo first and still have relationships of your own.'

'Ralph! Maman, look, it's Ralph!' Milo jumps up and down, takes a hop and a step, darts to one side to throw his now-empty cup in a bin before bolting into a crowd of people.

'Milo! Milo, come here now!' My voice growls with the volume of a lioness, but he's the adventurous cub who won't listen.

Heads turn but his isn't among them. I chase after him. Luckily, I spot him not too far away, hands now linked behind his back and looking up at Ralph who is gazing concerned at the faces in the crowd.

'Milo Marcel Durand, you do not run away like that. Come here now.'

'But look, it's Ralph.'

'I don't care if you saw a flying unicorn. You do not run away from me.'

'Sorry, Maman.'

Ralph says, 'You gave me a fright then, Milo. I thought you'd lost your mum.'

Bernadette coughs at my elbow and Luna stands in front of me.

'Ralph, this is my friend Luna. She's French. She doesn't speak very much English.'

'*Salut* Luna.' Ralph smiles down at the girl who's fiddling with the ends of her hair, glancing from him to Milo.

'*Bonsoir.*'

'And this,' I interrupt, 'is my friend from school, Bernadette. Bernadette, this is Ralph.'

'Yes, I could tell from Milo. Hello, Ralph.'

'*Salut.*'

'Sorry, I didn't mean to...' As Ralph has nothing to apologise for, he struggles to come up with an end to this sentence. '...distract Milo.'

'I wanted to tell you, I saw Père Noël.'

A rush of adrenaline runs down me like the undoing of a zip at the thought Milo might now tell Ralph what he wished for.

'Oh yeah? I bet that was good. The grotto looks amazing. And what did you ask for?'

'A bike and some other stuff too.' Milo's face is pink from the cold, but his coyness and the way he quickly shuts his mouth makes me wonder whether he's also blushing.

Ralph is a little pink too, we all are. He's just stepped out of Monoprix and seems to have a small bag of bottled water.

'Would you like to,' Bernadette waves her hand in thought, 'come with us to Glup's?'

Milo cheers a little but I quickly cut it down. 'No. Ralph has shopping to get home, and after running off, I'm not sure you should even have sweets.'

A whine of protest seeps from Milo's lips. 'I'm really sorry. Please.' The E in "really" seems to last for half a minute.

'If you put this in the bin for me, and promise never to run off again you can have a very small bag of sweets.'

'I promise!' Milo snatches up my used cup, Bernadette and Luna's too, before skipping to the bin.

As Milo vanishes out of earshot, Ralph narrows his pointed grey eyes on mine. 'Can I see you again tomorrow night? I thought you could prep me for Noëlle's birthday.'

'I'm really not sure. I'll message you.'

I haven't told anyone apart from Pierre, and asking Mamie if it was alright to invite him. With the guest list including Milo's papa, my papa and my ridiculous mother, it could be a very bad idea. I suppose at least it would be sink or swim.

As Milo returns from the bin, I do my best to give Ralph a please-don't-say-anything look.

'Ralph, will you come to Mamie's birthday? She told me you were, but I know she gets confused sometimes. Is it true?'

Ralph opens his mouth but only a confused *err* sound comes out of it.

'Mamie has invited Ralph, but he isn't sure whether he can come yet. Okay?'

'Please! You can meet my papa. He's very cool. I think you would like him also.'

'I'm sure I would, buddy. But for now, I best let you get some sweets. Have a lovely night all of you. It was nice to meet you, Bernadette, Luna.' Ralph dips his head and marches off in the direction of his Airbnb.

I let out an exaggerated breath, like his exit is a huge relief, which in many ways it is.

'Come on, kids, let's get to Glup's.' I grin down at them both and within a nanosecond they're holding hands and discussing Milo's new friend Ralph and how cool it is that he is English.

'He's very handsome. Milo likes him too,' Bernadette says in my ear.

'Milo likes everyone.'

'True. But Ralph was very good with him. He was smiley but not creepy. Does he have children?'

'Not as far as I know. He spoke of his cousin's children fondly once. I don't know him. Usually when you meet someone, they're connected to someone else. I have no idea who he really is.'

'That's why God gave you instinct.'

'Hmm.'

We stop at the red light ready to cross the road. Glup's waits on the other side with its multicoloured lettering and big letters on the windows. It's packed with dispensers of every kind of sweet and big colourful bags waiting to be filled.

As soon as the light turns green, we all march across and into the blinding colours of the sweets and the sickly smell of every flavour imaginable. The children grab striped bags and dart from one dispenser to the next.

'I think you should let him meet your family. Milo thinks he's a friend. And besides, you'd be making one of your son's Christmas wishes come true.'

Chapter 37

Félicité

'You must call him and tell him he isn't invited.' Carole has been following me around the supermarket so close to my elbow that whenever I stop to look at something she has to go onto her tiptoes to stop in time.

'Mamie said she wants him there. She's met him before.'

'She wandered off in the middle of the night. She doesn't know what she wants.'

'It wasn't the middle of the night.'

'And how would you know? You weren't even there.'

I could point out that she wasn't there either, and that I'm the one, and not her, who has moved in to look after Mamie. I'm the one who's always there.

There's no point in reminding her of this. She'll find a list of reasons, all that end with her being all but cut out of Mamie's will, or how she's always left out. Not that a child can be left out of a will in France. It's the law that they get a certain per cent, but with no estate left to give, it's not likely to be much. That means Mother will only get a share of money and belongings. The lion's share is something I didn't ask for – or want. I just want Mamie to be well.

I understand the practicalities of Mamie gifting her estate to me. I would be the same gifting Milo or his children whatever they needed to make life easier. That doesn't mean I want her death or illness thrust into my face. I'd rather be able to enjoy my time with her.

Now, with one slice of happiness dangled in front of me in the way of Ralph, all Carole wants to do is to snatch it away. I was already thinking I would tell him not to come. I don't want Milo to feel confused by some man I barely know being invited because of me. On the other hand, I've always been very welcoming and have told Milo it's good to make friends and to make people feel welcome. Ralph has nowhere else to be, and inviting him is a kind and generous thing to do. That's something Milo can most certainly understand. Kindness and friendship. Milo is wonderful at both.

My feelings are at the bottom of this pyramid and Milo balances at the top of it. Simultaneously, I really don't want Carole to be the one to tell me what to do. She's always been a strangely jealous creature who wants everyone to do as she tells them. She likes the control of it all, I'm sure. For her to be at the centre of everything that's happening in the world is a beautiful bonus of course. This is likely why I, Pierre and my father have all spent our lives travelling to be as far from her as possible.

'And what about Milo?'

'He's met Ralph already.'

'So, everyone apart from me already knows this man. I'm your mother.'

'That gives you no right to my life. Pierre hasn't met him, neither has Papa. He knows about him though.'

Glancing over my shoulder, I can see tension ripple over her slender shoulders and her jaw clenches shut. Good. That's what I wanted, her mouth to be closed instead of gaping and spewing ill-natured words.

'Perhaps if you'd been at home looking after Milo and your mamie, she wouldn't have gone missing.'

My fingers grip the trolley, making them look grey. I've changed my entire life to be there for them as best I can. I'm there for them all day every day. I can't let her suck me into endless guilt with her negative narrative and judgements on my life. She wants me to go for her so she can play the victim.

'Look, I'll think about it. How about you stay with Mamie and Milo tonight? I'll go and tell Ralph that it might be best he doesn't come tomorrow. I'll stay over at Pierre's after. Mamie will love it.' She won't but needs must. 'And Milo would love a sleep over with you and Jean-Claude. He's missed you dearly.' He doesn't and he hasn't. 'What do you think?'

Of course, she gives me a coy look, but this is what she wanted all along. To be needed. It's what the whole act is about: her personal insecurities. I'm yet to truly discover where they came from. I know it wasn't from her parents or my papa. Papa will defend her and say she had a hard time when she was younger, being bullied at school and attracting the wrong men before they met, and she's got worse as she has aged, but really, this is France. I thought people were meant to age like a fine wine. Clearly, she was corked.

'Fine, anything to help you, Félicité. I know you need all the help you can get, and, unlike your father I am here to help.'

My skin prickles like it's been rubbed down with a Christmas tree. I bite my tongue. This is all a ploy to spend a last night with

Ralph, and to decide whether I think it's a good idea for him to come tomorrow. Not for her to decide anything.

Chapter 38

Félicité

Ralph swings open the door with a beaming smile, but he doesn't look his normal put-together self, quite the opposite in fact. The smile is strained and the circles under his eyes are dark.

'What's wrong?' spills out of me instead of the obligatory hello.

The smile drops straight off his face and his arms slap down by his sides as he steps out of the way to let me in. 'What makes you think there is something wrong?'

'I don't know, I just know there is.'

This brings light back into his eyes. I meet this with a lift of my own.

'I like that you can do that, that you can read me. Most people can't, or don't bother.'

'Well? What is it?' I slip off my coat before working on my boots.

'Clarissa kept messaging. There were streams of the things; and then radio silence. I asked my mum to go round to her house and she wasn't there. The weird thing was, she'd left the dogs with newspapers on the floor, like, in case they mess on the floor, like she might be gone for a while. Mum could see in her window. Luckily, I know where the spare key is, so Mum let herself in. Clarissa wasn't there. I've asked them to call the police, but she hasn't been missing long enough and we just sound like nosy parkers over-reacting.'

Ralph takes my coat and hangs it next to the door. I follow him past the living-dining room and into the kitchen. There, he pulls out a bottle of white from the fridge and red from the rack and waves them both as he's talking. I nod towards the red and he gets some glasses.

'Why is this all on you? Is there something you're not telling me?'

I'm not sure why I ask this, but something about this girl gives me a tingling sensation that I don't like. Alarm bells buzz in my mind like his phone the other morning, and they won't switch off.

Ralph glugs the wine into glasses and hisses an exhale through his teeth. 'She kissed me.' The words are mumbled, but I hear them well enough over the pouring of the wine. 'I should've told you before. I didn't kiss her, she kissed me—'

'You don't owe me an explanation. I have no idea what we are or what we are doing, but one thing I do know is you don't need to explain anything to me. Particularly about the past.'

Ralph passes me my glass. In his distraction he's over filled them. To my mind they should be half full to let the wine breathe. He has filled them almost to the top. He is a man of food and wine, he knows this, and I've never seen him do it before.

'Was it recent?'

Ralph's frown deepens into cutting lines, 'Yeah, right before coming here.'

I let out a hum of acknowledgement. 'You want to tell Bennie, don't you? To explain to him your innocence in this matter.'

We move out of the kitchen. I sip at my wine to lower its level before pacing over to the window. People are wrapped up like the English pigs in blankets Lizzie makes at Christmas. They're fighting against the snow that's started again. At least in here it's cosy and warm.

I turn back to see Ralph, mouth slightly open and eyes narrowed at me. He hasn't moved from the kitchen doorway.

'Go on then,' I jibe. 'Tell me I'm wrong.'

'I can't. I just don't understand how you know me better than I do.' Tentatively, he enters the room and pulls out a chair at the dining table. No food filling its space today, only a small vase the colour of mulled wine with a single plastic flower poking out.

I stay leaning against the window frame, carefully sipping my wine and watching people hunched over walking against the blustering swirls of white. The Christmas lights glitter in spite of the beating they're taking. Although they're attached close to the window, it's blowing up so much they're almost moving like a skipping rope.

'I've been leading her on. Clarissa, I mean. Not on purpose. To be honest, I didn't even know that's what I was doing, not at first. Not until she kissed me.' Ralph throws his head back and looks up at the ceiling. 'Bennie would kill me, hurting his little sister. It's the last thing I'd want to do, too. I didn't mean to lead her on. I don't see her like that at all.'

'So, how did it happen?'

Chapter 39

Ralph

Three Days Before Leaving for France

'You're back!' Clarissa is all teeth before she leans in and kisses my cheeks.

Flopsy and Cottontail jump up and lick my hands as I make my way through the door. It's the standard greeting.

I've tried to be more supportive of Clarissa with the five-year anniversary of Bennie's death round the corner. I've been up and down the country between writing articles and filming bits here and there. I've even been offered sponsorship from a pasta company, and next year they want me to film some adverts for them. My new agent told me I can use it to up my per-word payments from the magazine. In between it all, I've been trying to be here. Keeping an eye on Clarissa.

We make our way to her grey sofas and their layer of dog fur. I sit down to be smothered in more dog kisses while Clarissa puts the kettle on.

Today is a big day for me and I want to tell her about it.

Today I booked the Eurostar to Paris and from there a train to Rouen. I'm going to see Félicité again. Her words sounded in my head every morning when I look in the mirror, using Benedict, as she said, as an "escaped goat". Even though that slip-up was cute and still makes me smile, it equally bothers me. Is Félicité right, am I using him as a scapegoat?

She even asked if I'm looking for Bennie's approval, I can't get it, can I? No matter how hard I try. I can't know what Benedict thinks about anything anymore. He can't let me out of this promise I made. It all sloshes around in my head in those quiet moments in front of the mirror when I brush my teeth or shave my face. Everything is reflected right back at me. Then I slip into the idea of holding Félicité again. I have to give myself the chance to know more about her and her life. Sometimes, when I smell vanilla, I can almost taste her skin on my tongue and the subtle smell that lingers around her throat.

Clarissa will be happy for me, I'm sure, and she's the only person I want to tell. I need to thank her too, because she's been a big part of helping me see that I need something meaningful again, and that Benedict would agree and be happy for me. She's unknowingly supported what Félicité had to say about me keeping this promise so I can protect myself from a life of pain.

My hands feel clammy at the thought of loss, at the thought of never saying goodbye, but Benedict's gone for good. I swallow the feeling down as Clarissa comes into the room, grinning over two mugs.

Almost two hours have passed. The dogs are asleep and we've moved to talking about Clarissa and Benedict's childhood. I don't know how we got here, and I haven't even managed to tell Clarissa about France yet. She launched into a conversation about the mugs and how she'd had them since she was a kid. They were from some theme park. It sparked a conversation I couldn't have expected.

'I don't know how much he told you about it all.' Clarissa pulls her knees up and rests her chin on them. Her navy joggers and navy tee make her look like she's in pyjamas.

'He told me everything, I guess.'

Her hooded eyes half close as her gaze narrows at me.

'Seriously?'

'Yeah, I mean, I was there, Clarissa. I remember what your mum and dad were like with each other.'

'Yes, but you never saw what Mum was like with him. She was never silly enough to let slip when people were over.'

I clamp my mouth shut. What Joy was like with him? With Benedict? I always thought Clarissa had it worse, always being ignored by her mother. At least she spoke to Bennie.

When Clarissa doesn't automatically give more information, I probe more. I say with an impatient exhale, 'How do you mean?'

Clarissa's right leg flops down. 'I thought you said he told you everything.' Her voice is riddled with churlish sarcasm.

'Well, yeah, that's what I thought too, but now I've got my doubts. You're making it sound like loads of shit went down when my back was turned and Bennie never said.'

Clarissa looks down at one of the dogs as it flinches in its sleep. Another moment passes before she begins.

'I don't know if it was because he was the oldest or because she had a down on men.' Clarissa's voice is steady but barely audible over the gentle snoozing of the dogs. 'Maybe both. Everything he did was wrong. She'd dig her nails into his wrists, or the back of his neck, and drag him from place to place telling him what he'd done wrong.' Her hands squeeze at her trackies like they are Bennie's wrists.

'What?' I'm trying not to leave my mouth hanging open as a million questions filter towards it, leaving only one word able to funnel its way out.

'Yeah, like, if his room wasn't perfectly tidy, she'd point out any speck of dust by pressing his face into it. Then she'd drag me in and tell me things like, *You need to make sure your man does as he's told, or you'll end up with a loser like your father or your brother.* One Christmas the bitch got him a duster and made him use it all day. She wouldn't even let him have dinner, because she said he was too fat for Christmas dinner.'

'What the hell?' I want to exclaim that Benedict was not a fat kid at all, quite the opposite, but it's a pointless thing to say; Clarissa knows that. Something else jumps out of me instead. 'And you and your dad, what? Just watched?'

Clarissa's eyes become thin lines of black, points of pain narrowed on me.

'You weren't there. He wouldn't want me to step in, and Dad really was a waste of space. She got that much right at least.'

My mind blurs with thoughts and questions, spiralling out of control. How didn't I know any of this? How much hadn't he told me?

'He didn't tell me any of this. How old was he?'

'That Christmas? Oh, I dunno, maybe, eleven.'

'That's insane.' My stomach feels like it wants to escape my body and my brain has gone numb. My hands and lips too. Numb. Nothing feels real all of a sudden. Then that poem of his, the one I found glued into his book, and that now lives next to my bed, seeps into my thoughts. The sheep that didn't want its lamb and used to nip and bite its neck. My mouth is dry and my fingers curl. He was the lamb. It wasn't imagined at all. It was a metaphor.

'I knew he didn't want to have a relationship or have kids because of your parents' crappy relationship, but this–'

'Oh yeah, it was really messed up. Bennie took most of it. Dad was seriously useless. If he said anything, Mum would go for him, so he kept out of the way and let her go for Bennie instead. Went for him with a knife once, you know. It was easier for them both to just do as they were told or avoid her as best they could. Best for us all.' Clarissa switches to a bright and pretty smile. 'But hey, we did a great job of pretending, right? Pretty sure the Oscar will arrive any day now.'

'Wait, what, she went for Benedict or your dad? With a knife?' I can't imagine either. She's a slight woman with too-perfect nails who never lifted a finger. Born into a fat inheritance and then married a man with a good job and, apparently, no backbone.

'Dad. She went for Dad. Maybe Bennie too. He wouldn't have told me if she had, because he knew I was terrified. I saw her go for Dad though.'

'What in the hell did your dad do?'

Her eyes roll and her face relaxes back to normal.

'Nothing. Weak and useless. They only split when she couldn't be bothered with him anymore. No, that's not it – he lost his job and wasn't a cash cow anymore, I guess. He'd still live with her now. God knows why. I don't understand it for a minute. Bennie was so strong, though. Nothing like either of them. You don't know the half of it, Ralph.' Her voice goes up and the light from the Christmas tree in the corner of the room reflects in the watery glaze of her eyes.

Automatically, I move closer to her and place my hand over one of hers that's resting on her knee. My fingers encase her vulnerable little hand, and I begin to gently squeeze.

'I'm so sorry I didn't do more for you both. I'm sorry I wasn't there for him all the times he needed me the most.'

'Stop it,' she snaps. Her eyes darken and fiercely meet my own. 'Without you I don't even know what would've happened to him. You were a ray of hope and light for him, and you never once let him down. You got him out of that dreadful house and pushed him to get an education. What happened wasn't your fault.'

Clarissa pauses. I keep my eyes on our hands, but I can feel her studying me and eventually I meet her gaze.

'You've changed,' she says. 'You make me want to be better too you know. You've been softer this year, here with me, helping me. I've decided to come off the antidepressants at last. That's all thanks to you. You make me feel like I could do anything.'

A smile brightens her face, but a tear that had been patiently waiting to fall takes centre stage and tumbles down her rosy cheek.

I swallow down everything I'm feeling, the strange and painful mixture of resentment and pride. 'That's brilliant news. I'm so proud of you. Bennie would be proud of you.'

Her worn fingertips graze my stubbled chin.

'He'd be proud of you. He'd be proud of us.'

Her mouth edges to mine. No, surely not? Her lips latch onto my bottom lip. This can't be happening. I don't want to push her away, because I don't want to hurt her, but I really want to push her away. Adrenaline pulses around my veins like the beat of a rave and I'm as still and silent as the night before Christmas.

She softly kisses me, and I try to both return the kiss and pull away. All this does is lead her forwards and onto me.

This isn't what I want to do, but I feel I have no choice. My feet lightly tap Cottontail's bottom. It's enough to make her sit up and look about with a bark as if it ask who nudged her. It's enough to give me an escape.

'What's up, girl?' I lean over her and scrub her head to make sure she's fully awake before loudly slapping my hands down on my thighs like I'm the dame in a panto. 'I'm really pleased for you, Clarissa, about the meds. You really can do anything. I believe in you.' I pull the sleeve of my jumper up and look at my watch. Every move feels stupid and exaggerated because I feel like a complete dummy. 'Gosh, is that the time? I'm going to have to go now.'

'Now?' Her skin bruises red.

I'm a massive idiot. I'm embarrassing us both, but I need to leave. If I stay, I'll say the wrong words and make the situation worse. I'm not good at letting people down easy, and she's the last person I want to make feel bad.

'Yeah, I was going to tell you. I need to go to France in a couple of days... for work. I need to get ready. Prep and such.' I shouldn't lie, but it's too late now. She's caught me off guard and I'd say almost anything to escape now. 'I'll see you when I'm back, okay? I'll come straight round. We can pick up where we left off.'

Now that was a really bad choice of words. Why in the hell did I have to word it like that?

Chapter 40

Félicité

I feel as though he is giving me broad brushstrokes of the story, telling me that he had been regularly visiting Clarissa over the past six months and that had led him to have the confidence to come back here to see me. Only she seemed to have taken it to be more than platonic. He's told me that before he left for France, she was telling him about her childhood with Benedict and then told him she was proud of how much he'd changed, then she kissed him. I play all this back to Ralph to see if I've got the story straight.

'Yeah. But the worst part is, I was so desperate to escape that I said "we'd pick it up where we left off when I'm back" or something. Why the hell did I have to say something like that? I should've been clear with her. I'd gone round there to tell her about you and... well, I fucked up big time.'

'It does sound that way, yes.'

'Now she's off her meds and she's missing. I should've been clearer with her. It's all on me. First Benedict, now Clarissa.'

'You can't control everything. She is a grown woman with her own life. Should you have been more honest with her? Yes. Are you in control of her fate? No. When you are back in England, you'll need to be honest with her. Friends should always share honesty.'

'If they find her. Maybe I should go back early.'

Ralph's phone begins to ring from the bedroom. He abruptly pushes his chair back and jogs towards it. I take another sip of my wine and look out to see a couple kissing in the snow.

Why am I here letting myself get tangled up in this man's messy life? He might be attractive with his ridiculously sharp jawline and swish hair neatly gelled to one side, but looks are of little importance to me when it comes down to it. I don't need more drama in my life. I walk to the table and put down my unfinished wine.

I should leave now, walk away and stop this insane charade. Last time I was here, he was hinting that I was the thing in his life that had changed everything. Or maybe he wasn't. Maybe I'm letting myself believe in this too much because I have nothing in my life that is just for me, and after years without a relationship, I've been caught up in the thrill of it all. Walk away.

My heart races as I move towards my boots and coat near the door. Then I catch his voice, the delight at whoever is on the line, perhaps Clarissa? More baggage than I can handle.

I duck down to grab my boot, and I'm tucking it onto my foot when I hear him say, 'That was my mum. Where are you? Oh.' I can't see him. He's behind me. I can only imagine his face and the confusion that's scrunching it up. 'Are you leaving?' And there it is. A sadness that brings me back to him in the strangest possible way.

Words slowly arrive at my lips as I stand and face him, 'Yes. I think perhaps this isn't right. You have a lot that you're going through with this Clarissa girl, and I have my family to think of. I think perhaps I should go.'

'That was my mum. Apparently, Clarissa's neighbour came home and said that she'd agree to take the animals to the kennels where Clarissa works. She had to leave in a hurry because her great-aunt had a fall. I didn't even know she had a great aunt. Point is, I can relax now. I can focus on us and figure out what the hell *us* is... or could be.'

He's moved to be close to me. His fingers curl under my chin to tilt it up for his mouth to lower onto mine. I can taste the wine on his tongue as it teases mine. I press into him, and all my concerns are silenced, because being held by Ralph is worth getting in trouble for. It's worth a little pain and heartache, because this has been all I've dreamt of for a year. He is my Christmas wish, my gift to myself. The only selfish desire I have in life right now. And I want to enjoy every moment of it before it ends. I'm no fool. I know it will most likely come to an end. But not tonight. Tonight, I'm going to take in every muscle and every curve of him.

We stumble as he steps back and we gravitate towards the bedroom. I think of the last time and the shift between us. The way everything seems to fall into place when we're together. It's as though we have known each other for centuries and can share the most intimate of things while everything is fresh and exciting all in the same instant.

The pragmatic side of me wants to see this as fulfilling a primal need, but I know it runs deeper than that as we slide our hands lovingly over each other's skin. Even that first time, even with no knowledge of each other's bodies, something felt so different. It was too good for a first time. It was like we knew each other even though we didn't. There were no clumsy moves, no awkward steps. We moved around each other like liquid.

Now we know what to expect, but surprise each other none the less, pushing each other as hard as we can. I want to ask him whether he's consumed with fear too, fear that this is temporary, fear that tomorrow he will meet my family and the bubble will be cut open with a knife and all we'll have left is memories and raw emotions.

My fingernails dig into his shoulders harder than I intended as he presses his weight on me, pinning me in place while sweat pours like tears over my skin. When we kiss it's as wild as it can be without bringing each other pain. We're already doing that, by wanting something we're too afraid we can't really have. Or at least, I know I am.

After a satisfying and tiring evening, I coil into his arms as we hide under the thick blankets and duvet. My relationship with Henri wasn't like this. It was different, but I can't say how or why. Perhaps because he was a selfish lover, selfish in his entirety if I'm honest with myself. Selfish enough to leave his child and live a life for himself and no one else.

Ralph says, 'I don't want to go back to England and be without you. I want to spend time with you, and get to know Milo too. I need to see if this could really work.'

I can't give him the reassurance he needs, however much I want to. Instead, I fill the room with an echoing silence.

'Please, give me a chance. I travel a lot for work, but when I'm off, can I come here instead of England? And see you?'

'I do want that. I want to say yes to it all, but Milo comes first. Let's see how tomorrow goes. If you can survive Carole, then I guess anything is possible.'

Chapter 41

Félicité

We arrive early at the restaurant. Really early. So early they're still making up the room for our party. It's an out-of-the-way place not central to the city, but in the suburbs. It's easier for everyone invited to avoid coming into the city. Here they can travel by car and park with ease.

Ralph and I loiter in the doorway to the side room as the staff put up the balloons I've ordered and decorate the tables with cloth napkins made into simple origami-style flowers. The room is already made up for Christmas parties with tinsel around the edges and a big tree in the corner that looks like it's been plucked from a magazine, with silver-and-navy decorations equally spaced, as though someone has taken the time to measure each spacing with a ruler to be sure. To finish the look of the room, one of the members of staff lights the fire in a big inglenook fireplace, wide enough and tall enough for a small

239

adult to move about under it. It's a Christmas-card-perfect room for the week before Christmas. Another reason I chose this place.

'I'm so nervous. I'm more used to talking to a phone than people. Unless I'm interviewing them. We've only known each other a total of, what? Six days? If you add up all the time we've spent together, I mean.' Ralph rubs his palms over the back of his jeans. He looks as rigid as the Christmas tree.

A laugh chokes out of me and I tilt my head towards his ear. 'We've slept together more times.'

'Félicité?'

I physically jump and nearly head-butt Ralph's cheek at the sound of my father's voice behind me. I feel like I'm fourteen and I've just been caught kissing my boyfriend after school.

'Papa!' I whip round and we kiss cheeks. 'Lizzie!' I then kiss my stepmother's cheeks. 'This is Ralph, my...' We haven't established what we are and I can't exactly say "person I'm trying on for size". It feels like so much more, but I can't let on. It's not the time. '... my friend. He's also English.' Then I switch to English. 'Ralph, this is my father, Louis, and his partner, Lizzie.'

'Hello, Ralph. My English is...' My papa wobbles his hand to indicate the uneasy status of his English. It's a complete lie. It's my father's humour to wind people up.

'And there was me thinking you were an English teacher like Félicité.'

They exchange a sturdy smile before I move to introduce Lizzie in more detail, explaining, even though I've already prepped him, that she is English too, although she and my father mostly speak in French.

'No Milo?' My papa's muddy eyes dart around the room. Heavy wrinkles fold into his forehead.

'Carole is bringing him and Mamie.'

Papa nods and slides his hands into the pockets of his jeans.

Lizzie and Ralph are discussing languages, and how many she speaks. The list is seemingly endless. She and papa still travel round together. Papa's love for language isn't as extensive as hers, but he will give anything a go. Lizzie is eight years younger than him, and she is as vibrant as she was when I met her all those years ago. She loves colour and dancing, staying up late then getting up with the sun. I can't imagine her soul will ever age. They're the picture I put in my mind when I think of a perfect couple. They, and my mamie and grand-père when he was alive. Even though my grandparents were homebodies, who only holidayed in France, they were happy. There's nothing more important than that. Except health of course.

Papa starts mildly quizzing Ralph. I wonder whether he heard my comment or not. It's too late now of course. Heat pricks around my throat under the decorative scarf I've wrapped around my neck. It's warm in here, with the fire. If I take it off, my outfit feels underdressed, but keep it on and I might sweat through my silk blouse. I'll risk it for now.

'Does your mother know we'll be here?' Lizzie catches my elbow and pulls me close so her pouty lips are next to my ear.

'I have not told her. I'm not sure whether Pierre has. Sorry.'

She raises one sharp eyebrow and I cover my lips with my fingertips knowing what she means.

'So she doesn't know.'

'No, probably not.'

'Perhaps we can hide at the end of the table.'

Lizzie is wearing a vibrant green blouse with a ruffled front and silver snowflakes all over the sleeves. Her multicoloured coat is thrown over her arm and her chestnut hair is pulled into a tight bun at the top of her head. It would be almost impossible to hide her even if the room were full.

The waiter indicates that we can come in now that everything's in its place. Soon more people will be arriving. Mum said she would bring Milo and Mamie. It's the perfect grand entrance for her, playing the role of doting daughter and grandmother. When she walks in and sees us four it'll be interesting to know whether she can keep her cool.

Lizzie and I follow in behind Ralph and Papa who are already settled into a conversation about work and what Ralph does. I'm not sure my father quite understands how he can make a living chatting online about food, but the shared love of travel seems to be sparking something. Ralph's crisp white shirt makes my papa look rather crumpled.

Lizzie joins the conversation, explaining she's from Lancashire in England, and of course, Ralph knows a great restaurant not too far from where she was born.

'How do you two know each other?' Lizzie waggles her finger from Ralph to me.

We look at each other and back at them. We should've planned for these obvious questions.

'We met last year,' I begin. 'Ralph helped me with Mamie. I told you at the time. This is the man who walked her back with me, before her fall. We went for a drink when Bernadette stood me up.'

'So, you're the knight in shining armour?'

Ralph's cheeks redden and he begins to laugh and stumble over words. 'Hardly. I mean, I think Félicité fits the bill for that. All I did was walk by her side for one night.' He brings his index finger up to emphasise the point. 'She's the one who's completely changed her life to look after Noëlle. I don't know anyone else who has done that for a grandparent. She makes me want to be a better person. She looks after everyone around her. And Milo, wow. What a smart and polite kid. When I met him, he welcomed me in like a best friend.' He hesitates and looks over us all before adding, 'Just call her Joan of Arc.' He says the last part in a goofy tone but it doesn't take away from his words.

'This is all very true, Ralph.' Papa twists his face into a crooked smile. 'I am very proud of my daughter and her intense loyalty.'

'I don't think she's just loyal. She genuinely cares.'

Ralph's right. It doesn't feel like duty or loyalty to me. I'm not looking after Noëlle because I feel I have to, although I'm aware that if I didn't, she would likely be in a care home. I love my mamie. Not knowing whether she was taking her meds or whether she was okay each day stopped me from being able to really function when I lived in Carnac.

Our conversation is interrupted as my cousins and aunt come in to join us. Even with the distraction of introducing Ralph to my aunt Aimée, her daughters Michèle and Rachael, and Rachael's boyfriend Wissam, I feel a warmth in my chest like never before. Ralph's pride in me is shining out of him. I don't need someone else to be proud of me, I'm not ten years old, but to hear someone talk about me in that way did make my chest and cheeks grow warm. I feel loved. It's ridiculous, we hardly know each other and neither of us had any intentions for any of this, but here I am, feeling the glowing heat of a love that is burning like the fire in the corner of the room. It feels safe and cuts across time.

I'm hardly able to keep up with the conversation going on around me and Ralph looks a little out of his depth as only Rachael has simple conversational English. They all laugh, so I laugh. I can't help but gaze at Ralph like I'm seeing him for the first time. Really seeing him. Even this stuff with Benedict's sister, alright, he got it all wrong on one hand, but on the other, he was trying to be kind, trying to be a friend. He is caring and thoughtful and loving.

'Maman!' Milo's voice squeals from behind me and a moment later I'm almost knocked off my feet as he propels himself into me.

We aren't apart very often, only when he sees his father, who will be here soon enough, and perhaps one or two other nights a year at most. I bend forwards and squeeze him before he lurches in to Michèle on my left and Rachael on my right. He catches sight of Ralph.

'Ralph, have you met Michèle and Rachael? This is my friend Ralph. He is Maman's friend also.'

'Yes, I–'

'Mamie-Carole! Have you met Ralph?'

With that, Milo has introduced Ralph to Carole and reintroduced him to Mamie before leaving us with only Carole's sour face coming towards us.

Oh well, I've accidentally fallen for this man now. Whether he sticks around or not, he is my friend and she's going to have to do her best to be polite. Although, the face she is making is likely also at the realisation that my father is here and Lizzie too. This will be fun.

Chapter 42

Félicité

Things are going well. Mamie is on form which is lovely to see. She's keeping Carole in check and Pierre and Ralph are getting on as well as apples in Normandy. Some of us are still mingling and others have taken a seat. We've been given Calvados as an aperitif while we wait for Henri and Naomi. They're the last ones to arrive. Which I could've predicted.

I'm standing talking to my Auntie Aimée, my Uncle Marcel's widow, about how life has been since we last saw each other a few months before, when Henri's husky voice appears in my ear and his hands rest on my shoulders.

'Félicité, how are you?'

I turn to face him and we kiss cheeks, then I welcome Naomi too.

Milo nearly knocks his father off his feet, hitting into him harder than he did with me. Henri releases an involuntary noise as the air is thrust from his lungs.

'Hello, *mon grand*. It's good to see you too.' Henri picks him up and throws him in the air, almost catching his head on one of the thick black beams above him.

A new hand rests on my shoulder as my auntie says a proper hello to Henri and Naomi. The gentle weight is Ralph, I know without even looking.

'Papa,' Milo says, 'this is Ralph, my friend.'

'Your friend? Aren't you a little young to have friends that old?' Henri sniggers.

'He's my friend too,' I say. 'This is Ralph. He is an English food critic.'

'Food critic, hey? Not good enough to make the food, only to put people down?'

This is new. Henri, still holding Milo like a shield, is firing sarcasm, or something, in Ralph's direction. He's stretched to his full height.

'It's nice to meet you, Ralph.' Naomi steps forwards with her hand out and shakes his hand, before kissing his cheeks.

'Yes, where are my manners? A friend of Félicité's is a friend of ours,' Henri says, almost with a grimace.

'And mine!' Milo beams. 'Ralph likes the word reblochon, because he thinks it's fun to say.'

'I do. It's nice to meet you both. I've heard all about you.'

'Funny,' Henri says tartly, 'we haven't heard a thing about you.'

'That's not surprising. I only got into town a week or so ago. Félicité didn't even know I was coming.'

Henri eyes me with suspicion. Henri is a big guy. His grandfather was from Cameroon, and apparently a well-built man, although I never had the privilege of meeting him. Henri is perhaps six feet with very broad shoulders, caramel skin, even if he did go to live in the Arctic Circle for three years, amber eyes and a wave of thick black hair spiked on top of his head. As always, Naomi seems as plain as paper that needs some attention. She's waiting for her moment to escape the tension. It's not that she's unintelligent, quite the opposite. She can hold a conversation well enough, there's just not much to her. She would never be the one to start a conversation even though I believe she speaks four languages.

'Where's the birthday girl? Oh, I see her, and your mother. I'd best say hello. Come on Naomi, let's say hello.'

Henri moves past us, still clutching Milo in his arms like a boy of half his age.

'So, that's Henri.'

'That is Henri.'

'I really wanted him to be ugly.'

'Ah, sorry to disappoint you. I have had some ugly boyfriends in the past. Would you like me to go and find one to make you feel better?'

'Nah, it's alright, I'm not too bad, am I?'

I look up with the urge to kiss him, until I realise where we are and that I've introduced him as a friend, not a boyfriend.

'You're annoyingly perfect, and I really, really wish you weren't.'

Chapter 43

Ralph

Félicité's mum couldn't be more different from her. There are only aggressive edges to her mother, even when she smiles and agrees. They look similar in the face, but Carole's lines tell of dissatisfaction, which couldn't be further from Félicité. She looks much more like Noëlle. All three have the same slight cleft in their chin and deep, dark eyes, although I think maybe only Félicité's are navy. But that's where the comparison stops. Noëlle and Félicité have a lot of other similarities, laughing at the same stuff even when I don't know what it is, and helping those around them even in small ways. Noëlle, for example, was trying to pass Milo an extra napkin across the table when he got garlic butter from the snails all over his smart navy shirt. He didn't see her in time, and Félicité passed him one. Noëlle was watching and taking it all in. She was there, ready to be of use.

I think Noëlle is overwhelmed as well as amused by all the people and attention. There are moments she's as mute as I am in it all. We've caught each other's eye once or twice and exchanged smiles. She tried to talk to me at one point before she was quickly and sharply reminded by Carole that I don't speak French.

It's interesting how much of a back seat Félicité has taken with Noëlle while everyone else vies for her attention. I'm not sure whether they're trying to prove who loves her more, or who is the most helpful. Don't get me wrong, the cousins all seem nice enough as far as I can tell anyway. I guess they're just trying to make the most of their fleeting time with their grandmother.

Félicité on the other hand subtly checks on her mamie's needs. She tops her water up without asking or making a big show of it. She gets to see her every day, which also means she instinctively knows what she might need and how to just be normal with her instead of treating her like a toy that's allowed out for only one day to be played with.

I lean into Félicité's ear. 'Which one is Michèle and which one is Rachael?'

Her cousins don't actually look much like sisters even though they are. It's just that when they all came in, I was overwhelmed with names and now I can't remember who's who.

'To the left is M,' Félicité whispers in my ear as I place the last piece of my almost-blue steak into my mouth. Lightly I nod to confirm I've heard her.

I swallow my bite. 'I can't believe I have to leave for England in a couple of days.' The thought sinks into my stomach along with my food, only it hits much harder. I don't want to leave. I'm sure of that now. It was the right choice to come here and take this risk. It's now all down to Félicité, and how she feels. I clear my throat before plucking up the courage to ask what I need to, while making it sound as relaxed as possible. 'So, what do you think? Will you give me a chance? Maybe let me come and visit and see how it goes?'

She looks down at Milo who's the other side of her gobbling up a bowl of pasta. Her eyes skim the other people around us too. As she glances at Henri, he catches her eye and a reflexive smile is shared between them.

Félicité turns back to look me over. Her eyes dancing over the lines of my face make me worry that I might have food on my chin.

'Yes. I want to see where this goes. But I need you to make me one last promise.'

Her hand finds my knee under the table, and we look into each other's eyes with an intensity that doesn't fit with our surroundings, but it's impossible to let go of it. A deep-set smile soon becomes hard to suppress too. I place my hand over hers.

This is my chance.

She is my chance to move on with Benedict's blessing. I can feel it.

'Oh really?' Nerves swell in my chest like a balloon, but I do my best to keep a calm exterior. 'What is it?'

'*Désolé,* sorry to interrupt, is there a monsieur Ralph here?'

The only two things I understand from the waiter are sorry – *désolé* – and my name. As silence falls over our room, an irritated voice can be heard. Fingers point in my direction and I push my chair back with the intention of standing, as the waiter politely nods, says something, then pops his head out of the door and nods again. Félicité is still holding my hand, so I stay seated for a moment as we exchange looks and shrugs.

The stomping of feet sounds from the hallway beyond, then Clarissa stands in the doorway. Her hair and eyes look wild, like she hasn't slept in a year.

'Ralph, thank god! There you are!'

Chapter 44

Félicité

The woman in the doorway is enough to stop conversations throughout the restaurant and twist them into new ones with hushed tones and snide looks. I can't see them, of course, the people glancing over their menus; we're in a private room. But I can hear a difference in volume from the restaurant beyond, and the same is being echoed in this room too.

This woman looks like she has been held upside down and rattled around for loose change.

Automatically, I grip Ralph's hand harder as she glides like a shark towards us, coming to a halt behind our chairs.

'Clarissa,' Ralph says, 'how are you here?' Before she has a chance to answer he turns to my family, still gripping my hand as he stands, displaying this moment of quiet affection to all who aren't already staring at the woman behind us. 'Sorry – *désolé* –

this is my friend's sister, Clarissa.' I slip my hand from his and feel Milo at my left elbow.

'Maman, should I get Ralph's friend a chair?' Milo pushes his own chair back from the table, ready to be of service. This leaves him hovering out on a limb closer to the back of his father's chair.

My sweet baby is wide-eyed but always eager to make a new friend.

'No, chéri, I think she'll be leaving.' Replying to Milo's English with my French is an intentional act. I don't want this odd woman to know what I've said to my son.

'So, this is why you didn't tell me where you were going? You've found someone else?' Clarissa's long nails claw at the sides of her jeans. 'I bet you've all been laughing at me, haven't you?'

Ralph climbs over his chair. He cautiously steps forwards with his palms open, the way you might with an unfamiliar dog, letting them settle themselves with your scent. 'I'm sure we can sort this out. Let's talk outside.'

In one darting movement, she steps away from him.

'Because I need you. Remember, you said I could always find you if I needed you. Remember that, Ralph?'

Ralph shakes his head. 'Yeah, I do remember.' Ralph raises his face to the ceiling scrubbing his forehead before continuing directly to Clarissa. 'This wasn't what I meant, Clarissa. Come on, let's go outside.' Ralph makes for the door and stands by it, waiting for her to move. She looks from me to him.

'Félicité.' Mamie's voice is strangled from the other side of the table, her tension resonating in the air.

'Not to worry. All will be fine,' I coo.

In turning to look back at her, I can see the agitation in her face. Milo's caught sight of her too and goes to stand. I know what he's thinking, he wants to comfort her, but I don't want him to have to edge any closer to Clarissa than he has to.

'It's okay *mon grand*, I'll see to her. You stay with your father.' I stand and skirt the table as Ralph moves closer to Clarissa, asking her in a polite, but clearly strained tone to come outside with him. What the hell have I brought to my family's door?

I catch sight of Henri on the other side of Milo as I settle myself next to Mamie. His jaw is clenched tight shut, and a fake smile has turned into a grimace.

'You're a beautiful boy. What did the old lady say? And such good English. Is he yours? This whole time you've been lying and he's yours, isn't he?'

'Thank you.' Milo says this like it's a question as confusion makes his eyes dart toward me and mamie at the opposite side of the table.

Clarissa stabs her dagger-like nail at Ralph, who is doing his best to accost her. Her anger at this flips and falls off a cliff, and she begins to sob into her hands. 'Why are you all laughing at me? Why? Ralph, why are all these monsters laughing at me?'

As Clarissa peeps out from her fingers, I can see her eyes dripping with streams of tears. They're so fast and so abundant that I'm almost impressed. I can't imagine being able to cry so much liquid in such a short time.

'What's wrong with her? I don't like her.' Mamie's lips move close to my ear.'

'Ralph,' I begin to shake my head because I don't know what words to say that won't run the risk of escalating the situation.

'I know,' he turns back to Clarissa. 'You shouldn't be here. It's time to leave. Now.'

Ralph moves to take her arm, but she swiftly moves away, lurching from his grasp to land behind Milo's chair, arms rigid at her sides.

'You have broken me, haven't you? This is all your fault. Everyone you ever love you break, Ralph. First Bennie, now me. Every part of you should die.'

'What's this woman saying? I don't like her, Félicité.' Mamie's voice is shrill as she openly objects to Clarissa's presence.

My father and I try to comfort Mamie and calm her. He and Lizzie have some of the best English at the table and have been able to understand what Clarissa is saying.

'Tell the creatures I don't like that sound, Ralph. Their croaking hurts my ears.' Clarissa loudly over enunciating and taps her index fingers to her ears.

Ralph's already sharp features lock into place as he takes a measured breath and calmly steps towards her again, this time curving around her. 'Clarissa, when did you last take your meds? I think you need to see a doctor.'

'Am I embarrassing you in front of your pet?'

I snatch an angry breath but Ralph snaps first, 'Don't talk like that.' His voice stays calm but his fingers twitch at his side. 'Let's go outside and talk now. I'm sure we can sort this all out.'

'Why? I came here because I love you. But now you're one of them. You're not Ralph at all. You're one of these creatures.' Clarissa begins to stroke Milo's hair. 'This one is still innocent isn't he? Isn't he?'

I want to rip her dirty finger from my son's hair. Tension ripples over my arms and shoulders; poised for action.

He's just out of my reach since I moved to be with Mamie. Henri's arm awkwardly slips over Milo's shoulder, his grimacing is now a snarl aimed at Clarissa. His English is almost as good as mine, only more accented, and like everyone else in the room, it wouldn't matter if it wasn't, because this woman is making everyone feel uneasy.

'Out! Now, Clarissa, or I'll drag you out. You're scaring the poor boy.'

My cousins' quiet, confused chatter makes Clarissa's eyes dart around.

He reaches a hand tentatively towards her again, 'Let's leave Milo's hair alone.'

Her eyes flick to the table before her body lurches forwards. The moment is enough to make Ralph and me both jump. I see his body ripple in front of my eyes and there's nothing I can do.

Clarissa's fingers scramble to grip the handle of a sharp Laguiole steak knife. My knife, from my steak.

She slashes it around wildly while words jumble out of her mouth. 'I'm doing this because I still love you. And these monsters, no, can't have you.'

At first, I'm frozen with shock at her deranged movements, and scrambled garbled words, so much so that it takes me a whole moment to understand them.

Then I'm not quick enough. I can see what she's about to do, but I can't do anything to change it.

My fingers, arms, body, glance off everything they touch like it's all made of glass as I scramble, reaching over the table.

I'm helpless as she launches herself and the point of the steak knife towards my son, who is only exposed because he was politely going to get this devil a chair.

I can't breathe.

Time stops.

Life in my lungs and my heart stops.

I see Henri desperately trying to drag Milo into him, but he has nowhere to go, only pulling him open and exposed in the chair.

Then there's Ralph.

Faster than me.

Faster than her.

Faster than humanly possible, securing himself onto the end of her blade as his hand attempts to push her back.

His crisp white shirt drowns in a crimson red only found in the draining of life. So dark, so thick, it makes Santa's suit seem pink.

Clarissa pulls back the knife and sighs his name before dropping the blade and being manhandled in a mountain of people.

I push and shove to get over and round the table.

'Ralph!' It's a scream on a distant wind. Milo's crying and saying my name, but he's being wrapped in Henri's arms. Ralph falls back into Milo's now-empty seat.

'I'm sorry,' both Ralph and Clarissa repeat. She to him, he to me.

Chapter 45

Félicité

I'm not family, but he has no family here with him, so I lie.

I tell them we are partners and I'm all the family he has.

I sit in a waiting room. A couple of nurses, I think they're nurses, talk about their upcoming Christmas celebrations out in the hall before their voices lower into hushed tones that reach my ears even so. They're talking about a Christmas party in a nice out-of-the-way place where an Englishman was stabbed. They don't know the details. If they did, they would know it was an eighty-six-year-old's birthday party. They would know that he saved my son. That he didn't deserve this.

When the doctors are done with him, I'm allowed in to watch him sleep.

The anaesthetic has induced a state of oblivion, but the doctors tell me soon he will wake.

Soon.

Milo's voice rings in my ear. Almost a scream cutting through the chaos. *He saved me Maman, he saved me.*

I had wanted to stay with both Milo and Ralph, but my six-year-old has a kind and full heart. Through floods of tears, he demanded that I look after Ralph, that Ralph had saved him from this crazy woman and someone had to look after him. He begged me to go with Ralph and keep him safe. I kissed him a thousand times and gripped him in my hands before tugging Henri in, tears streaming faster than Clarissa's, to press our foreheads together while I implored Henri to keep Milo safe.

Now, I grip Ralph's hand. I wait forever to hear his voice.

Machines pound like war drums in my head. A perfectly rhythmical death song.

This isn't a death song.

She stabbed the side of his torso, but the doctors told me he was lucky. A lot of blood was lost, and he'll have a very nasty scar, but no major organs were affected.

Everyone else is safe in Mamie's town house now. Milo was checked over by paramedics and deemed well enough, but they suggested he be taken to a counsellor to talk about the shock as soon as possible.

This is my fault.

Trying to find happiness when I should've been focusing on my son and my family, I brought a stranger and his baggage into our life.

Milo's voice sounds again in my head, telling me to keep Ralph safe. As though, if I don't, I will be in so much trouble. This is my job in Milo's eyes. I will be the only one to bring news of his health. I know Milo will want to see him again to congratulate him on his bravery.

Tears bite and emotion claws under my skin. Ralph put my child's life before his own, with no question. Love and anger curdle in my stomach until all I feel is the burning of acid in the back of my throat.

I pick up my phone from the little table next to the bed. I've checked every minute even though I know everyone is safe now. Clarissa was taken away by the gendarmes.

That's all a blur now.

I remember squeezing Milo and Ralph.

I remember that Ralph told me not to worry about him, but to check on Milo and Milo wanting me to look after Ralph. The waitstaff, my father, Pierre, all helped to detain Clarissa while she was like a cat trying to climb up curtains. Screaming and clawing. Begging Ralph to get the monsters away from her.

I slip my hand back into Ralph's over the rough fabric of the hospital blanket.

'I don't know what'll happen now. You saved him when I couldn't. You saved Milo and put him first. If you hadn't, I dread to think–' I snatch a breath and wipe away another tear that's weaving down my cheek.

'You'll have to say that all again in English.'

The croak of his voice makes me physically jump in my chair.

'Ralph! Thank the stars.'

His hand goes towards his side. 'It wasn't a shit dream then? She really got me?'

I bounce my head through tears that are beginning to flow over my face and drip from my jawline.

'I'm so sorry, Félicité. I had no idea–'

'This is not your fault. You can't blame yourself for the actions of others. Only your own, and your actions saved my child's life. You protected Milo.'

Our hands knit together at the same time as Ralph's brows do.

'Of course, I did.'

Chapter 46

Ralph

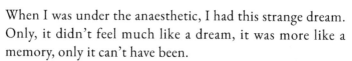

When I was under the anaesthetic, I had this strange dream. Only, it didn't feel much like a dream, it was more like a memory, only it can't have been.

Benedict was sitting in his Uni room on the bed. That room was filled with posters of cars and topless girls. You couldn't move an inch without someone's eyes being on you. Some of the girls he'd been with complained about the girlie posters, but he didn't care, and it never stopped them coming back to him either.

He was slumped over his PlayStation controller with his back pressed into the wall. The dream was so vivid. So real.

He swore, then chucked the remote to one side. He stretched out his expanse of chest and back until his spine cracked before looking right at me from under his mop of curls. 'You alright, mate? You look like you've seen a ghost!' There was that cheeky grin of his. The one that hooked all the girls in. Playful and carefree, like he had seen it all and none of it mattered.

'Yeah, I feel like I'm looking at one, bud.'

'What?' Bennie wrinkled his nose, but the smile lingered.

'Nothing.'

Benedict picked up a TV remote and shut down the screen on the desk. I did what I aways did back then. I sat in his office chair and swiveled it from side to side.

'You never told me about your mum... what she was really like.' Even in a dream, I couldn't look him in the eye.

Bennie shook his head and rolled down onto his bed, hands behind his head.

'Don't want to spend my life thinking about the past. What's the point in living in the past when you have all of the future to live for?'

If only this dream-Bennie knew. If only I could've saved him and tell him everything I know.

'Sometimes,' I said, 'you have to leave people you love in the past and you don't want to forget them. The past shapes us.'

Bennie propped himself up on his elbows and looks across at me with one eyebrow firmly lowered. 'You can't change the past, but you can change the future. Yeah, the past fucks you up, it fucks everyone up, but the future holds all the promise to keep us going. It's all about the fun. You gotta live your life for you. Not for anyone else...'

His youthful face faded away from me, and I began to hear a disembodied voice speaking French. Félicité's words replace the image of Bennie.

Benedict hasn't been holding me back. I've been holding me back. I've been afraid and using him like a shield. Then I used Clarissa as a therapist when clearly she needed one of her own. I've let them both down, because I couldn't face up to it all.

Not anymore.

Seeing Clarissa like that was a wake-up call. There was no way I could let her hurt anyone, especially Félicité or Milo... But I stopped her. That's what matters.

I just hope Félicité can forgive me for putting them in danger in the first place.

The only thing that's bubbling up over the pain meds are questions. And I know exactly where I need to start.

Chapter 47

Félicité

Warmth fills me up like I've taken a deep swig of the soup Ralph made me last year, heating me through. When I said to him that he had protected Milo, he replied, "Of course, I did." Those were his words. Of course he would put Milo first.

'Félicité, before Clarissa, you were going to make me promise my life away again. What were you going to make me promise?'

A laugh splutters under my tears that won't stop rolling and dripping off my chin. 'It doesn't matter now.'

Ralph frowns and shakes his head. 'It does matter.' He attempts to sit up only to wince on realising that he can't. 'I don't want this to be over.'

'I didn't say that.' I wipe the tears away with the back of my hand.

'Then tell me what you were going to say.'

I exhale and look up at the tiles on the ceiling before bringing myself back in line with his gaze. 'I wanted you to promise to put Milo first. I mean, to understand that he will always be the priority in my life. That his feelings will come first, and that if you two didn't get along then that would be that. I wanted you to make a promise for Milo. But, I think you've proven you understand the importance of my son. An inch of two differently and you might've given your life for him.'

'So, I passed the test already, and I didn't even need to make the promise?'

'I could always come up with a new one, if you like?'

'No. I think I'm done with the big promises, at least for a while anyway.' Ralph grips my fingers a little tighter. 'How is Milo? He must've been terrified. I'm so sorry.'

'Stop apologising. It wasn't your fault. Milo is doing as well as can be expected, as far as I know. He is desperate to see you. I think he believes you're a superhero now.'

'And what do you think?'

'There are no straight lines in my mind. Everything is a tangle of emotion. Logic is stuck in a web-like-knot from shock... But I agree with Milo,' a smile curves my lips, 'you *are* a superhero. And I can promise you there will be a tomorrow. I want there to be a tomorrow for us.'

'More promises?' Ralph's features relax a little, 'I'm grateful there will be a tomorrow, for me, and for us.'

'Oh yes, there'll be a tomorrow. One with Milo, if you can handle it.'

Ralph laughs then squints with pain. He grips my hand. 'Seeing as you don't need me to make one last promise, can you make me one?'

Trepidation catches on my nerve endings, but I nod my head and hope for the best. He did just save my son after all.

'I promised Bennie I would have fun. And after a while I wasn't having fun, running around and trying to be like him. Maybe it was never fun, not really. Acting like that was never who I was meant to be. You were the first person to make me feel that. To feel anything. It was the starting point of realising that the promise I made Bennie ever going to bring him closer to me, because I can't replace him. I had way more fun chatting with you and Milo than chasing one more girl just for the sake of it.'

'You need to get over the fear of losing someone else, and just live.'

'So do you.' I screw my face up in confusion. 'Your mother leaving, then Henri. They might not be dead, but they may as well be for the scars they've given you. I'm trying to move on from my fear, but this isn't about me, it's about you. Or maybe it's about us all. You and Bennie got one part right with that promise; there needs to be fun in life. You love to travel, and so do I. I think Milo seems like the kind of kid who loves adventure too. Do you know what he told me?'

I shake my head, still dumbfounded at his comment about Carole and Henri. He's right. I don't know how he is, but I know he is. I've been hiding it in my love for Milo and Mamie, just as Ralph has been hiding in his promise.

'He told me he wanted to go to England one day, and maybe he could meet my family because I got to meet his. He told me he would like that very much.' Ralph's cheeks swell and his eyes crease at the corners at the memory. My face lifts too at the thought of Milo saying this. The heat of love radiates from my bones. 'He's a sweet kid. It's your turn to promise me you'll do your best to start to have some fun. To travel, and enjoy life.'

'I can only promise to try.'

'Good enough.' Ralph lifts my hand to press his lips to it. 'More than good enough.'

A nurse comes in and reprimands me for not alerting them that Ralph has woken up, before telling me I'll need to leave now. Our time is up. I translate for Ralph, before leaning in for a gentle kiss. 'Until tomorrow.'

Chapter 48

Ralph

As soon as Félicité leaves, I'm isolated in a foreign language. None of my words are their words. Some have my words, and all that do are trying to help me.

Nothing about my body feels like mine. My nerves tingle a little, I guess from the pain meds. Or maybe not. Maybe it's from being overloaded with too much information, or from being stabbed with a dirty knife and having my left hand hooked up to a drip, which probably has antibiotics in. I've got no clue and no desire to find out. I have other things on my mind that dig deeper than the wound in my side.

The first being, Clarissa's face. Her eyes wide and darting about the room. In the clouds of my mind, I try to recall her words. Nothing about it made much sense. There were times in the past that she'd been a bit wild, a bit off the wall, but never dangerous.

All I can think is, it has to be something to do with coming off her antidepressant medication. But that surely doesn't make sense. The medication is for anxiety and mood. She was more like a lunatic. What was she thinking going for Milo like that? Cold anger drips over my skin, encasing the concern I feel for her. I want to shake her and ask her what the hell she thought she was doing. I need information.

I ask one of the doctors about Clarissa, someone whose English seems good enough that they might know where she is and whether she's alright. They don't know anything, or if they do, they're not telling me. My first thoughts and concerns were, and are, for Milo. He's a kid, a good kid at that, and what Clarissa did was insane. But the question of, "what the hell happened for that to happen?" won't leave me.

Eventually, I get around to asking where my stuff is, because I'm in some flimsy hospital gown. A slender nurse, with a stern face but helpful words, gets my phone and wallet for me. Now I have the fun of calling my parents, and telling my mum exactly what happened, or as much as I can fathom anyhow.

Ringing from France to a landline in England means that strange, elongated calling tone sounds in my ear rather than the usual chirpy tone. Eventually it rings off with no answer. I try again. Still nothing, so I ring Mum's mobile. No point ringing Dad's; if they've gone out there's about a one percent chance he has remembered to take his phone with him.

'Hello, dear. How are you?' Mum sounds genuinely pleased to pick the call up, which makes me feel a bit rubbish because I'm about to squash that fresh tone right out of her. That's the fun of being an only child, it's all on me. Happiness, sadness, drama, calm... I'm king of it all in their house.

'Now, don't freak out but–' I take a breath because even I can't believe I'm saying this –'Clarissa stabbed me.'

'Sorry, Ralph, it's a bad line. I'm in the shops and your father's getting some steak for tonight's dinner. It sounded like you said something stabbed you? Hello? Did you hear me?'

'Yeah, Mum, I said: Clarissa, Clarissa stabbed me.'

'No, no. What? It sounded like stabbed again. Len, Ralph's calling, I can't hear him all that well. What sounds like stabbed? No Len, what rhymes with stabbed? I'm trying to guess what Ralph's saying on the phone. Your dad says hello. Asks how the market is.'

'Mum, Mum! I *am* saying *stabbed*. I'm in hospital. In Rouen. I'm fine, no need to worry or anything. It was just a small stabbing.'

'Is this a joke? I don't appreciate this sort of humour and you know that–'

'Mum. This isn't a fucking joke.' Pain is starting to hammer in my side. Either the pain killers are wearing off, or Mum is managing to wear my nerves so thin they're all beginning to break.

'Tell me where you are, and we'll be there soon.' She manages to sound both flustered and calm all at once. Her tone being the calm part and her speed being flustered. Normally she tells me off when I swear, so at least I got away with that, I guess.

'No don't–'

'Ralph. Now.' The tone. The parent tone that's hard to argue with at any age. She doesn't pull it out all that often, she's not the best at it, but it's still there. I could ignore it better when I was thirteen, right now I don't have the energy. I give her as much detail as I can muster. Brief, brief detail before I'm sort of regretting telling her at all.

Chapter 49

Ralph

"Until tomorrow," was the last thing Félicité said to me, and hell, that's all I've been looking forward to. That is until my parents rocked up on the scene.

The ward I'm on has five other blokes with injuries, as best I can guess anyway. None of them have any English and no way my French is good enough to ask any questions.

Mum sent me messages last night until my phone died. Luckily, I was able to slip in a few to Félicité who said she'll try to get me some stuff out of my Airbnb by contacting the owner for me. I managed to send them a message too, thankfully, to confirm she wasn't scamming them.

Between it all, I worked out that Mum made Dad leave his steak behind and they pretty much got in the car straight away and drove to Portsmouth to get a boat to Le Havre. I hope they went for their passports at least. My phone died before I found out if they've made it here or not, although I did manage to sort of explain on the phone that Clarissa stalked me and that I got in the way of her stabbing a child. That was all I got to tell them on the phone.

Félicité's messages were much softer, unlike the fear and hard edges from my mum. Félicité asked what I wanted, what I needed, and wanted to check that it was definitely okay to bring Milo along to see me. Her messages kept light shining on my face until it had to stop.

Tomorrow is now today, and I've been having a disjointed chat with a police officer about Clarissa. One that's left me rubbing my temples.

His English is pretty good, but this conversation has some trickier language involved. She's seen a psychiatrist and I think my mum might've tried to get some information across for them. I'm still not sure on that one. There have been parts of this conversation that have left both me and this very tall chap politely squinting at each other, wishing that in doing so we could squeeze knowledge from the other one's head.

Eventually we give up; he has enough witness statements from other people and I have no desire to punish her for what she did to me. I just want to get to the root of what the hell made her do it in the first place. It's up to Félicité, Henri and Milo to decide if they want to take action against Clarissa now, I guess.

A new fear scratches along my bones when I think of that one, because it's a conflict. My past and my present colliding in a way I could never have imagined.

The sound of hurried footsteps, ones I know all too well, tap along the corridor not far from my bay.

'Oh Ralph, there you are.' My mum piles in on top of me, kissing my face.

Dad waits patiently for his turn and he leans in and kisses my forehead. 'How are you doing, son? They treating you well?'

'Yeah, I'm fine, Dad. Nothing serious.'

'Nothing serious, he says!' Mum echoes me but with a condemning eyeroll. 'No, nothing serious. Only surgery and a stabbing.'

'Other way around actually,' I correct with a laugh in the back of my throat. I throw in a playful look at my dad for good measure, and they both relax a little. I'm me. I'm alive. I'm normal. Dad's lips twitch into a smile and Mum audibly exhales some of her fear.

Dad pulls up a chair as Mum begins to apologise for not seeing me before this moment in time; they weren't allowed to, because of visiting hours and they only managed to book a hotel nearby for one night. They need to look for somewhere else now, apparently.

Mum places a stuffed shopping bag decorated with pictures of brightly decorated cakes on the bed at my feet. She gets out a European plug adapter, a phone charger, finds my phone, plugs it in, gets out my childhood favourite chocolate bar, a massive Toblerone, passes me the chocolate and my now-charging phone, then pulls out a brand-new packet of the worst grey underwear imaginable, and brand new PJs, takes her coat off and puts that in the bag instead, all while telling me about their ordeal getting to me.

It's one of those moments when I can actually appreciate what a superhero my mum is. She thinks of everything. Yeah, she might not execute it perfectly, but who the hell does?

'Thanks for all this, Mum.'

'Thank your father. He had to do all that driving. We wouldn't be here without him. My hands were shaking much too much to drive anywhere at all.'

Now Mum's hands are free of bag-related items, she busies them by smoothing my hair back into its normal position, swept over to one side in a neat and old-fashioned chic kind of way. My attempt at classic styling.

'Right, tell me everything that happened. And from the start. I still can't believe Clarissa of all people would do such a thing.'

As I open my mouth to explain, I catch sight of movement just past Mum. I do my best to shift without hurting myself and realise that Félicité, Henri and Milo are hovering just behind my parents at the foot of the bed.

'Hello?' Félicité's voice is enough to make my mum whip round from her hair-smoothing task, and for warmth to run from my toes up to my spine. 'I hope we're not interrupting.'

I want to tell her that interrupting would be impossible, her presence is welcome near me for as long as she's happy to stay. But I manage to keep it simple.

'Not at all. This is my mum, Margret, and my dad, Len.'

My mum starts swiping her hands over her black cashmere jumper – I know it's cashmere because I got it for her for Christmas last year – then through her hair. My dad on the other hand jumps up and starts shaking hands and scrubbing his fingers into Milo's thick, spiky hair. My dad's that guy who's great with kids and will patiently play games or kick about a ball for hours. He was a teacher for years and if we ever bump into students, they always say hello or call him a legend. If my parents had known the real deal about Benedict and Clarissa's home life, there's no doubt they'd have offered to adopt them.

My mother steps forwards, deceptively shy behind Dad, and introductions pass around before Mum turns back to me. Her eyebrows are raised and there's a smile hiding in her eyes as she asks the question, 'And how do you know these lovely people? Is this the little boy you saved?'

Chapter 50

Félicité

It feels only fair, after everything that Ralph has been through, for me to give a detailed answer when Margret asks exactly how Ralph and I know each other.

As I explain what originally happened last year with Mamie, it soon becomes clear that she knows nothing about me, and next to nothing about what happened to Ralph, only that Clarissa stabbed him.

I begin to cobble together with Ralph the basics as I stand at the end of his bed, wishing I could say hello with an embrace and a kiss. At first, Milo tugs at my sleeve, before giving up on me completely and going to Henri to ask if he can go up to Ralph now. As soon as Henri agrees that it seems to be fine, Milo bounds past me and up to Ralph, telling him he's a superhero and would he like to come to ours for Christmas dinner. Henri begs him to slow down, but while my mouth is still moving, explaining to his parents how we got to this point in time, my insides are as warm as a Christmas fire watching Ralph's face light up at Milo's enthusiasm.

Then Henri pipes up over Milo's buzzing voice.

'I wanted to thank you in person, Ralph, for putting yourself between that woman and my son. I can see you have important guests here, but I want to wish you a strong recovery.' They shake hands with short nods of acceptance between them.

As Henri goes to leave, he says to me, 'I'll be in the car. If Milo is getting too much, just message me and I'll bring him down to sit with me or take him for a walk.' He takes a slow breath through his nose, and lowers his voice, even though we are speaking in French and only Milo can understand us. 'I know I haven't been... the most present parent, and I have no right to say anything, but I think this man,' his head subtly flicks in the direction of Ralph, 'perhaps this man is one to keep around.'

While I'm left slightly wide-eyed at Henri's statement, he turns and says to Ralph's parents that it was nice to meet them and then makes a swift exit.

As soon as Henri is out of earshot, Margret leans closer to me and says, 'Is that your husband? He's very handsome.'

A short laugh spits out through my lips. 'No, no. We were a couple once. He is Milo's father, but that is all.'

Ralph's father turns to a patient nearby, who's watching a video on their phone, and asks in broken French if we could use the chairs that are next to their bed. I smooth the conversation along and bring the chairs over to Ralph's bed, so that Marget and Len are sitting on one side of Ralph and Milo and I are on the other. It's now that I take the opportunity to say a proper hello to Ralph, as proper as I can get away with. Two simple kisses, one for each of his softly stubbled cheeks. He still smells of sterile surgery and bleached sheets.

'Your English is very good, Milo. How old are you?' Len presses his glasses back up his nose as he smiles across at Milo.

'I'm six, almost seven.' Milo wiggles to sit straighter in his chair.

'And it sounds like our Ralph was a bit of a hero. You're okay now though, are you?' Len's lightly creped skin wrinkles further into concern.

'Oh yes, I'm fine. Ralph saved me from that bad woman.'

Ralph's eyes dip and his lips disappear as he sucks them in. This has to be hard for him. He told me he feels responsible for Clarissa, and then this happens. He must be knotted in conflict. Even I am. I want to feel sorry for her, and I'm trying my best to be empathetic, but feeling it is still tricky when I close my eyes and see her going towards Milo with a knife.

'*Mon grand,* just because people do bad things doesn't always make them bad people. Clarissa obviously has some problems she needs help with.'

'Yes, but Ralph is a hero, although Mamie told me not to say that too much, because I'll make Ralph's ankles swell and then he won't be able to walk out of the hospital.'

A tickle wriggles in my chest as Len and Margret simultaneously open and shut their mouths, before tilting their heads in opposite directions, likely they usually mirror each other. As it is, they look like curious bookends.

'In French we say compliments make your ankles swell. In English you say you get a big head, no?'

This information reassures them enough to relax into smiles and chuckles.

'Have you heard anything?' Ralph's eyes search mine. 'About Clarissa, I mean?' His mind isn't letting him relax into the frippery of language and the individuality of nations. It's rightly stuck on a strange situation we're in, and I can't help but feel sympathy for him.

The night before, I couldn't sleep, and I ended up sitting up at four in the morning talking to Mamie, who also couldn't sleep. We had a good conversation over fresh cups of strong black coffee, mostly about what had happened. She had retained her recall well about the events of that evening, as though something so dramatic was easier to etch into her memory unlike the day-to-day life we carve out for ourselves. I suppose that at least makes sense, although we shall see how much of her memory has worn away a few months from now.

As it was, she held a lot of sympathy for Clarissa, when I told her what I knew, as well as for Ralph for being in the middle of it all.

She had said, 'This reminds me of Pierre, although much more extreme than him. Do you remember how he struggled to come off the medication they gave him? And when he did it too quickly, he said he needed to run from the devil.'

'That's a bit different though. He was just running.'

'You realise at first he meant it literally? He was seeing the devil and thought he could only keep him at bay if he ran. It took some time to realise that, of course. He had to go back on the drug at a low dose to give his brain time to move away from it. He thought he had to run. Don't you remember?'

I didn't want to admit that I hadn't realised Pierre had taken up running because he thought he literally had to run from the devil. The distractions in my own life had kept me from seeing exactly what was going on in Pierre's. I hadn't wanted to see. I had wanted everything to be alright, and for my brother to be happy and healthy. It wasn't that I wanted to ignore his pain, but perhaps that's what I'd been doing without realising. I'd been too afraid to show my fears in the light.

I do my best to conjure a reassuring smile for Ralph. Although his angular face and bright eyes are as handsome as ever, today he looks as worn as some of the old decorations hanging on Mamie's tree.

I try to reassure him, 'Pierre is working to get Clarissa the right help. He knows more of the right people to help her. We have said we are not taking action against her as long as she can get the help she needs.'

Milo pipes up. '"Everyone needs a second chance." That's what Uncle Pierre said.'

'Milo, would you like some chocolate? If that's alright with your maman?'

I give Ralph the nod, and he begins to unwrap an enormous Toblerone. His bed is stacked with new clothing his parents have obviously brought with them. It reminds me to place the carrier bag of things I retrieved from the apartment next to his bed. Milo eagerly waits for a triangular slice of chewy chocolate before Ralph offers some to the rest of us.

A nurse comes into the ward to inform us that we have exceeded the visitor quota, and it's not fair to those who are sticking to the rules. I take this moment to quiz her about Ralph's condition on his behalf. As soon as I reply to her broken English with my French, her jaw unclenches and her tired dark eyes brighten a little. She's probably happier that I've removed the stress of speaking English from her mind. I wonder whether we've been able to break the rule for this long because no one wanted to come over and ask us to move in English.

With a few well-placed questions, I find that she heard the doctor say Ralph is likely to be discharged in four or five days. Just in time for Christmas. That is, as long as there's no infection or complications, none of which are expected.

I confirm to the nurse that we will be on our way; we just have to say our goodbyes.

I turn to Ralph. 'I would like to offer you my bed to look after you while you recover.' As soon as the words are out of my mouth, I try to find a way to step back over them and create something new, because the raised eyebrow from Len on the other side of Ralph's bed is enough for me to hear my words in a very different light. 'I mean, I will stay with Milo in his room, and you can take mine. You are welcome to be at ours for Christmas, too, instead of trying to travel home. You're all welcome, of course.'

Chapter 51

Félicité

Christmas Day

I wasn't sure how it would work, having Ralph in our home over Christmas. His parents have taken over the Airbnb he was renting and extended their stay there. Papa and Lizzie are staying nearby and arrived very early this morning, but in a completely bizarre turn of events, Pierre won't be joining us. Instead, when Carole left – apparently because she was too traumatised to stay – he took in Clarissa. She doesn't have any decent family back in England, and he didn't want her to be left alone at this time of year. I'm proud of the way he has looked after her. A doctor confirmed that her violent episode was down to her suddenly stopping her anti-depressants. According to Pierre, they were impressed that she'd followed her phone from Devon to Rouen. In many cases, stopping neurological medication abruptly can cause severe psychosis and other dreadful side effects, even medication as readily prescribed as antidepressants. Pierre has relayed that she genuinely thought we were all monsters there to capture Ralph.

Ralph's parents are going over to see her before they come to us for dinner. They've known her as long as Ralph has after all. Ralph still isn't quite ready to see her yet, neither's Milo, although they both seem happy to know that since getting back on her antidepressant medication, she's doing a lot better.

In a quiet moment before saying goodnight to him last night, Ralph and I managed to have thirty minutes alone together in my, or his, room. It was a moment where he expressed how grateful he was for everything my family have done for him and Clarissa. That's before we had a teenage moment of snatched kisses.

The last two days have gone better than I could have expected. I'm quite glad that Ralph's arrival aligned with Henri and Naomi's departure; that's one less thing to worry about. Although in some strange way the Clarissa incident has done my and Henri's relationship some good. Perhaps the thought of losing Milo woke him up. Perhaps it woke me up too.

Ralph has stepped with ease into a role as Milo's play companion. He's been patiently playing games with him, and has even asked Milo to teach him some French.

I was worried the whole thing might be a bit of an overload for Mamie, and although she has had a few moments, wondering who everyone is and why they're here, Milo has been amazing at keeping her grounded. Although I hate that he has to grow up to deal with her ageing, I'm also so proud of his maturity with her. It's like a switch flicks in his brain and he keeps everyone happy while still maintaining his bouncy ways.

Papa and Lizzie have been in to see us a lot in the lead-up to Christmas. Lizzie spent all of yesterday making our town house a little extra special for Christmas, while helping Milo to teach

Ralph French and instructing me what she needed from her big cardboard box of fun. She has done this every year since we were children. No matter where we were in the world, certain things had to be found, or drawn on paper, and put around where we were staying. She has pinned up bunches of mistletoe in places where people loiter, there are ruby-red holly berries in the corners and doorways, and oranges encrusted with cloves have been put above the fireplace so that when the fire is lit they will fill the room with the warm fragrance of citrus and cloves.

Throughout this, Lizzie demanded, as she always does, that a soundtrack of Christmas carols should play while we worked. That is after listening to "Last Christmas" until we forced her to change it.

At one point yesterday, Lizzie even had Ralph, Milo, Papa and Mamie making brightly coloured paper garlands at the kitchen table, and promptly hung them on every spare inch that she hadn't already decorated. Finally, she pulled out a box of red-and-gold British Christmas crackers for our dinner. Mamie still finds this particular tradition a strange one, and vocalises it every time crackers are mentioned.

My biggest issue in the past week – if that's even what I can call it after everything that's happened – was what to get Ralph as a gift. We've been acting as a secret couple, unquestioned by family members even though I'm quite sure they're aware. We've been sneaking around because I don't want Milo to get too excited. I know he would because he adores Ralph. Although, I already feel confident that no matter what happens in our future, Ralph will always be around for Milo. He's that sort of person, loyal to such a degree that he'll even keep a warped promise to a friend for five long years.

None of this helped with the sweaty panic of what to get him for Christmas.

I managed to take Milo shopping, because he too wanted to get Ralph something special. Within the shortest time he chose a card game, some chocolates from the market shaped like snowflakes and the biggest Christmas card in the shop to write "thank you for saving my life" in. But then it was my turn to pick him the perfect gift, and nothing was good enough.

For the man who is willing to take a knife for my child, whom I've certainly fallen in love with completely by accident, what on earth could I get?

After Milo had picked out his special gifts, he was suitably bored of trudging about the shops listening to the same jingly Christmas music in every store, while I was getting sweaty and irritated, strangled by my coat in the burning heating each time we walked into a shop.

As we marched through Printemps, past all the designer jewellery and clouds of perfume, Milo demanded in his most whiney voice that I pick something. In a panic, I was drawn to a white box of CK One that was on offer, some overpriced gloves, and I picked up and put down some socks three times before leaving them and being ushered to the counter by Milo. As I placed my items in front of the cashier, I discovered the gloves were a size small, and so I left them behind too.

Needless to say, as soon as I left the shop with only a bewildering bottle of CK in my bag, I could've screamed. Instead, I went home to find Pierre and Mamie watching gameshows in a content silence. Smiles sprang to their faces for Milo and me as we walked through the door.

As soon as I sat down with them, I scoured the internet. Hours passed before an idea came to me. Ralph had asked me whether he could visit us in-between his travels. He had told me that I should travel too, so I thought perhaps a bracelet with a compass might be a thoughtful idea, and that's how I found the perfect gift.

There on the screen, carefully placed in a box, lay a thick, laced-leather bracelet with a small gold disc marked to look like a compass. Inside the lid of the box was a golden embossed image of two hands linked at the little fingers, just like the promise image that is tattooed on Ralph's left arm, together with these words:

No matter where you go,

No matter what you do,

You'll always be there for me

And I'll be there for you.

Next-day delivery, and the perfect simple gift had arrived before Ralph came to stay. Now it's nestled under the tree, waiting for the after-breakfast madness to begin. Lizzie and Papa arrived early to keep up the tradition of cooking his homemade *pains au chocolat* for us all. We're all happily devouring the sweet crispy delight as Milo tells us what he found in his stocking from Santa.

'So, is that what you asked for then, Milo?' Ralph is sitting next to me, looking over at Milo who is on the other side of the round kitchen table.

A nip of adrenalin radiates out through my chest at the memory of what Milo actually asked for from Santa, not the bike, which is hiding outside, but about Mamie, and my "good friend".

'Not exactly, but if I'm really good, sometimes he tells Maman to get me things too, and they work together as a team.' Milo's amber eyes and chocolate-smeared face are aglow with excitement and wonder. 'Finished!' he exclaims, before scraping his chair back. 'Is it time to open presents now? Can I give Ralph his?'

I glance around the table and everyone seems to have finished breakfast. Before allowing Milo to sprint into the next room to scramble under the tree, I make him wash the chocolate from his hands and face.

Ralph is still moving carefully from one place to the next, and sometimes we use this as an opportunity to make contact with each other, as I let him use my left arm, even though I know he doesn't overly need to. When I'm not available, he doesn't ask for help from anyone else, as it's an unspoken connection between us that comes along with furtive looks and glancing smiles. Although, with or without me, he moves with caution.

Every time we touch, or manage a solitary conversation of our own in amongst the Christmas decorations, roots of *us* dig further into my soul, and I wonder whether I should give Milo one of his Christmas wishes and tell him that Ralph and I are a new couple. The practical side takes over, of course, and I know we should wait until we're more established. Ralph doesn't live here, and when the bubble of Christmas pops, we need to find out how things will work between us.

We all move into the living area, and I sit on the floor at Ralph's feet as he shuffles carefully into the armchair next to the Christmas tree. Milo begins to read names on labels then hands out both perfectly and imperfectly wrapped parcels. I helped Mamie to get her gifts for everyone some time ago, and added in some chocolates for Ralph from her, and Papa and Lizzie got Ralph a nice bottle of malbec. They asked me what he might like and I know that's a wine I've seen him pick.

Paper is scrunching, and being littered like confetti all over the floor. The air fills with the sounds of gratitude just as Ralph gets to the gifts from me. He reads the silver label with my name at the bottom.

'Please open this one first, it was an–, what do you English call it? Lizzie, what do you call it when you buy something because you don't know what to get but anxiety takes over?'

Lizzie and Ralph answer in unison, 'Panic buy.' They share a laugh just before Lizzie pulls out a gold bracelet with multicoloured stones that only she could make look wonderful. On anyone else in the world it would look as garish as wearing tinsel in the summer.

'Yes, I can't explain what made me pick this one up, let alone take it to the till. I have the receipt.'

'I'm sure it's great.' As Ralph tears along the line of the paper I bite at my lower lip, scrunching up my face as I wait.

'Maman, look what Grand-père and Mamie-Lizzie got me!' I look away from Ralph for a second to see Milo waving a hefty Lego box with a picture of a dragon on the front. 'Can I open it now?'

'Open all of the presents, then you can get it out.'

Above me, there's the sound of a snatched breath. I look up to see an expression on Ralph's face that I can't place. His eyes are glistening and there's a lift in his cheeks as he presses the unopened box to his nose.

'This was Bennie's scent.' His voice snags on the words. 'He wore it all the time. I think he really did send you to me.' Although no tears arrive, Ralph gently sniffs like he's holding something in. 'Thank you. For everything.' Without more words, I can't know for sure, but I get the distinct feeling that this is a sentence of weight, because we both want to express more feeling than we are allowing ourselves.

'Hey, Milo.' Ralph clicks his tongue to gain Milo's attention, 'Kiddo! Can you do me a favour and grab that red box from under the tree and give it to your maman? Down there,' he points, 'right near the–, yeah, that one.'

'When did you have time to shop?' I enquire with keen interest. I hadn't expected a gift, after everything that's happened and being so close to Christmas. We hadn't actually discussed anything.

'That's what the internet, and parents, are for.' Ralph all but winks at me and playfully pouts his lips before turning back to Milo. 'Thanks for doing that, Milo. And look, see at the back? Right under the tree? That one's for you. Look, in the green paper. And there's some for everyone back there too. Can you pass them out for me? Thanks, little dude.'

Milo eagerly does exactly as Ralph has instructed, and while everyone else is distracted with their gifts, Ralph opens the present from me, and I open the one from him.

The sizes of the boxes are similar, square and firm. I wonder what might be inside this neatly wrapped shiny, red package with its petite bow on the corner.

We both unwrap our gifts and each of us finds a small box. We flick open the lids.

Inside my box, neatly curling around a small black velvet cushion is a gold bracelet, with a disc in the centre of its thin gold chain. The disc is engraved with a compass, so similar to the one I chose for Ralph it's uncanny. Only my bracelet is delicate and glitters with a stone, likely a crystal, at its centre.

With wide eyes and mouths agape, we both stutter words of disbelief, before Milo trots over and announces to the world that we got each other the same gift, which isn't accurate, but they're almost impossibly similar.

Soon after, Milo's bike is piled in, and the array of coloured paper is put into the recycling. Ralph and I can't help but sneak out to the bottom of the stairs for a moment of quiet.

'How did you know?' I whisper up at him.

'I didn't. I just saw it and–'

'Had to get it.' I look down at the bracelet on my left wrist and carefully move it to see the stone glitter. 'I love it.'

'Bennie wrote this poem, a sad poem, but in it he said, "Because where there's life then love can be too." I've found life and love in you. You're my fun.' I look up to see the serious look on his face, his eyes glittering as much as my crystal. 'You know, we're standing under mistletoe that Lizzie put up here yesterday.' Ralph lifts his hand to point to the ceiling.

I tilt my head up further still to see the fresh sprigs hanging over our heads.

Ralph's fingers lift further to curl past my face and into my hair as he brings me in for a soft kiss. We try to keep it brief, but the moment lingers as we carefully press together, wishing to continue.

A squeal cuts us in half. 'My Christmas wish came true! Mamie! My Christmas wish for Maman and Ralph came true!!'

Chapter 52

Félicité

Epilogue

Another *ting-ting* of a spoon against a champagne glass rings in the air. The *ting-ting* sound is followed by Clarissa gently coughing into a mic she's clutching with both hands. Ralph squeezes my hand under the table.

'Thank you isn't enough. I love you isn't enough. I'm grateful isn't enough. And I want to come back to all of that. But first, I want to start with a story.' Clarissa's voice trembles and cracks as she speaks.

'Oh no, this is what I've been worrying about.' Ralph smacks his hands to his lips. His eyes dart across the scores of people in front of us, but I can spy the playful smile behind his hand.

As Clarissa recounts childhood pranks of Benedict and Ralph, and her part to play in it all, I look out and watch the smiles on the faces of those around us. So much has happened over the past couple of years. So many people have entered and left our life.

In my minds eye, I can see Carole's painted lips, as red as the holly berries decorating all the tables.

A knot used to pull and twist my innards whenever I thought of her, but now I'm free of that feeling. I don't have to worry about seeing her and the ways she would put down my life without a second thought.

After not congratulating us on our engagement, it wasn't long before she stated she did not want to attend our wedding. That's when I gave up. I'd tried for many years to incorporate her and welcome her despite the fraying knot.

Sometimes I told myself it was for Mamie, which in part it was, but sadly there was also that slice of me that always held the belief that my mother did love me. That in being harsh she was showing that she cared enough to push for more from us. Perhaps that's true, but if she couldn't be happy for us, how would she ever be happy for Milo? No. She couldn't.

It was the right choice to remove her from our life. Not to mention she wanted to make today all about her. Apparently, she couldn't stand to be in the same room as Clarissa, let alone see her as Ralph's best man, or best woman as it were. Carole was already not speaking to Pierre, and so he has happily joined me in cutting her out completely. I'm proud of us both for taking a stand.

Clarissa is sitting at our top table with Lizzie one side of her, and Pierre the other. Milo is next to me, with Ralph's parents on the other side. They've swept Milo up to be one of their own, showering him with love the way my papa and Lizzie do. They even took him to the Nausicaá aquarium, the largest in Europe, with Ralph and Papa. I was trying on wedding dresses with Bernadette and Lizzie that day, and it was their idea to take him for a special day out.

It made my time picking out my dress even more relaxed knowing that Milo was off having fun with his new family. That was the day I settled on my simple cream dress, with long sleeves and a puddle train. My favourite part isn't the dress I chose though, it's the long maroon cloak with a fur trim, which I very much needed today when it began to snow earlier on. The cloak reminds me of a coat Mamie bought for me when I was four years old.

My heart is crushed at thoughts of Mamie. It was hard to pick out a dress without her opinion. I can't help but wonder how she would feel, what she would say. I briefly indulge myself by closing my eyes to see her and Grand-pére with arms joined walking slowly through the Christmas market, under the sheet of twinkling fairy lights and down towards the cathedral.

Today would've been Mamie's birthday. She would've loved this. She always loved a family party. I am glad that she knew Ralph and adored him at least. We all raised a glass in her honour before the speeches. I thought it was another way to keep her here with us today. She was the reason I was even in Rouen, and in that restaurant, and started talking to Ralph. Without her, there would be no us.

After Ralph's and my engagement, not long before she passed peacefully in her sleep, I told Mamie I was afraid of the future, and the idea of Ralph leaving me the way my mother had, the way Henri had. This was one of the deep-rooted reasons I hadn't wanted to tell Milo, or anyone else, about our relationship. If Milo hadn't caught us kissing, I don't know how long I'd have made Ralph wait for our relationship to be public.

Mamie said to me, 'You don't see the way he looks at you when you're not looking at him. Henri never looked at you like that. He and your mother, they only regard the mirror with such admiration.'

FRANCESCA CATLOW

As always, she was right. Ralph is nothing like Henri or Carole. When he makes a promise, he'd do anything to keep it alive. Today, in front of everyone we care about, he promised to love me forever.

Raucous laughter snatches me from my reverie. I lift my head from Ralph's shoulder with a light sniff to pull back any tears hiding behind my lashes.

My eyes sting at the swirling emotions of this precious day, as Ralph's lips press against my neatly swept back hair.

Clarissa, still laughing at her own story, adds, 'If Bennie were here, he would have so many tales to tell.'

Clarissa has a lingering smile at this thought, then looks across directly at us. 'He was lucky to have you, Ralph. And now I am lucky to have you and Félicité. I would like to express how you have both changed my life. Nothing I could say or do could ever repay the kindness you have both shown me. With everything that happened, you could've both banished me forever. But you didn't. You helped me when so many people didn't want to know. I know everyone here will know about the...' Clarissa shakes her head as though trying to dissipate the thought. Her Christmas bauble style earrings wildly dance about her face. '...what happened. What I did. I don't really remember it myself, and what I do remember feels like watching a strange cartoon. Anyway, enough of that. I want to say how grateful I am for all the care you've shown me. I wish you both all the love and happiness in the world. You deserve it all. I'd like you to all raise your glasses to the bride and groom.'

Champagne glasses are raised into the air as people celebrate us with another sip of bubbles. I glance back to say thank you to Clarissa, but she's already been enveloped into the loving arms of Pierre. Their happiness is one of the most beautiful things to come from all the mayhem. They found each other, and her bringing light to Pierre's life has made me eternally grateful to her too.

Ralph tilts his head down towards me as Christmas carols start again from the corner of the room now that the final speech has been given.

'I love you, Félicité. Thank you for everything you do, and all that you are. Not many women would've forgiven Clarissa and accepted her into the family.'

'Oh come on, you know how I feel about this. That wasn't her. Not really. It could've easily happened to Pierre, or anyone. And look how happy they are.' I nod over Ralph's shoulder. He briefly glances back to see Pierre squeezing Clarissa into his chest. 'I can't believe they're engaged.'

'Ralph? Ralph?' Milo interjects, 'Was that *really* true? What Auntie Clarissa said? Nanny Margret said she'd never heard those stories before but could quite believe them.'

As I wrap Milo up in one arm, and Ralph in the other, I'm encased with joy. Ralph starts to laugh next to my ear as I squeeze him in.

'Yeah, it is. We did some stupid stuff, and most was a *really* bad idea.'

Milo continues to ask questions across me, and Ralph indulges him as he always does. We've been living as a family for quite some time now, and in three weeks from today, we'll be leaving France for a year. We've decided to world-school Milo, and travel. Ralph will be documenting the adventure for his ever-growing social accounts as well as a new TV offer he has had. I'm not quite sure how I feel about a crew turning up with us at random intervals, but work is work, I suppose.

I will be working in various schools teaching both English and French, whatever is needed, as well as teaching Milo as we go. We'll even be meeting up with Henri and Naomi for a time too.

In a week it will be Christmas, our last big celebration in the townhouse before it'll become an Airbnb for a year. It feels strange leaving Mamie and Grand-pere's house to strangers, but Clarissa and Pierre will be keeping an eye on it for us. He has given up travel for a while. Instead, he has taken over my role, and is teaching from his laptop.

A voice sounds in the speakers around the room; first in French, as we are in the heart of Normandy after all, then in English. 'Please welcome the new Mr and Mrs Williams to the floor for their first dance.'

I kiss Milo on his sweet smelling hair. As we stand, Papa comes over to sit next to him.

Ralph takes my hand and leads me to the middle of the empty dance floor, my puddle train flowing behind me as I pass everyone we know.

Ralph draws me in, and holds me close.

'You are so beautiful, Mrs Williams. There isn't a promise in this world I wouldn't make to keep you happy.'

'I'll hold you to that, Mr Williams.'

'As long as you hold me.' Ralph's lips move close to my ear, 'Do you know what happens tomorrow?' His tone has a playful slant which rouses a deep warmth in my chest.

'No.'

'Tomorrow, I'll have the best memory of my life, at last.'

'I thought you wouldn't know until you were old.'

'I don't need to be old to know marrying you is the best decision I'll ever make.'

A blanket of fairy lights just like the ones in the Christmas market glitters above us, and Ralph and I begin to sway in our peaceful embrace as Nat King Cole's rich voice sings softly, "Merry Christmas to you..."

I have loved creating this book stuffed with a lot of big issues. I try to do this with a light hand, keeping hope at the forefront of my work. But there was one topic I thought I should touch on as myself and outside of fiction…

Antidepressants

Let me start by saying I have no personal experience with taking anything other than the most simple medications (I didn't even have pain relief when giving birth and I'm still crying about it). I am not a doctor and I cannot give any medical advice. I can only talk about my experiences and my research for this book.

My husband, on the other hand, has suffered from the use of prescription anticonvulsants. Some of which are also used to treat bipolar and other disorders. I have lived through and cared for him in psychosis, Alice in Wonderland Syndrome and other such terrifying issues. One time, for example, he could see everyone around him with animal heads. Each person was a different animal.

Myself and my husband were in London for a conference when we watched BBC Panorama about antidepressants at the hotel we were staying in. So many of the patients' stories rang true with our experiences, and I wanted to shine a light on this topic as a whole.

Those of you who know me will also know how passionate I am about nutrition being a big factor in individual mental and physical health (you might be surprised to find out how many people can't process Folic Acid... and how it can cause postnatal depression). Medications are right for some people, but the propaganda of the past is still seen as fact to many.

If you are struggling with mental health, know that there are lots of wonderful professionals who are willing to help you.

I will leave you to your own research on these topics, but if you ever want a chat (not medical advice!!) then feel free to contact me and say hello on socials or via my newsletter.

Much love and good mental health to you all.

Francesca xxx

The Little Blue Door Series in order:
Book 1: The Little Blue Door (2021)
Book 2: Behind The Olive Trees (2022)
Book 3: Chasing Greek Dreams (2023)

Greek Standalones:
Greek Secret (2023)
Found in Corfu (2024)

French Standalones:
The Last Christmas Promise (2023)

Novellas:
For His Love of Corfu (2021)
One Corfu Summer (2022)

All of Catlow's books enjoy character crossover.

Printed in Great Britain
by Amazon